The Library Game

Also by Gigi Pandian

The Library Game

A Secret Staircase Novel

Gigi Pandian

MINOTAUR BOOKS
NEW YORK

First published in the United States by Minotaur Books, an imprint of St. Martin's Publishing Group

THE LIBRARY GAME. Copyright © 2025 by Gigi Pandian. All rights reserved. Printed in the United States of America. For information, address St. Martin's Publishing Group, 120 Broadway, New York, NY 10271.

www.minotaurbooks.com

Designed by Gabriel Guma

Library of Congress Cataloging-in-Publication Data

Names: Pandian, Gigi, 1975- author.
Title: The library game / Gigi Pandian.
Description: First edition. | New York : Minotaur Books, 2025. |
   Series: The secret staircase mysteries ; [4]
Identifiers: LCCN 2024043451 | ISBN 9781250880239 (hardcover) |
   ISBN 9781250880246 (ebook)
Subjects: LCGFT: Detective and mystery fiction. | Novels.
Classification: LCC PS3616.A367 L53 2025 | DDC 813/.6—dc23/
   eng/20240920
LC record available at https://lccn.loc.gov/2024043451

Our books may be purchased in bulk for promotional, educational, or business use. Please contact your local bookseller or the Macmillan Corporate and Premium Sales Department at 1-800-221-7945, extension 5442, or by email at MacmillanSpecialMarkets@macmillan.com.

First Edition: 2025

1   3   5   7   9   10   8   6   4   2

For everyone who loves libraries

The Library Game

Chapter 1

Tempest Raj was late.

A former stage performer who relied on split-second timing, Tempest didn't *do* late.

Yet here she was. So ridiculously late that even Gideon had texted her to make sure she was all right. *Gideon*. A man who'd only grudgingly been dragged into this century and bought his first cell phone this year.

She had no excuse. She couldn't even blame traffic. The Bay Bridge had been astonishingly empty for a weekday afternoon. She had only her curiosity to blame. Even that hadn't been satiated. What had happened was *impossible*.

Tempest specialized in creating mystifying illusions—once for spectacular stage shows and now through architectural misdirection for her job at Secret Staircase Construction—yet she had no idea how an invisible intruder had ransacked former client and friend Enid's library. She'd spent far too much time attempting to help Enid already—and, if she were being honest with herself, to satisfy her own curiosity. *Nobody was invisible.* Yet the security cameras showed objects in the library being tossed around—with nobody in sight.

Pulling up in front of Gray House, she flew out of the car so quickly that her wrist twisted painfully as she yanked out the key. Her long black hair came within an inch of getting slammed in the door before she hurried up the cobblestone path. But as soon as she caught sight of the home she was working on turning into a library, the magic of the house cast its spell.

Gray House looked as if it had been plucked from a European countryside of centuries past, or perhaps out of an illustrated fairy tale. A steep roof with narrow peaks stretched into the cloudy sky, punctuated by narrow dormer windows shrouded in shadows. The rooftop shingles formed a warped pattern that resembled a medieval thatched roof. You could easily imagine Hansel and Gretel being lured into this house. Cozy and welcoming on the outside, but hiding many secrets inside.

A wrought iron weather vane on the roof squeaked from the light breeze as she opened the mahogany front door. Exposed beams of wood stretched across the ceiling. A wide, arched doorway showed the separation of the large living room from the kitchen and dining room. Next to the arch, a small half bathroom was tucked discreetly next to the wide stairway that led to the second floor.

"You're late." Ivy Youngblood stood from where she was crouched at the baseboard molding near the stairs. As usual, Tempest's best friend and coworker was dressed from head to toe in shades of pink, including short fingernails painted bubble gum pink. The only *not* pink thing about her was the nail gun she brandished in her hand. A natural redhead, even her hair was pink adjacent.

"You were at Enid's library again," Ivy added, "weren't you?"

"If I said no, would you believe me?" Tempest kept her eyes on the nail gun.

Ivy raised an eyebrow before pulling the battery pack from the nail gun and setting it down. "I thought I was going to have to replace this old model with a boring new one when I misplaced it the other day. It's rather intimidating, isn't it?"

"Not nearly as fierce as you."

That got a smile. "Don't change the subject, Tempest. I can't believe you not only left us to finish up on our own *and* missed lunch, just to figure out who played a practical joke on Enid."

It was more than a practical joke. Tempest was sure of it. But nothing had been stolen from the library, so Enid was ready to move on. Ivy was right that there were more important things to do today.

"It won't happen again."

"No need to lie to me." Ivy pointed a pink-tipped finger at Tempest. "But you *can* help with the sliding bookcase that's stuck. Your dad got called away to work on another site, so he's not here to check it out."

This evening was their dress rehearsal for an interactive murder mystery play taking place at Gray House. The broken bookcase was part of the show. It needed to slide open to reveal clues to the solution of the mystery play. Tempest and Ivy had written the script that three local actors would be performing.

The murder mystery play was part of Hidden Creek's summer stroll, as was a literary-themed escape room that was housed on the second floor of Gray House. They'd already tested the escape room clues several times, so the "Escape from the Haunted Library" room was ready to open to the public this weekend.

This fairy-tale house was perfect not only for the book-themed mystery play and escape room, but also for what Gray House would become later that year: a library comprised exclusively of classic detective fiction.

Secret Staircase Construction had been hired by Harold Gray earlier that year to renovate the house. Like all projects the Secret Staircase team worked on, it aligned with their mission of bringing a touch of magic into homes. There was nothing remotely supernatural in their offerings. Their magic was made through woodworking details like hidden compartments in a built-in bookcase, or secrets carved in stone like a gargoyle whose wing was a lever to an underground room.

In Harold Gray's case, that meant helping him turn his home into a library brimming with books from British queen of crime Agatha Christie and hard-boiled American Dashiell Hammett to famed Japanese writer Seishi Yokomizo and little-known pulp authors that he'd collected for more than seventy-five years.

Harold was in his early nineties when they began the project. He wanted the Gray House Library of Classic Detective Fiction to be his legacy. He got the idea from Enid Maddox's Locked Room Library across the bay, which he'd frequented until his health declined. The Locked Room Library focused on impossible crime fiction, an even more specialized niche than Harold's dream. Harold hadn't lived to see his own library's completion, but his grandnephew was seeing it through.

Renovations to the house weren't yet completed, but the opportunity to get initial publicity by being part of Hidden Creek's once-a-year summer stroll was too good to pass up. Tempest had been tasked with creating the library's literary-themed murder mystery play and escape room for this coming weekend's stroll, which promoted local small businesses.

"It would be great to have this bookcase fixed for tonight," Ivy said, "but my own checklist is a long one."

"I'm on it." Tempest was good at this type of fix. It was the kind of thing she often needed to troubleshoot at the last minute before going on stage.

"I'll be testing the invisible ink on those faux-antiquarian books." Ivy held up three books that Tempest's grandmother, an artist, had hand-bound for them to use as clues in the interactive mystery play. None of them had liked the idea of defacing vintage books, so they'd created their own.

After Ivy departed to check the props, Tempest flipped into a headstand to look at the bookcase casters, which was probably where the problem lay.

In jeans, a fitted gray T-shirt, and ruby-red sneakers, Tempest was well dressed for flipping upside down to inspect a broken sliding bookcase, but decidedly unglamorous compared to her previous life. After years dressing in elaborate outfits and multiple costume changes for each show, she could now wear casual attire for her job at Secret Staircase Construction. The adjustment still felt surreal in many ways, but she'd surprised herself by how satisfying it was to work with her hands in a different way.

She would have gotten a better view if she'd flopped onto her belly and looked, but the aforementioned belly wasn't nearly as taut as it had been when she needed to leap from one spot on stage to the next with precision. She didn't get nearly as much exercise these days, so she added it where she could. Flipping upside down and balancing with the strength of her arms and abs—that was the key to proper form for a headstand—her body protested the exertion.

She didn't mind the blood flowing to her head. She was used to that. In some ways, it helped her focus on the matter at hand. Like now. She might not have spotted it if she'd looked from a normal angle. But here, from her focus, she saw the sharp marks on the bent casters. From a flathead screwdriver? This wasn't normal wear and tear, and definitely not shoddy workmanship—her dad would never have allowed that.

Before she could look more closely, a pair of black boots covered in dust came into view. Not just any dust, but stone dust. Which could only mean Gideon.

Tempest flipped right side up to see him properly, but immediately stumbled backward. Not because she was lightheaded or had lost her balance. The problem wasn't her admitted loss of physical stamina. It was that it wasn't Gideon's face in front of hers.

Facing Tempest was a wax bust of Agatha Christie. At least that's what she guessed it was. Half of the face had melted like a figure from a horror movie.

"Where did you get that monstrosity?" she asked.

"Tucked behind a stack of those uncataloged books in the garage. I was looking for a few more old books to add to the set for tonight."

There was, of course, no room for even one car in the detached two-car garage. Only thousands of books. Most likely, more than ten thousand. And, apparently, a ridiculous wax replica of Dame Agatha's head.

Gideon lowered the dusty bust. His dark brown eyes met hers with an intensity that she'd never encountered before she'd met him last year. There was something about him that made Tempest feel like he belonged in another century, before the world was full of so many distractions. Gideon didn't know the meaning of multitasking. If he looked at you, his attention was entirely focused on you.

"That head isn't only half melted." Tempest pointed at the bust resting in Gideon's arms. "It's also broken on top."

"Which is too bad, really." He set it on the mantelpiece above the hearth. "It's so creepy that it would make a perfect addition to a display in the horror-mystery section, but I'm worried it's about to break apart completely. People should really use more stone."

Tempest grinned. "Says the stone carver."

"What?" asked Gideon in all seriousness. "Stone is what lasts."

A stonemason by training and sculptor by passion, Gideon Torres was one of the Secret Staircase Construction crew members. Over the past year, with what they'd been through together, he'd become one of her closest friends. There were moments when she wondered if they were becoming more than that, but later this week, he was leaving for a three-month internship with a stonemason in France. Because when was life ever simple?

"Don't distract me." Tempest scowled at him. "I made an important discovery."

"You fixed the broken bookcase while standing on your head? Impressive."

"I didn't fix it," she said. "But I figured out what's wrong with it. And it's not good. This wasn't an accident. Someone wrecked it on purpose."

Chapter 2

"Sabotage?" Ivy scratched a pink fingernail over the jagged grooves cut into the casters. "Why would someone do this on purpose? It has to be a fluke."

They'd dumped all the books from the noir and hard-boiled detectives section onto the floor so they could lift the bookcase and properly examine the damage.

Tempest attempted to spin the wobbly wheels, but only got a half-spun squeak in return. "This isn't a fluke. The wheels were fine when we built this."

"But *who* could even have done it?" Ivy's eyes swept over the books strewn across the floor and over to the other bookshelves in the room filled with classic mysteries.

Tempest knew exactly what her friend was thinking. Ivy Youngblood had been her best friend since childhood, when they'd bonded over their shared love of mysteries. Ivy was the most well-read person she knew, and Ivy firmly believed that the solution to any real-life mystery could be found in the pages of a classic mystery novel or short story. Ivy intimately knew the twisty plots of the golden age "Queens of Crime"— Agatha Christie, Dorothy Sayers, Ngaio Marsh, and Margery Allingham—but her favorite author was John Dickson Carr, the master of the locked-room mystery, and Tempest suspected Ivy not-so-secretly wished to be as clever as Carr's most famous sleuth, Dr. Fell.

"Someone invisible," said Tempest.

Ivy snapped her gaze back to Tempest.

"Enid is officially in charge of the Gray House Library as it gets up and running," Tempest continued, "and last week, her own library was ransacked by an invisible intruder." She didn't like the connection.

"Anyone could have wrecked these casters," Gideon said. "We've had the house unlocked during the day while we've been working on it. A bunch of subcontractors were coming and going. I doubt we'd have noticed if someone else slipped in."

"A bunch of people don't want this library to open." Tempest looked toward the front windows. "One person in particular."

"Mrs. Hudson?" Ivy asked. "You think she snuck over here to wreck the sliding bookcase?"

Tempest shrugged. "There was also the water damage last week that we wasted a bunch of time looking for the source of. That could have been done on purpose as well."

The front door handle turned, and the door squeaked open. In walked the new owner of the house, Harold's grandnephew, Cameron Gray. Fair-haired with gray eyes that matched his name, those eyes grew wide as he took in the sight of his once-beautiful living room.

"I know Uncle Harold always said these books contained

lives of their own," he said, "but will someone please tell me how they flipped that bookcase upside down?"

"Didn't you notice it's the bookcase that was holding noir novels with brooding detectives?" Ivy asked with a straight face. "Unfortunately, they found our drawing room décor too cozy and comfortable. They needed some extra drama."

Cameron grinned. "I'm glad they've broken free, but will they be back in place by tonight?"

"As soon as we fix this bookcase," Tempest said. "It won't take long."

"We just need to get a new set of casters." Ivy straightened a stack of books they'd removed.

"And what is *that*?" Cameron's eyes fell to the Agatha Christie bust now resting in between two piles of books.

"A broken Agatha Christie head," Tempest said as she lifted the half-melted terror from the floor.

"We'll toss it onto the junk pile," Gideon added.

Ivy rolled her eyes. "You two are ridiculous. It's not broken. Only a little melted. That hole on top is obviously for flowers. It's a vase."

"No way," said Gideon.

Tempest turned the bust in her hands. *Huh.* Ivy was right. The edges were smooth. "No doubt meant for flowers from a poison garden."

Agatha Christie had been Harold Gray's favorite author, and she was well known for using poison expertly in her books. Harold's interest in poison was close enough to an obsession that before Secret Staircase Construction began work on the house, they'd hired a local botanist to look through the backyard garden to make sure there was nothing poisonous. Harold found their concern amusing, but he hadn't objected.

The botanist told them the most poisonous thing in Harold's

garden was oleander, a surprisingly common plant for home gardens. Most people didn't even realize it was poisonous. They hadn't renovated the garden area yet, but they wanted to remove the oleander before the library officially opened.

Ivy squinted as a bright flash of light shone across her face. Less than a second later, the blinding light was gone.

Tempest sprinted to the front window. She reached it in time to see binoculars disappearing from a window across the street. Beige curtains fluttered shut.

"Our spy is back."

The woman spying on them from across the street wasn't actually a spy. Well, probably. But her frequent use of binoculars certainly made it feel like it.

"What does Mrs. Hudson hope to see?" Ivy asked as she joined Tempest at the window.

"Gathering more evidence to use against me, I expect," Cameron answered, his voice in between anger and resignation.

"But we're not doing anything wrong." Tempest abandoned the window, anger welling inside her. "The library games were approved for the summer stroll, and we haven't begun the bigger renovations to make the second floor one big room for the library."

Why was it that one negative person could ruin something that was otherwise going so well? Tempest was all too aware life wasn't fair—the deaths of two people she loved dearly and the sabotage of her career had already taught her that—but why couldn't she get a break? This job at Gray House was supposed to be the one *without* drama. Tempest pushed past Ivy and Cameron to head across the street.

This was a residential street, but not straight or narrow. The town's layout was as quirky as its residents. Eighty percent of it was on a steep hillside, and a long-ago earthquake had caused the land to shift, and the creek moved underground—giving Hidden Creek its name.

Structural engineers made sure each house that was built would be structurally sound if there was another earthquake. That meant leaving plenty of room for vegetation so rainwater would flow down the hillside naturally, and building a lot of retaining walls. Therefore, the houses of Hidden Creek weren't as close to one another as they were in nearby cities. There were no houses behind or close to Gray House on either side, but Mrs. Hudson's house sat almost directly across the street.

The official architectural term for Harold Gray's home for the last sixty years of his life was *provincial revival*, but the unique design was referred to more casually as a "storybook" or "fairy-tale" style of house. The cozy style of architecture was briefly popular in Northern California in the 1920s, but here in Hidden Creek, it was the only house like it that Tempest had seen. Mrs. Hudson's home was a more standard bungalow, much like Tempest's house had been before her parents had renovated it into the labyrinth it was now.

"Where are you going?" Cameron asked Tempest. "You're in the middle of figuring out what to do about my wrecked bookcase."

"That's exactly what I'm doing." Tempest gripped the door knob. "It's time we had a proper conversation with your neighbor—to make sure nothing else like this happens again."

Cameron's eyes bulged, but it was Ivy who spoke. "Are you sure that's a good idea?"

Tempest raised an eyebrow. It was a skill she excelled at. It looked fierce, and it triggered whatever chemical it was in the body that made her *feel* fierce as well. "We've been tiptoeing around that woman for months. You haven't done anything wrong. None of us have. You can stay here, but I'm going to talk with her."

And, ideally, persuade the woman to confess.

Tempest didn't exactly plan to intimidate Mrs. Hudson. But her height and muscular frame, which she got from her dad, couldn't hurt. Her stage shows had always been physical, with illusions that involved acrobatics to pull them off. Pirouettes, leaps, and flips all contributed to her misdirecting the audience and telling heartfelt stories with more music and movement than dialogue. Her strength came in handy with construction work, but that was only her secondary role. She was the story-teller for Secret Staircase Construction, translating her theatrical skills into creating magical elements like the library games scripts and accompanying interior design.

"I'm with Ivy on this." Gideon took her hand in his to stop her. "I don't think this is such a good idea, Tempest."

She looked down at her strong hand in his warm, calloused one. The late spring and early summer had been so busy that she and Gideon had barely seen each other even when working on overlapping job sites. He hadn't been scared off by the multiple murder investigations Tempest had roped him into, which was a good sign for both friendship and the possibility of something more. And her hand felt so *right* in his. She didn't mind the permanent calluses. Still, she found herself pulling away. She was always pulling away. Life was safer that way.

"We have to do *something*." She twisted the doorknob, but Cameron stepped forward and blocked it with his foot.

He shrank back as she raised her eyebrow even higher and added a hand on her ample hip.

"What?" She turned back to face them as she swung open the creaking door. "Why are all three of you so opposed? What's the worst that can happen?"

Chapter 3

I n retrospect, uttering the words *What's the worst that can happen?* aloud is never a good idea.

Mrs. Hudson—whose first name had never been volunteered—stood in the doorway of her house, raising an eyebrow right back at Tempest. Tempest wavered, but only for a fraction of a second. Mrs. Hudson had decades longer than Tempest to perfect her eyebrow intimidation. It was good. *Very* good. But Tempest would not be cowed.

Mrs. Hudson hadn't invited Tempest into her home when they'd first met, and she didn't seem poised to do so now. She'd lived across the street from Cameron's great-uncle, Harold, for decades. Tempest had met her briefly when she'd first visited this street to interview Harold and find out his desires for renovations. But she didn't know much about the woman beyond the fact that she'd been close to Harold Gray until the last year of his life, when he had the plan to turn his home into a library.

"Yes?" Mrs. Hudson said when she finally spoke after eight seconds of staring at Tempest with that piercing raised eyebrow. Even though Tempest wasn't currently performing any shows that required timing that worked down to a fraction of a second, she still kept perfect time in her head. For some unfathomable reason, people usually didn't appreciate her innate timekeeping when she pointed out how wrong they were about how much time had passed.

Tempest couldn't intuit much about Mrs. Hudson, including her age. Her shoulder-length hair was white, and she wasn't a young woman, but it was impossible to guess her age. She was as tall as Tempest, with a similar muscular build. She held a paperback novel with a *Banned Books Week* bookmark poking out from its pages. It was a popular new mystery that had come out earlier that summer. Behind her, the living room was lined with bookcases brimming with books. Which was rather ironic, since she was the face behind the movement to stop the Gray House Library from being opened.

Tempest knew she should have responded with something nice. Placating. As she'd marched across the street, she'd been prepared to start off saying how she was sorry they'd gotten off on the wrong foot and wanted to put that behind them. But after her first hello was met with that cold stare and raised eyebrow? Tempest couldn't bring herself to apologize. That's how she found herself saying, "What do you hope to gain by your childish nuisance of spying on us at Cameron's house?"

For a fraction of a second, Mrs. Hudson looked impressed. But when she spoke, her cold demeanor was back. "Harold Gray should never have been granted planning permission to create those library games for this weekend's summer stroll, and Cameron shouldn't have moved forward with it after his great-uncle's death. It skews public opinion toward getting his library approved."

"You're a book person." Tempest nodded toward the book in her hand. "And a fan of mysteries. Why is having a library across the street so bad?"

Mrs. Hudson set the book on a side table that also held a pair of binoculars. She crossed her arms and leaned in the frame of her doorway, blocking Tempest's view. "You wouldn't understand."

"If it's the noise you anticipate—"

"It's not the noise," she snapped. "Which I doubt will be much anyway, even if book club gatherings include wine. I'm not interested in debating with you."

"Would you like to tell your side of the story about the property damage you did to our bookcase," Tempest said, "before I call the police?"

Mrs. Hudson's lips wrinkled as she pressed them together before she spoke. "I certainly don't know what you're talking about. Feel free to do whatever you wish. It'll only look bad for you. I haven't set foot inside Harold's house in years. Now, did you want something besides to berate me for bird-watching from my own home?"

"We both know you're not bird-watching."

Mrs. Hudson gave a thin-lipped smile. "Of course I am. Would you like to see the photos of bluebirds and sparrows on my phone? No? Oh, that's right. If you look at my phone, maybe you'll accidentally see all the terrible things they're saying about you online."

Tempest stiffened, but otherwise didn't react. *Don't feed the trolls.* The same advice for online interactions applied in real life. After horrible rumors about her had been volleyed at her a year ago, she'd gotten rid of all her social media accounts. A smaller flurry of activity had taken place a couple of months ago, with horrid people flinging accusations at her until she'd solved a mystery at Hidden Creek's Whispering Creek Theater. People still tossed her name around, online, hiding behind the faceless anonymity it afforded, but she also knew it was a lot healthier for her to stay out of it.

Mrs. Hudson's smile grew wider. She sensed that she'd struck a nerve. "Will that be all? Good luck getting those silly little games set up. They won't save the library, you know."

"Actually, the other residents of Hidden Creek aren't as anti-book as you are. I hear your petition to stop the library is failing spectacularly." Tempest had no idea if her words were true. She wouldn't know for two days, until the city council meeting. And even then, the petition wasn't the deciding factor as to whether the council voted to approve the library plans or not. Though she expected public opinion would sway them.

But her words had the intended effect. Mrs. Hudson's smile faltered.

Tempest didn't wait to have the door slammed shut in her face. She turned on the heel of her ruby-red sneaker and skipped down the steps of the front porch. She was on the last step when she heard the front door slam behind her.

Could she have handled that better? Definitely. Had she made things worse for their strained relationship with Mrs. Hudson? Perhaps. But it certainly felt satisfying to get in the last word.

Tempest paused on the sidewalk before crossing the quiet street. The storybook façade of Gray House was perfect for a book collector. Harold Gray had amassed a collection of thousands of books, but none of them were purchased for their monetary value. He wanted to read the books, not have them sit in pristine condition on the shelf.

Harold had been the type of person more comfortable around books than people. He'd quit a job as a bookseller because he didn't enjoy speaking with customers, and turned down a promising career recording radio dramas in the 1950s because he hated working in the recording studio with others. It was no surprise that he'd never married or had children. Though he hadn't liked spending time with people during his life, he liked the *idea* of people. As the end of his life approached, he hatched the idea of sharing the vast collection with people in his beautiful home. And he had the perfect person for his inheritance: his grandnephew, Cameron.

Cameron had recently finished his master's of library and information science degree and was working as a librarian at a small public library a few towns away, while renting a bedroom in a shared apartment with several roommates. On a librarian's salary, Cameron couldn't afford to buy a house in the area, so he was saving up to build a tiny house to have a place of his own. Cameron understood his uncle Harold better than the other members of his family and was happy to come over twice a week to read to him. Harold knew about Cameron's real estate woes, so they'd come up with the perfect plan to share the book collection and give Cameron a home: The first two floors would be turned into a library, and the spacious third-floor attic could be converted into an apartment with a floor plan like one of the tiny homes Cameron had been looking into building himself.

Harold had hired Secret Staircase Construction for both the attic renovation and the library renovation. The attic apartment was completed, and Cameron would be moving in once the library renovations were approved and completed. Nobody else had put up with Uncle Harold's eccentricities, so Harold wanted to repay the young librarian with this kindness.

The problem was that Gray House was on a residential street, not a commercial one. It was only a three-minute walk to the center of town. Easily walkable, and the local public library welcomed having a specialty library nearby. Librarians don't see other libraries as competition, and nobody thought it was a problem—until Mrs. Hudson raised an objection and began a campaign to stop the library.

Cameron Gray had put everything into realizing the vision he'd begun with his uncle when Harold was alive, but thanks to Mrs. Hudson, the city council might not approve the library plan. With a last glance back at the library-wrecker's house, Tempest walked up the cobblestone path to Gray House.

"Mrs. Hudson still has a grudge against Harold," Tempest said to Cameron as she came through the front door. "She didn't admit to messing with the bookcase, but she's definitely transferred her grudge to you."

She was about to add that perhaps Mrs. Hudson was simply the type of person who didn't like to see anyone else enjoying themselves, when she noticed the grave expressions of not only Cameron but also on Ivy's and Gideon's faces.

"What's happened?" she asked. Something was clearly very wrong.

"It's tonight's murder mystery play," said Cameron. "One of the actors is missing."

Chapter 4

L ucas Cruz, one of the three actors in their murder mystery play, wasn't technically missing. The actor simply had a conflict come up at the worst possible time. He was going to miss their dress rehearsal.

Typical. Lucas had grown up in Hidden Creek, a class clown who was a year behind Tempest and Ivy at school. As soon as Tempest made it big in Las Vegas, he'd gotten in touch with her to ask for an introduction for an acting gig. She made the introduction and he got the role, but he dropped out within a few months to pursue becoming a star in LA. He'd moved back to Hidden Creek about a year ago when his mom got sick. She'd died not too long ago, so Tempest was inclined to not be too hard on Lucas.

At least he'd located a replacement for today. Someone who was a skilled-enough performer to pull off a dress rehearsal on short notice.

"Since when does the Hindi Houdini consent to an amateur theater troupe performance?" Tempest asked Sanjay.

Sanjay Rai, known as "the Hindi Houdini" on stage, was the only one of Tempest's magician friends who'd stuck by her when she'd been accused of setting in motion a dangerous illusion that had wrecked her career and her entire life in Vegas.

She'd fixed the bookcase at Gray House, it was now late afternoon, and Sanjay was in Hidden Creek at Tempest's house. They were inside the secret turret above her bedroom, accessible only through two secret staircases. Tempest loved this small octagonal room. It was hers, and hers alone, which was a rarity in this sprawling, magical house she shared with her dad and her grandparents after moving home last year. She only invited her closest friends to join her here.

"At least he didn't ask me to perform a fake séance." Sanjay swept his bowler hat off his head and twirled it on his index finger. "You know those never go well for me."

"Or anyone else involved," Tempest murmured, wishing she could forget the bizarre death that had occurred during his last fake séance performance.

"Don't remind me." Sanjay flipped the bowler hat so high it nearly tapped the vaulted ceiling above. He caught it easily with his right hand, and as it came to rest in his palm, a puff of paper butterflies flew out of the hat. The paper creatures fluttered in the wind he was creating by blowing gently. If she hadn't known what to look for, it would have appeared as if he was simply smiling with parted lips.

Even knowing some of the steps involved in creating the illusion, it was every bit as magical. Six paper butterflies floated to their feet.

"Really," Tempest added. "Why did you agree to step in for Lucas? Procrastinating when you should be practicing?"

Sanjay shrugged. "I should always be practicing."

"Seriously, then. Why?"

He steepled his fingertips together. "I have my reasons."

"Fine. Be that way."

Sanjay wasn't the kind of magician who performed close-up magic and humorous patter, but a stage illusionist who commanded large audiences across the globe. He was selective in the gigs he accepted. Tempest had once been even more successful when she headlined a show in Vegas, but that meant she had farther to fall—and her career came crashing down in a heartbeat. One night, which wasn't her fault, had ruined it all.

She didn't begrudge Sanjay his success on any level. He was hardworking, talented, a great guy, and a loyal friend.

Plus, she didn't miss her old life on stage. Back home in Hidden Creek, working for her dad at Secret Staircase Construction, adding the magic to their renovation projects like her mom had done before she died, Tempest had found her calling. Here, she used what she loved most about magic, but on a more personal level. Occasionally, she'd get pangs of regret at how her career had ended, but she didn't want to be back on the stage full-time.

Until last year, she'd been living in a sprawling McMansion in Las Vegas, with Abra the rabbit her only roommate, easily paying the huge mortgage with her income as a headliner. But as soon as her show was sabotaged, the people she'd thought were her friends abandoned her. Only her family and friends back home believed in her innocence. Among her peers, Sanjay was the only magician in the country who'd wholeheartedly stood by her. He believed in her and defended her without question.

Moving home to her childhood bedroom hadn't felt great, but only because she'd been forced to do so as a failure whose house had been foreclosed upon. She didn't miss the generic house that was far bigger than one person and her pet rabbit needed. It was the fact that the move had been forced upon her through an unjust accusation, rather than a choice, that rattled her.

Sanjay ran a hand through his thick black hair, and a pang of something both pleasant and confusing stirred in Tempest. The most frustrating thing about Sanjay being back in her life was figuring out where exactly he *fit*. They'd dated once, years ago, when their careers were taking off, and they'd never been in the same place for long.

Now, it was the first time they were in the same geographic region for an extended period of time. But after everything they'd gone through this past year, Sanjay was more like her BFF number two, second to Ivy. She expected he felt the same about her. He was always casually dating someone or other. He steered clear of women from his fan club, the Hindi Houdini Heartbreakers, and none of his relationships lasted longer than a couple of casual dates. She loved him dearly and hoped he'd find the right person one day. She hoped they both would.

"Come on," said Tempest. "Let's grab a bite to eat and get back to Gray House."

"We have somewhere else to go that's more important than food."

"We do?"

Sanjay waved his bowler hat in front of Tempest's face. He repeated the movement a second time. The third time, it vanished.

She knew how the trick was done—it was all about perception and expectation—but she couldn't deny that Sanjay did it brilliantly.

"We have to get back to a different library," he said as the hat reappeared on his head from thin air. "You still haven't figured out how a thief remained *completely invisible* as they burglarized the Locked Room Library."

Tempest raised a skeptical eyebrow. "So the master escape artist and illusionist can see through the impossibility that little ol' me failed to spot?"

"Don't worry about missing it. Sometimes it takes an expert eye to see these things."

Tempest forced herself to remain calm on the outside, but her jaw clenched so tightly at his condescending assumption that a stab of pain shot through one of her molars. She amended her opinion from a minute ago. *This* was why she and Sanjay had never worked out as a couple.

"Fine," she said. Though she had no idea how Sanjay would get any further than she had. An intruder was captured on camera entering Enid's library, an old Victorian house in San Francisco with the library on the first floor and Enid's apartment above it. From there, the interior security cameras showed lamps, books, and the library's motion sensor raven being disturbed by the intruder—but the burglar remained invisible. "I'll let Enid know we're heading over. Let's see what the great Hindi Houdini can do."

Chapter 5

Three hours later, when Cameron opened the door of Gray House for Sanjay and Tempest's late arrival for the dress rehearsal, Sanjay was pouting. He hadn't solved the mystery of the invisible intruder either.

It was nearly half past eight, and a cappella jazz played on the speakers, setting the mood for the murder mystery play they'd set in the 1930s.

They wouldn't have been quite so late, except Sanjay had insisted they run an errand after visiting the Locked Room Library. Hopefully, loud, upbeat music meant the others were enjoying themselves as they waited.

As they stepped inside, Tempest realized that it wasn't music playing on the speakers at all. Kira Kendrick, one of the three actors hired for the play, stood in front of the fireplace, holding a prop cigar like a microphone. She belted out the jazz standard "Summertime," both looking and sounding like Billie Holiday as she did so.

Kira finished the last line of the song and took a bow. As her audience of six applauded and whistled, she donned a tweed jacket resting on the arm of the nearby love seat.

"Sorry we're late," Tempest said. "That was amazing, Kira. I'm sure Lucas will be disappointed he missed it."

She introduced Sanjay to both Kira and Milton Silver, the other actor they'd hired. Sanjay hadn't been involved in the library's escape game or murder mystery game until Lucas had canceled, so Lucas was the only one of the cast he'd met.

Sanjay already knew that night's audience members.

Enid Maddox had come over after locking up the Locked Room Library. Even with the increased demands on her time this summer, Enid had dressed up for the show. She was impeccably attired in her signature early twentieth-century style, which she'd adopted when she opened the library that specialized in books from that era. At first, she'd put on the vintage clothes like a uniform while working at the library, but as time went on, glamorous outfits from the 1920s to the 1940s became her daily attire. She'd changed from a Gatsby skirt to an A-line gown with a shoulder cape.

Cameron Gray was there, of course, and Ivy had come along as well tonight, since she'd written the play with Tempest. They'd invited Gideon, but he was packing up all his possessions from the house he rented, so he was short on time.

"We were wondering if you two would bail like Lucas," said Milton as he swirled a glass of red wine in his hand. "Everyone else has been here for half an hour. Even Enid, and she said you two were right behind her. At least your absence gave us time to try a glass of the bookshop's new cabernet."

Milton smiled, but it didn't reach his eyes. He was truly

annoyed that they were late. Matching his surname, thick streaks of silver ran through the fiftysomething actor's hair and well-groomed beard. In the tweed suit that made up his costume, he looked like a stereotypical version of his real-world profession of a rare books expert.

"My fault we're so late." Sanjay was dressed in a black sweater and slacks they'd found at a thrift store where he insisted they stop to shop, and it had taken three thrift stores to find something he deemed suitable. "Lucas gave me details of his costume, and I figured if I'm in, I'm all in. Even though I feel so strange performing without my tuxedo."

Sanjay tugged at the soft fabric of the collar. He was the only person for whom a cashmere sweater was *less* comfortable around his neck than a tuxedo's starched collar and tight bow tie. The only part of his standard stage outfit he hadn't given up was his bowler hat. The hat had been custom made for his stage shows, but it had become such a part of him that he wore it almost all the time. It was lined with hidden compartments, so Tempest admitted it came in handy.

"Want a drink before you get started?" Enid asked.

She didn't look happy tonight either. Not because Sanjay hadn't figured out what had happened at her library, but simply because she was busy. One of Harold's last wishes was for Enid to oversee setting up his library, since she had the experience of starting her own library. She took the responsibility seriously, rather than leaving it to inexperienced Cameron, and he was grateful for the help.

"Wine?" asked Milton.

"A glass of water would be much appreciated." Sanjay stopped fiddling with his costume and gave them all a charming smile that Tempest noted made Kira blush.

Kira was the youngest of the bunch. In her midtwenties, she

was an assistant librarian at the Hidden Creek Public Library. Stylish oversize glasses rested on the thin bridge of her nose, gold bangles adorned both wrists, and a tweed jacket hung loosely on her small frame.

Milton, Kira, and Lucas Cruz were all members of the Creekside Players, an amateur theatrical troupe. Hidden Creek's solitary theater was filled with a murderous past, a supposed ghost, and uncomfortable seats, so the Creekside Players sought out other venues, like this one.

"I'll grab the water," Cameron said. "Tempest?"

She nodded. "Thanks."

"There'll be a big block of ice here on the bureau on the nights of the performances," said Kira.

"For verisimilitude, since it's the 1930s," Milton added unnecessarily. "So there will be an ice pick here, too."

"I thought you were only serving this wine from the Hidden Winery." Sanjay pointed at the half-empty bottle.

As part of the murder mystery play evening at the library, attendees would first be served dinner at beloved local restaurant Veggie Magic, with Hidden Winery wines accompanying their food. After walking five minutes to the Gray House Library for the murder mystery game, they'd have the option of an after-dinner glass of wine or a nonalcoholic beverage.

The winery was a passion project for the couple who ran the Hidden Bookshop, the small bookstore on Main Street where Milton worked. He was close to the bookshop owners, so he wanted their new side-project launch to go well. The winery wasn't mass-producing wine, but instead would be serving at the Hidden Wine Bar, their new addition next door to the bookshop. Tempest wasn't a patron of the bookshop, because it specialized in rare and antiquarian books, but Secret Staircase Construction had built the book-themed secret entrance that ran between the two shops, and she looked forward to trying its new wine bar extension after its grand opening this weekend.

"It's the only brand of wine being served," said Milton. "But attendees will have other options. I don't see the vintage ice pick right now, but you can see the aged glass bottle with the gasket that's just like the ones they really used in the early 1900s. It's so important to get the little details right, don't you think?"

"Which reminds me—" Kira rummaged through a cute little backpack covered with colorful pins until she found a glasses case. She slipped off her large glasses and swapped them for a pair of small round wire-framed glasses with no lenses. She grinned at them. "That's better. Much more style-appropriate for the 1930s." She blinked at them and laughed. "But I'll have to make sure I remember to put in my contact lenses before the first real show."

Sanjay pulled out his phone and began looking up glasses styles in the 1930s.

Milton cleared his throat loudly. When it failed to solicit a response from Sanjay, he did so again.

Tempest tapped Sanjay's shoulder. "I think he's trying to get your attention about your cell phone."

"The play is set in 1935." Milton held out his hand, with the palm facing up. "No cell phones."

Sanjay gaped at him. "You're Method actors? Wait. You're seriously confiscating my phone? Like we're in high school?"

Tempest handed Milton her own phone. "Rules of the games. Following the clues of the play and finding a way out of the escape room are much more fun without phones. That way, you can't look things up like you're doing now—"

"This isn't a clue!" Sanjay insisted. "I'm simply curious—"

"There's a secured cabinet in the kitchen," Ivy said, "with numbered bags for phones."

"But I'm not a participant, I'm one of the actors." Sanjay blinked at Ivy and Milton as if they'd each grown a second head.

"I think you'll survive the next hour without your phone." Tempest plucked the phone out of his hand. If he'd wanted to, he could have made it vanish into thin air before she got to it, but in spite of his protestations, he was a good sport.

"You all ready for a full run-through?" Cameron asked as he returned from the kitchen with their glasses of water.

"I've got my part memorized already," said Sanjay. "Good thing I don't need my phone."

Cameron accepted the two phones from Tempest and locked them up in the kitchen with the other phones. He gave them each a thick rubber band with a number on it. It wasn't necessary for such a small group, but it would be needed for the larger groups that would be there that weekend.

Milton clapped his hands together. "Places, everyone."

Tempest took a seat in one of the wooden folding chairs that had been set up behind the rest of the furniture, which was organized in a U shape, so that everyone could see the actors where they'd be performing in front of the unlit fireplace. Ivy and Cameron were sitting on the rented futon. Enid looked dainty in the oversize armchair that had been Harold's favorite reading spot. The love seat remained empty, but Tempest thought it best to try out the folding chairs to make sure they were comfortable enough for the dozen attendees who didn't get one of the eight comfiest spots in the spacious living room. They'd belatedly realized they needed to rent the folding chairs and futon after figuring out that Harold didn't have enough furniture to accommodate the audience they had in mind. Luckily, Kira's cousin managed a furniture rental company,

Storage Solutions, which was able to rent them the extra furniture at the last minute.

The folding chair gave only a slight jiggle as Tempest crossed her legs. It wasn't cushioned, since the design was a good one that let the wooden chairs fold flat and thus be a good storage solution as the name of the company implied. The chair was surprisingly comfortable, but something else was bothering her.

She scanned the room, trying to identify what it was. As Kira stepped into the room to begin the performance, she knew what it was. The futon in front of her was low enough that she could see the coffee table in front of it. This wasn't the original coffee table. It had been replaced by a steamer trunk. One she recognized, but not from here. She would have noticed it right away if they hadn't arrived late and been rushed.

The steamer trunk that now sat in the middle of the room wasn't Harold's or Cameron's—it was *Sanjay's*. One he used for his magic show performances. What was it doing here now?

Sanjay had an ulterior motive for accepting this last-minute request. Just what did he have in store for them at tonight's performance?

Chapter 6

A crash of thunder sounded. The soundtrack of the evening had begun.

"Welcome to the Hidden Creek Manor House," said Kira Kendrick. She was playing the role of Dr. Keys, a research librarian working at this "manor house."

"I know the circumstances aren't ideal." She paused and wrung her hands together. "This fierce storm has brought you here. The creek has overflowed, and your tour bus can't get past. You'd think in our modern age—1935—after we've survived the war and the Depression, that we'd have better roads. It's almost as if our town is cursed."

Thunder crashed once more over the speakers. This time, more loudly.

Enid jumped. She hadn't seen their staged reading earlier that week.

"I'm Dr. Keys," Kira continued. "Not the medical kind, but a research librarian. I hope you'll forgive me if I seem a bit distracted as I welcome you to this isolated estate and its library." She swept her arm in front of her body, indicating the bookshelves that lined the walls. "I completed my PhD in library science only last year, but I've already made an exciting discovery. And it happened right here in this very library! Oh, but none of you are interested in these dusty old shelves. I won't bore you with those details—"

"Go on, Dr. Keys." Milton Silver stepped into the room from the kitchen serving as backstage. "It's an important discovery."

"This is my colleague and mentor, Dr. Locke," Kira said. "He's a world-renowned archivist. He helped me authenticate the discovery I made here at the library. A centuries-old document that confirms the existence of something *very special* here in Hidden Creek."

Tempest had learned that Kira and Milton had a similar mentor-mentee relationship in real life, so she and Ivy wrote to that dynamic. Kira was around the same age as Ivy and Tempest, and Milton was around the age of Tempest's dad. The pair had bonded during the first Creekside Players show they'd performed together several years ago.

The idea was for this to be an interactive murder mystery at a country manor house straight out of an Agatha Christie novel. Dr. Keys, Dr. Locke, and their assistant, Archie V.—played by Kira, Milton, and Lucas—were doing archival research in the stately home and had made an important discovery in the library.

Members of the audience entered the house as if they were members of the stranded tour group. But when one of the characters is murdered, the audience members are the witnesses who must uncover the culprit. In this house filled with thousands of books, creating clues had been a delight for Tempest and Ivy.

The background sound of a violent storm played on a speaker from the moment the audience arrived. After everyone had been given drinks and a short time to chat and look around the room, the actors would perform a ten-minute scripted skit, and then the more interactive portion of the games would begin.

"Dr. Keys called me as soon as she made her exciting discovery," said Milton. "Go on, tell them all about it."

Kira beamed at the audience. "This old manor house is filled with secret passageways. They were added because the man who built it needed more space for all his books. Keep in mind that this house isn't far from the creek. Down in his labyrinthine secret hallways, he also had a secret desk where he kept a diary. In it, he recorded sightings of a mythical creature known to live in the water. A *kelpie*."

"Yes, a kelpie from Scottish folklore!" Milton wriggled his eyebrows like a villain from a silent film. It was more than a bit over the top, but it caused both Cameron and Enid to laugh, which was the point. The audience was supposed to have fun.

Tempest wanted to have fun with it, too. She based the play on the folklore she'd learned from her Scottish grandmother.

"Kelpies," said Kira, "are shape-shifting spirits that haunt lochs and other waterways. They appear as large black horses. If you see one, you might notice there's something not quite right about them. Maybe they're a little too big. Or strike you as too human. Which makes sense, since they then shape-shift into human form."

Milton rubbed his tweed-covered arms as he shivered dramatically.

"Don't confuse kelpies with the selkies of Scottish mythology," Kira continued. "Selkies appear in the water as seals and transform into beautiful women on land. But kelpies look like horses, are more often male—and are *far more dangerous*."

"As Dr. Keys also discovered in documents here in the library," Milton said, "a kelpie has been sighted at the water's edge in Hidden Creek for more than a century before our town was founded. Our very own Dr. Keys here discovered the documents after her curiosity was piqued by the diary."

"The evidence was here the whole time." Kira paused and looked wistfully at the sliding bookcase, causing the audience to follow her gaze, as she intended. "I only thought to look in the archives where others hadn't. The original owner of Creekside Manor was an immigrant from Scotland. He believed he was cursed and that he unwittingly brought the spirit with him to America. *Was he right?* This is what I'm still researching in these archival materials. There are still many secrets to be found in this house."

"Perhaps our guests would like to help with our research?" Milton asked. "We believe there are secrets hidden in the pages of the books in the library of this manor house."

"Oh, you'd like that, wouldn't you?" Sanjay charged into the room, glowering at the librarians.

"Archie V.," said Milton, his voice clipped. "I don't believe you've met our guests yet."

Archie V.'s name was a play on the word *archive*, but the joke of the rearranging of the letters of the word was too subtle to pick up on verbally. The real audience this weekend would be handed a simple one-page program that included the cast list along with hints for where to look for clues.

"Our unexpected guests are a convenient cover for you to slip forged historical documents into the library," Sanjay continued. "Perhaps one of them will accidentally stumble across something you've planted."

"Don't be ridiculous," Milton sputtered, stepping protectively in front of his protégée. "How dare you accuse Dr. Keys of impropriety in our noble profession!"

Kira's glasses slipped down her nose. "Don't mind him, Dr. Locke. Archie is simply jealous that I'm the one to have made the discovery. That I'm the one who'll get the credit. That I'm—"

The lights went out, and the room was plunged into nearly complete darkness.

The cap gun popped. The gun thudded to the floor, as did a body. *Another* thud sounded. Another one? Had Sanjay shifted position for some reason?

There was a sliver of light, but Tempest's eyes hadn't yet adjusted for her to see what was going on when the lights came back on.

Sanjay lay on the carpeted floor, but he was on his stomach, not his back as he was supposed to be. In the role he'd taken over from Lucas, he needed to be face up to say his last line as Archie V., and to point at the bookshelf to give the audience a "dying clue."

For four seconds, everyone was silent, waiting for Sanjay to say his next line. Which he'd clearly forgotten.

In the script, the actor playing the now-dead character would take on the role of the detective. With the detective trapped at the isolated manor and unable to summon backup, they were all in it together. The audience would need to follow clues to catch the guilty party.

"You forgot your line." Milton stepped away from the light switch he'd been in charge of turning off and on, and kicked Sanjay's shoe.

His shoe . . . Tempest frowned. Something wasn't right about his shoes. They weren't his. Why had he swapped his shoes in the darkness? There must have been some purpose for his trick, but she couldn't think of what it might be.

"Come on, Sanjay," said Kira. "You're supposed to be face up so we can see your fake bullet hole and you can point to the bookshelf while you say your line." She looked at Tempest. "We can't fault him for not remembering the staging or his lines, since he's just filling in."

"Something's wrong." Tempest knelt down and shook his shoulders. "Sanjay?" He didn't move.

Even more disturbingly, as soon as she'd touched his shoulders through that thick fluffy sweater, she knew something was very wrong. His body felt nothing like the Sanjay she knew. Her heart thudded more frantically than it ever had on stage in front of thousands. Something was very wrong.

His body was a deadweight. Had he hit his head on the steamer trunk? Something both looked and felt entirely wrong about his body. Tempest had the most horrifying thought that Sanjay's soul had left his body and that's why he felt so wrong. She flipped him over.

A bullet hole was in the center of his chest.

But that wasn't the most shocking thing about the body in her arms.

This wasn't Sanjay. It was Lucas, the missing actor who'd recently moved home to Hidden Creek. And he was dead.

Chapter 7

Kira and Cameron screamed. Their voices jolted Tempest out of her stunned inaction, and she scanned the room carefully. It was almost exactly as it had been before the lights went out. Except for the dead body of Lucas Cruz that lay next to the steamer trunk.

No, that wasn't the only difference.

"Sanjay?" Tempest called out. There was no answer. *Where had he gone?*

Ivy stumbled backward and crashed into Cameron.

"He's dead," Kira whispered.

"He can't be dead," Milton said. "He's an actor. He's acting. Lucas, this isn't funny!"

Enid swore and knelt at the body. "*How?*" she murmured, looking up at them. "The gun . . . It wasn't real, was it?"

"Of course not," Tempest answered. Could she be sure, though?

"I fired the gun," Milton whispered, his face a pale imitation of the peppy actor he'd been minutes before. "God, it was me. I swear I didn't know it could kill someone. It's a toy!"

The gun lay on the floor a few feet away. It was the same prop gun Tempest recognized. A cap gun. A real bullet couldn't have been used in that little plastic gun. It wasn't possible, even if someone had murderous intentions.

"That gun doesn't take real bullets," said Enid. "It's impossible."

What was even more impossible was that only moments before, Lucas had been Sanjay. That's why he'd insisted on finding the perfect sweater. He'd planned this swap.

"Sanjay?" Tempest called out again. "Something has gone horribly wrong with your trick." Her mouth was dry. *What had Sanjay done?* "Where are you hiding?"

This had to be a trick gone wrong. What had the two men been up to? If this had been a bullet-catch trick, they'd have wanted an audience. Not this. Who had shot Lucas? It couldn't have been Sanjay. Not even as an accident.

"Sanjay!" Kira called with a much sharper tone. "Get your ass out here!"

"The police," said Cameron. His voice shook. "We need to call—"

"You took our phones," said Milton as he patted down his pockets and realized they were empty.

"So people wouldn't cheat and look up clues online." Cameron spoke the words like a zombie. He was in shock.

Ivy shook his shoulders. "It's all right, Cam. You have the key to the cabinet. You can get our phones."

Everyone filed out of the living room and into the kitchen.

Tempest knew that swaps could happen so quickly on stage that the audience would never suspect a thing. But why did Sanjay and Lucas arrange this? Both men had similar thick black hair, and similar medium builds, both around Tempest's five foot ten, so it made sense they'd work together as stage doubles. But *why?*

"I'm going to be sick." Kira gulped. She rushed toward the bathroom, but Milton grabbed her arm.

"We shouldn't go anywhere alone," he said.

"You want to go with her to the *bathroom?*" Enid looked sharply at him.

"Well, er, no, but none of us should be alone. I didn't kill him with that prop gun. Meaning—"

"Oh God." Kira broke free and ran the last few steps to the bathroom adjoining the kitchen, barely making it before she threw up. She hadn't taken the time to close the door behind her. Which seemed to satisfy Milton for her safety, but wasn't great for Tempest's own stomach.

"We can see her." Enid winced. "And hear her. Satisfied?"

Milton still looked concerned. Did he think they had to keep an eye on her because he was worried she could be next, or because he thought she could be a killer?

Cameron's keys clattered to the kitchen floor. His hands were shaking, so it wasn't surprising he was having trouble unlocking the cabinet that contained their phones.

Milton steadied himself on the counter. "I fired the shot." He took three loud, short breaths. He was hyperventilating.

Enid spotted it, too. "No, you didn't." She spoke gently and put her hand on his shoulder. "You used the toy gun as planned. A plastic prop. It wasn't your fault."

"You're kind to say so," he said, his breathing still clipped, "but do you think it's possible I could have fired a real bullet from that thing? Why did I ever think becoming an actor to impress my daughter was a good idea?"

"Let's sit down on one of the dining chairs over here," Enid said gently, though her voice had a faint tremor as well. The kitchen opened up into the dining room through another open archway. The living room wasn't visible from the dining room, but everyone was now in the kitchen or dining room within sight of one another. Even the bathroom door was in sight of the kitchen.

Cameron fumbled the keys once more. They jingled as they dropped to the kitchen's linoleum tiles.

Tempest turned her attention away from Milton and back to the cabinet. "Do I need to smash that lock?" It wouldn't take much to open it.

"A landline," said Enid. "I know Howard had a landline somewhere around here." She stood up and started rummaging through the large bureaus of the dining room. Tempest didn't remember seeing a phone when they'd worked on the house, so perhaps it was tucked away? She opened a wood-and-glass cabinet displaying dishes and knickknacks.

Cameron called after them without looking up from the locked kitchen cabinet, "I got rid of Harold's old phone. The line was shut off after he passed away."

"I'll open it." Ivy took the dropped keys and had the cabinet door open within five seconds. She hastily distributed phones while Enid and Milton came back into the room muttering about the foolishness of younger generations giving up landlines. At least the common cause seemed to have stopped Milton from hyperventilating and passing out.

"I'll call." Enid snatched her phone. "Everything at Gray House is my responsibility."

They all looked expectantly at Enid as she dialed 9-1-1, their heavy breathing broken up by Kira's dry heaves. She joined them with a sour expression as Enid explained the situation to the dispatcher.

"They'll be here in a few minutes," Enid said.

"Where the hell is Sanjay?" Kira asked.

Where, indeed. They trudged back to the living room—an *empty* living room.

The body was gone.

Chapter 8

L et me get this straight," said the police officer who'd arrived quickly. "There's no body, no blood, a fake prop gun, and the 'dead man' you saw was an actor in a murder mystery play?" He looked expectantly at the group.

"Well, when you say it like that," said Enid, "it sounds like a joke."

"Sanjay wouldn't play a joke like this," Tempest snapped.

"When someone is shot," said the officer, "there's blood. It's not like an old black-and-white movie where they fall down clutching their chest without even a bullet hole in their clothing."

"But there *was* a bullet hole," Ivy whispered.

The officer's expression softened as he looked around at their freaked-out faces. "Look. I can tell you're all really shaken. But what you're describing is impossible. There's no blood here." He pointed at the cream-colored carpet. "And no bullet hole."

"I hate to say it," said Milton. "but I was the one who fired the gun. He was standing, so the bullet would be somewhere in the wall."

"No bullet could be fired from this toy gun," the officer said. "I'm afraid your friends are playing a joke in very poor taste."

"It's not a joke," Tempest insisted. "Sanjay wouldn't—"

"If it's *not* a joke," the officer cut in, "your missing friend is the main suspect."

That shut Tempest up.

The officer took a cursory look around the living room, but without finding a body, blood, or a bullet hole, he departed shortly thereafter.

As the door creaked shut behind the officer, Tempest grimaced. How could she have failed to see the obvious? "We never heard the front door open and close."

"Um, are you trying to say the police officer was a figment of our collective imaginations?" Milton asked.

"Before that." She pulled the front door open. It creaked once more as they all heard the police car driving away. "It was also bolted from the inside when we opened it for that officer. Lucas didn't leave through the front door."

She thought back on when they'd all gone into the kitchen and the body had disappeared. *No creak.* Swinging the door closed as silently as she could, Tempest still heard a loud creaking that included a squeak, followed by a satisfying *click*.

"This door makes noise. It both makes a click when it closes and creaks when it swings open and closed."

"Oh, of course," said Ivy. "I should have thought of that."

"What?" Milton asked. "What should you have thought of? What are you *of course*-ing?"

"*Lucas and Sanjay didn't leave the house*," Tempest explained. "We had the back door in our sights the whole time, and the front door never opened."

Tempest ran to the sliding bookcase she'd fixed that afternoon and slid it open.

Nothing. Only a second bookcase behind it, with a clue the guests would find during the interactive portion of the evening. There wasn't room for Lucas or Sanjay to be hiding in that spot. What was she thinking? The problem was she *wasn't* thinking. She was freaked out, which was a problem if they were going to figure this out.

"They're hiding in the house," Ivy said.

"Where could they—" Tempest thought aloud, then bounded up the stairs. Unlike the front door, the stairs were completely silent. Anyone could have gone up the stairs without being detected.

"I'm going to kill Lucas when we find him," Kira muttered as she followed Tempest up the stairs. The others were close behind.

"Enid, Cameron," said Tempest as she reached the second-floor landing. "You two stay here."

"Is there something to search here?" Enid ran her fingertips over the wallpaper. "A well-hidden door?"

Tempest shook her head. "From here, you can see both upstairs and downstairs. You two are the lookouts—in case they're on the move. The rest of us will search."

Exposed wooden beams adorned the ceilings of each room, even when not structurally necessary, but the steeply pitched roof didn't leave room for many hiding spots inside. Neither did the fact that most of the nooks and crannies had been filled with books. Books, books, books. And Lucas hadn't shrunk down to fit between the covers of a book.

Their search through the storybook house felt more and more like they were in a dark fairy tale. One with a ticking clock.

Tempest bumped her head on the small table in the library escape room game, causing the book resting on the table to fall to the floor. *The Corpse in the Waxworks* by John Dickson Carr. One of their escape room clues.

She rubbed the sore spot on her head. Why did she feel such urgency? She knew the answer. Sanjay wouldn't be part of such a distasteful joke. Not willingly.

"They're not upstairs hiding in Cameron's soon-to-be apartment," Ivy said, poking her head through the door.

"And none of the windows were open," Milton added from behind her.

"The attic is too high to get down safely," Tempest said. "But I checked the windows in the second-floor rooms as well. Locked from the inside."

"Find anything?" Enid's voice called.

"Might as well regroup downstairs," Tempest said, hating to admit defeat. She gave one last glance at the library escape room before following the others downstairs. They didn't need to search the garage, since it was detached from the house, but for good measure, they took a look. Stacks upon stacks of books were piled into semiorganized towers, leaving only narrow aisles and nowhere for anyone to hide. In the living room, Tempest peeked inside the steamer trunk, lifted the removable cushions of the love seat, and looked underneath every piece of furniture.

"I don't understand." Cameron sank into his uncle's old armchair. "I'd swear Lucas was dead."

Tempest stood in front of the hearth and surveyed the room's bookshelf-lined walls. "And they *both* vanished."

"The officer was right that there wasn't blood." Ivy bit her nails. "Maybe they escaped out a window?"

Enid drummed her fingernails nervously on a book she clutched in her hands. "I didn't see blood oozing from the hole in his shirt either. Maybe it really was a joke." Enid's voice shook, belying her words. "We're all well versed enough in detective fiction to realize that people at the scene of a crime are terrible eyewitnesses."

Before Tempest could see what book she was holding, Enid tucked it into a hidden pocket of her skirt.

"Are you feeling all right?" Tempest asked.

Enid smoothed her dress and looked at her hands. "There's a school of thought that says you should always trust your gut. That it's an instinctive survival mechanism. That even before your conscious, rational brain can process a piece of information from your surrounding environment, your brain knows something is wrong. It knows the truth."

"The lizard brain," said Kira. "Sure."

"I've always fought against that," Enid said softly, still looking at her hands. "I never believe my eyes. We know eyewitness testimony is reliably wrong. We *can't* trust what we see."

"What did you see, Enid?" Tempest asked softly.

A sad smile spread across Enid's lips, and she looked up at Tempest. "It's not what I saw today. It's what I saw when—" She broke off, her eyes glazing over again.

"What did you see?" Tempest's voice was nearly a whisper.

"It doesn't matter."

"It matters," Cameron said softly. "What did you see?"

Enid shook her head. "In the classic detective novels I love, there are clues hidden in plain sight, but we just can't see them. If witnesses are convinced they've seen a ghost or a miraculous event, they haven't really seen what they think they have. It's simply the culprit temporarily outsmarting the detective. There's always a rational explanation at the end. I've always been *so sure* that's how the world worked."

She paused and looked around the room at each of them. Tempest stood closest to her. Cameron sat in Harold's old armchair and Ivy on the nearby futon. Milton and Kira stood together near the sliding bookcase.

"What if . . ." Enid said finally. "What if I was wrong? What if it's not a living person who did this? You know what happened at my library last week. My invisible intruder. I've tried to tell myself it was just a prank and it doesn't matter, but nobody has been able to explain the lamps the invisible man knocked over, the fact that my motion sensor raven cawed at him, and the books I found turned upside down. And now this?"

Ivy crossed her arms and scowled. "Are you really saying a ghost made Sanjay and Lucas vanish? Enid, you run the Locked Room Library! A place where rationality prevails, even if it takes a while to figure out what really happened. You love those books."

"I do," Enid agreed. "They're what I wish the world were really like. Rational explanations. Justice at the end. But real life *isn't* like that. We don't get a neatly tied bow at the end."

"Enid," Tempest said. "*What did you see?*"

With a shaking hand, Enid removed a slim paperback from the pocket of her skirt. *The Wheel Spins* by Ethel Lina White.

"Never heard of that book," Milton said. "Any good?"

"Where have I heard that title?" Kira asked, but she looked as if she were asking herself.

Cameron swallowed hard. "Oh no . . . You don't really think . . . do you?"

Enid met his gaze. "It was one of your uncle's favorites."

"I know." Cameron looked pale once again. He blinked and looked up at the rest of them. "It's the book that Hitchcock's film *The Lady Vanishes* is based on. Harold always loved a good vanishing."

"Let me get this straight," Kira said. "You two believe that because Cameron's uncle Harold loved old books and films about vanishings, he's come back from the dead to haunt his house, kidnap Sanjay and Lucas, and hide both of them somewhere so ingenious that we can't find them?"

"*Or worse*," said Enid. "Can't you feel something off about our surroundings?"

"Are you sure we can't get you something to drink?" Milton asked. "A glass of wine would take the edge off."

Enid shook her head firmly.

"Enid," Tempest said softly. "The house feels creepy and mysterious *on purpose*. Because we fixed it up for the library escape room game and murder mystery party."

"I've been to my share of murder mystery parties," Enid said. She walked across the room and slipped the book back in place on the shelf. "There's something else going on here."

"I need a drink," Milton said, a bottle poised above his glass.

"No!" Enid grabbed the bottle out of his hand.

"Poison," Cameron whispered. "Harold loved books with poisons. As long as they were done right, like Agatha Christie's poisonings."

"I don't know about the rest of you," Enid said, "but I'm getting out of here. Harold! If you're listening, I really did enjoy knowing you in life, and I hope you're at peace now, but I hope we don't meet again."

Enid slammed the bottle onto the bureau and pushed past Ivy. Milton and Kira followed.

"I, um . . ." Milton fidgeted in the doorway. "I suppose I'll be off as well. Good luck with . . . uh, whatever this is."

"It's been an interesting evening, Cameron," said Kira. "If this isn't actually a ghostly invasion and our missing actors come clean and repent, I'll see you tomorrow night for one last chance at a dress rehearsal."

The front door squeaked once more as Enid, Kira, and Milton departed.

Tempest took *The Wheel Spins* off the shelf. There *was* a rational explanation at the end of the story. Why was Enid so shaken? What *had* she seen?

"What do you think Enid is keeping from us?" Ivy asked.

"I can't imagine she's involved," Cameron said. "But why was she acting so strangely? She was so convincing she almost had *me* convinced Uncle Harold is haunting—"

A rap on the front door made him break off.

Cameron looked through the front window and gasped.

"Who is it?" Ivy whisper-screamed. "Why did you react like that?"

"I can't see them." Cameron swallowed hard as the knock sounded again.

"What do you mean you *can't see them?*" Tempest asked. How could he not? If there was an invisible man on the porch, she was going to scream. She nudged Cameron aside to look through the window. "What the . . ."

"Who is it?" Ivy clasped her hand over her mouth after she spoke.

"I don't know," Tempest whispered.

It was true. The person's face was obscured by a huge bouquet of roses. The delivery person reached up and knocked on the door once more. His hands gave him away. She knew those hands. Half of her worry vanished. But she had a hell of a lot more questions.

"I have no idea what's going on," said Tempest, "but the person at the door can tell us."

She flung open the door.

Chapter 9

Sanjay strode into Gray House with a broad smile on his face.

"For you, m'lady." Sanjay's smile fell away. "Hey, where's Kira?"

"Kira?" Tempest grabbed the flowers and flung them to the floor. A mangled rose petal landed on her red sneaker. "You and Lucas staged this macabre joke for *Kira*?"

Sanjay sputtered, "I know I'm late, but the florist Lucas wanted me to go to was already closed. I didn't have my cell phone to call and let him know. Where *is* everyone? I didn't take that long, did I?"

Ivy reached Tempest's side and stomped on the flowers in solidarity.

"Hey." He frowned at the crushed petals. "Those were expensive."

"Forget about the flowers." Tempest glared at him.

"Yeah," said Cameron. "How could you and Lucas play such a cruel joke on us?"

Sanjay blinked at them. "Swapping places? A surprising twist, yes, but I wouldn't characterize it as a *joke*. It was a pretty good quick-swap routine, if I do say so myself. Where's Lucas?" He looked around the living room and peeked into the kitchen and dining room.

"How the hell did you get out of the house?" Tempest asked. "And don't act like you don't know where Lucas is."

"If he's still alive at all," Cameron said.

Sanjay chuckled, then broke off as he saw that Cameron wasn't joking. "What? *Really?* There was an accident after I left? I'm so sorry. Is he in the hospital? Did the others go with him? That's why you were all so mad at me! You could have filled me in."

"The bullet hole was part of the joke?" Cameron asked.

"*Bullet hole?*" Sanjay stared at them. "Someone *shot* him?"

"You're the magician," Ivy said. "How did you miraculously vanish both yourself and Lucas? Or is he actually dead? Was it a bullet-catch trick gone wrong? I'm sure the police will understand if it was an accident—"

"What the hell is happening?" Sanjay tugged on the rim of his bowler hat. "It's like I've stepped into an alternate dimension."

"You'd better start at the beginning," said Tempest.

"Me?" He gulped.

"*You,*" Tempest and Ivy said at the same time. Cameron nodded but looked incapable of speech. It was far more likely he was about to punch Sanjay. Which would have been very bad both for his ego and his upcoming performances.

"How am I supposed to know where Lucas disappeared to? All I did was walk out the back door during the darkness when Lucas and I switched places."

They stared at Sanjay in silence for five seconds.

Tempest groaned. "The actors were all making noise in the dark, and with us in the living room, it wasn't yet impossible for you to leave through the back door. All you had to do was walk out in the dark. It was only *after* Lucas was lying on the floor a few seconds later that we saw what was happening and then ran to the kitchen so nobody could have left that way."

"You were running after me?" Sanjay asked.

"We were getting our phones to call the police," Tempest said. "Since we found Lucas dead."

"This wasn't part of the plan," Sanjay wailed.

"You two had a plan?" Cameron asked.

"Of course. Why else would I switch places with him and show up with roses?"

"Get back to your explanation," said Tempest. "*Now.*"

Sanjay picked up the open wine bottle.

"I wouldn't do that if I were you," said Ivy.

"That bad?"

Tempest took the bottle. "I don't really believe it was poisoned by a ghost, but probably best not to take any chances."

Sanjay's eyes widened for half a second, but he quickly recovered and strode to the central point of the room: the fireplace. Always the performer. "I was doing a favor for Lucas," he said, "to woo Kira."

"To *woo* her?" Tempest repeated.

"That's the expression he used," said Sanjay. "But you get the picture. He really likes Kira."

"Really?" Ivy asked.

"He called her singing 'heavenly,'" Sanjay said, "which I know is a bit cliché, but it conveyed a heartfelt thought. Anyway, he didn't know how to go from friends to more, so he thought of this grand gesture. We swapped places when the lights went out, and I left through the back door to get roses. Like I already said, the nearby florist Lucas suggested was closed, and I couldn't call since I didn't have a phone, because of your murder mystery party's stupid rule. Rather than show up empty-handed, I went in search of another florist. Which is harder than you'd think without a phone."

"Hang on," said Tempest. "You glossed over the most important part."

"What's that?" Sanjay blinked at her.

"How and when did this even begin? Something else is going on, so we have to figure out when it started."

"Right. Makes sense. It was today, around lunchtime, that Lucas got in touch to ask for my help tonight. As a favor."

"I didn't know you two knew each other," Cameron said.

"They didn't," Ivy cut in. "Lucas asked me for Sanjay's number. I didn't think anything of it. We all know one another, and they're both performers."

"Which is why he got in touch," said Sanjay.

"You don't normally help out random people you have a tangential connection to," Tempest said. "And you definitely don't do it on a small stage."

Sanjay's cheeks darkened. "I'm a romantic, Tempest. I couldn't resist helping. The two of us have similar hair and builds, so he thought we could pass as each other in the dark. He called it a *quick change*, but really, it's a swap or more technically a transposition—"

"Sanjay," Tempest interrupted.

"Right. Point is, he wanted my help performing an impressive magic trick."

"*Why?*" asked Cameron. "Why did you want to mess up the play?"

Sanjay narrowed his eyes. "Magic *elevates* all forms of art. But never mind. Like I said, he wanted to impress Kira. He has a major crush on her." Sanjay pointed to the crushed roses Tempest had discarded. "That's how he convinced me to do it. For love. It's hard to move from platonic friends to a romantic relationship, so he needed to try something different."

He stole a quick glance at Tempest and reddened. "He thought it would be fun to surprise Kira and show her he could do magic in addition to acting, and then he'd pick up the rest of his role as the detective in the play. It wasn't going to mess up the practice show, since he was supposed to resume his role right away. Then I'd show up a few minutes later with roses from the shop down the street. Only it didn't go as planned."

"What did you do to him?" Cameron asked.

"Nothing! The swap went as planned. He was hiding in the trunk we're using as a coffee table. It's one of mine, so it has plenty of air holes and there's no danger of suffocation. So when the lights went out, I let him out . . . but then everything went off the rails because I didn't have my phone. I told you taking people's phones was a bad idea."

Cameron glared at him.

"I went down the street to Veggie Magic," Sanjay continued. "Lavinia let me use her phone, so I found a flower shop that was open, got flowers—it was a good thing I had a credit card in my wallet, since I didn't have my phone to pay—and arrived back later than I'd hoped. The back door had locked behind me, so I knocked on the front door . . . And you all know the rest of what happened."

"You have to know more than that," Cameron insisted. "You vanished and then *he* did."

"While you were all in the kitchen?"

"When we came back into the living room a few minutes later," said Tempest, "he was gone."

"Before you ask," said Ivy, "we were all in sight of one another the whole time."

"And the house is locked up," added Cameron, "including the windows being locked from the inside."

"So Lucas is playing a joke," said Sanjay, "and he roped me into it?"

"That's what the police said," Ivy said.

"There you go. Did you search—"

"We searched," said Cameron.

"Maybe he's *good* at hiding." Sanjay eyed his magic trunk.

Tempest followed his gaze. "We already checked in there."

"In the second false bottom?" Sanjay asked.

"There's a *second* one?" Even Tempest didn't know about that one.

She didn't know if she was hoping to see Lucas inside the trunk or whether she was dreading it. She held her breath and opened the lid of the trunk.

Chapter 10

The trunk was empty.

Ivy flopped into Harold's favorite armchair. It was definitely the coziest piece of furniture in the house. "We've already searched the house. That means he must have been alive and left through the front door while we were in the kitchen."

A sharp knock sounded at the door.

Cameron looked through the front window and swore. "It's Mrs. Hudson."

"I'm guessing she's not being neighborly and bringing us cookies for our rehearsal," said Tempest.

"I'll just be happy if she's not here to deliver a subpoena for a civil lawsuit she's threatened to file," said Cameron.

"Or that petition to cancel the library," Ivy added.

More raps sounded on the door, this time more forceful.

Cameron took a deep breath and opened the door.

"I saw the ruckus with the police." Mrs. Hudson looked accusingly at him. "I told you this is a family neighborhood. We've never had the police show up before now."

"It was all a misunderstanding," Cameron said. "There's nothing—"

He broke off as she pushed her way inside.

As Tempest caught Ivy's eye, she was transported back to the connection they'd shared as kids obsessed with mysteries. They were thinking the same thing: *Could Mrs. Hudson be a murderer?* It would definitely be a good way to get the library shut down. And if anyone would know a secret way into the house, it would be a neighbor who'd lived across the street for decades.

"Is there something you wanted, Mrs. Hudson?" Cameron asked. "The police are no longer here. There's no problem."

"Nobody called the police on us," Ivy added. "We were the ones who called them."

"Whatever for?"

The normally bold Ivy shrank behind Cameron at the sight of Mrs. Hudson's piercing gaze.

"Someone was playing a joke," Tempest explained. "We were worried that he'd gotten in trouble, but we see now that he just left without telling us."

"This one?" Mrs. Hudson pointed at Sanjay.

"Me?" Sanjay balked. "What did I do?"

"You," she said, "were the only one who left the house. I assume you're the one who made them call the police."

"Hang on," said Tempest. "You were spying on us just now?"

"Well," Mrs. Hudson huffed, "I've been across the street *watching* this charade. Before the police officer arrived, I saw this man sneaking out of the house." She thrust her finger at Sanjay's chest.

"Me?" Sanjay shrank away.

"Between the time this ridiculous murder mystery play began and when three people left together a few minutes ago, you and that twelve-year-old police officer were the only people to come into or leave this house."

"Nobody else left?" Tempest asked. "You're certain? There aren't any hidden ways out of here?"

"I'm quite certain."

"That can't be right," said Ivy.

Mrs. Hudson frowned at her. "Are you questioning my competence?"

"Of course not," Ivy stammered. "I didn't mean that. I only meant . . . I mean, you can't have been watching the house the *entire* time."

"I was, and I'll swear to it in a court of law. But you don't need to take my word for it. My sister, Jane, has been with me all evening."

"You roped your own sister into spying on us?" Tempest raised an eyebrow at Mrs. Hudson.

Mrs. Hudson raised her own eyebrow right back at Tempest. "Jane smokes a pipe. I hate the odor of that remnant of her misspent youth and refuse to let her smoke in my house. We were sitting on my front porch with a perfect view of this house."

That meant Lucas couldn't have escaped via the back of the house either, so he couldn't have slipped out a window. The two women would have seen him leave along one of the sides of the house. Directly behind the house, there was nowhere to run. The house butted up against a steep hillside, with a high retaining wall that not even an expert rock climber could scale without equipment. The murder mystery party group's movements meant he couldn't have gone out the back door. Mrs.

Hudson and her sister would have seen if he went out the front door or a window.

"I think you all need to tell me what *has* happened tonight," Mrs. Hudson said. "This isn't part of your games. What's really going on here?"

"Nothing you need to be concerned about," Tempest said hastily, before anyone could show their hand to her number one suspect. "Just an actor who thinks he's a comedian. Thanks for stopping by, Mrs. Hudson, but we've got the situation with our mischievous friend under control." Tempest gave her the sweetest smile she could muster.

Mrs. Hudson returned the fake smile. "We'll see what the city council thinks of this unprofessional motley crew running this would-be library."

Tempest's smile vanished.

Mrs. Hudson's smile remained as she turned and left.

After she was out of earshot, Sanjay whispered, "I can't tell if it was just my imagination, but didn't it sound like she muttered, *Kids these days?*"

Cameron laughed. "Thanks. I needed that. This whole situation is . . . I don't even know how to describe it."

"Impossible?" suggested Ivy.

"Mrs. Hudson was right about being able to see every possible way out of the house," said Tempest. "Why did Lucas set up this elaborate hoax?"

"I'd suggest he had stage fright and didn't want to perform in the play," said Cameron, "except that's the opposite of Lucas's personality. If anything, I'd have expected him to poison one of the other actors so they wouldn't upstage him."

"I don't think I like being a pawn in his game," said Sanjay. "Although it does rather make me feel like I'm a spy." He tugged at the collar of his cashmere sweater. "Though not in this fluffy monstrosity. My tux is outside in my truck. Back in a sec."

"Later," Tempest said. "You can put up with soft natural fibers for a little while longer."

Sanjay fidgeted but complied. Tempest had thought it was only the specially made bowler hat he was never without that served as a security blanket. Apparently, it was his attire as a whole that gave him confidence.

"Fine," she said. "But we don't know what's going on, so be quick so you can help us figure this out."

The front door creaked as Sanjay slipped outside.

"Why does someone want to ruin me?" Cameron picked up an Ellery Queen novel and fanned the pages.

"We don't know what's happening yet," said Tempest.

"But we should, shouldn't we?" He stopped at a page close to the end of the paperback book in his hands and tapped his finger on the page. "The challenge to the reader. This is where Ellery says he and the reader have all the clues. Well, we have all the clues, don't we? We were all here tonight and saw the gag that Lucas played that's going to ruin me. How did he vanish? Why can't we find him? And why is he messing with me and my library?"

"Why are you so sure it's personal, about you?" Tempest asked.

He shrugged and gave a sad chuckle as he looked at the bookshelves. "This library is supposed to be *my life*. I've already given notice at my job and told my roommates to start looking for someone to rent my room to. It sounds so stupid to say that now. I got ahead of myself, but I was just so excited—"

"This is only a minor setback," Tempest insisted. "We just need to figure out what Lucas is up to."

Ivy sat across from Cameron and leaned forward with her

elbows on her knees. "The library will be approved. A lot more people are signing the petition in favor of the library than Mrs. Hudson's petition against it." She spoke in a comforting tone, and Tempest detected a hint of something else in her voice. *Ivy had a crush on Cameron Gray.*

"But if the library doesn't get approved—" Cameron broke off as the door creaked open once more and Sanjay walked inside, but this time, he was dressed in his tux.

"I'm sorry to break up this heated debate about whether or not your library will get to open," said Sanjay, looking as if he was anything but sorry. "But Lucas is *missing*. And he didn't tell me what he had in mind. I don't even know if he's really interested in Kira, but don't you all get the feeling this is about something else entirely?"

"How did you get changed so quickly?" Ivy asked. "You were gone for less than a minute."

"Magic." Sanjay gave her a charming grin.

Tempest wondered if Sanjay or Lucas would win out as the one who liked being the center of attention more.

Sanjay flipped his bowler hat onto his head with a flourish, but nobody was smiling. They all knew that something was very wrong at Gray House.

"The question," said Sanjay, "is what would make an actor who thrives on attention vanish?"

"And when," Tempest added, "will he reappear?"

Chapter 11

Light streamed into Tempest's bedroom through a slit in her curtains. For the blissful few moments between sleep and consciousness, she didn't remember the events of the previous night. Then the image of the dead body of Lucas Cruz popped into her mind. In those first few horrid moments, she'd been so sure he was dead. Had she overreacted because she was scared it was Sanjay?

She kicked off the mess of blankets and opened the curtains, blinking at the bright light of the midsummer morning. As she was shaking out a tangle in her hair, her phone dinged with a text message.

Plenty of breakfast at the tree house.

A message from her grandfather. It was simultaneously delightful and horrifying to be temporarily living in her childhood home as an adult. Her grandparents hadn't lived with them when she was growing up, but she'd spent many summers with them in their Edinburgh flat and as a teenager had lived with them in Scotland for a couple of years after her aunt died.

These days, it was she and her dad in the main house and her grandparents in the in-law unit in the backyard. Their main deck had a perfect view of one of Tempest's bedroom windows. Three people who loved her unconditionally and fed her the best food she'd ever eaten . . . versus privacy and adulting.

Instead of choosing between those options, she was building her own home in a private corner of the property. It would allow her to be close to her family, but not within their line of sight. She was using an existing partially built stone tower that her mom had begun building, so it would also let her feel close to her mom even though she'd lost her. She knew she was lucky to have a small plot of family land to build on. It was ridiculously expensive to buy a house these days, and she knew how fortunate she was.

The stone tower was the only true folly on this land that Tempest's parents, Darius and Emma, had christened Fiddler's Folly. Follies were ornamental structures without a formal purpose, and her mom's favorite instrument had been the fiddle, so the couple had liked the whimsical name. It perfectly represented the hodgepodge of buildings filled with secret doors and hidden rooms that they were experimenting with for their fledgling business. Fiddler's Folly now consisted of the main house where Tempest and her dad lived, the tree house in-law unit where her grandparents lived, a barn that served as the workshop for Secret Staircase Construction, and the partially built stone tower Tempest hoped to one day turn into a small home for herself.

Be there in 10, Tempest texted her grandfather.

On her way across the steep path to her grandparents' tree house, she stopped by the stone tower to check on Abra. The stately, six-year-old lop-eared rabbit was fifteen pounds of fluffy therapy. Abra was far from sweet, but he was the smartest rabbit she'd ever met, and he was an excellent judge of a person's character. He was very particular about who he'd let hold him—a feeling Tempest shared—but he loved cuddling with Tempest. Abra was house-trained but most of the time preferred the domain of his labyrinthine hutch in the shelter of the partially completed stone tower in a steep corner of the yard.

"Want some company?" Tempest asked him as she scooped him up from his hutch. He nuzzled her cheek, so she took that as a yes. She carried him to the tree house.

When the tree house had first been built by Tempest's carpenter dad, it was a simple structure for a child to climb up a tree and have a secret spot high in the branches of her backyard. But as Tempest's parents experimented with various architectural creations, the initial tree house became a proper two-story in-law unit built in between two oak trees. Its decks surrounded the massive oaks, making it feel like a proper tree house.

Tempest reached the top step of the staircase that delivered people into the heart of the home: its kitchen.

Ash looked up from the stove, where he was stirring a pot of fragrant jaggery coffee. "Have you eaten?"

Ashok Raj, known to both Tempest and most of Hidden Creek's residents as Grandpa Ash, wore a fedora on his bald head and a look of concern on his face.

He didn't share the same Scottish accent of his wife of fifty years. He'd moved to Scotland from India as a teenager, ostensibly for medical school but in truth running away from a family tragedy, and to Tempest, his accent sounded approx-imately 90 percent South Indian, 9 percent Scottish, and 1 percent Californian.

"Grandpa. It's seven o'clock in the morning. When you saw my curtains opening, that was me having just woken up."

He clicked his tongue. "Your father left for work an hour ago."

The hours of a general contractor, carpenter, and owner of a home renovation business were early ones. Especially when all those roles were filled by the same man. Tempest's previous career had her heading to bed around two a.m. and getting up around ten. Life at Secret Staircase Construction had been an adjustment.

"Gray House is my main project right now," said Tempest as she set Abra down on the deck next to the kitchen. "We're focused on getting it set up for the library games."

"That 'Escape from the Haunted Library' room you had us test was pure brilliant." Ash poured her a mug of the sweet, steaming coffee. "How did the mystery play rehearsal go last night?"

"Don't ask."

He frowned and picked up a plate of food, then led the way outside to the dining table on the deck. "The cast didn't learn their lines?"

It was nothing short of a miracle that Ash hadn't heard ru-mors about what had happened. He knew everyone in Hidden Creek. He was the epitome of the friendly grandfather whom everyone loved and shared their secrets with. After a first ca-reer as a stage magician alongside his famous family, he'd been a medical doctor for forty years before retiring. Imagine a doc-tor with the bedside manner of a country doc you'd see in a Hallmark family movie, and that was Ash. He still received

Christmas cards from dozens of former patients. He'd practiced medicine in Scotland, but since moving to Hidden Creek
six years ago, he'd made friends so quickly it was almost magical. He rode his bike everywhere and would stop and chat with
people from all walks of life. Regardless of whether you were
nine or ninety, Ashok Raj would know your life story within
five minutes of meeting you, and he'd be feeding you something delicious within ten.

"Something like that . . ." She didn't want to worry him. Besides, how could she explain what happened, since she didn't
even understand it herself? "There was a problem with one of
the actors who bailed on the rehearsal. Now we don't know
where he is."

"Hmm. Surprising. Actors aren't nearly as volatile as people
would have you believe. It's the singers you need to watch out
for."

"Noted."

They sat down at the deck dining table, and Ash set the plate
in front of Tempest. "Normally, I wouldn't give you only a
sweet option for breakfast, but I want to make sure the bramble cobbler is perfect."

"I tried it a few days ago. It's already perfect. My only critique
is that you need to call it *blackberry cobbler*, since nobody outside of Scotland thinks of blackberries as brambles."

"*Bramble* is a much better name for them. You know how
much I regretted letting them grow in our small yard in Edinburgh, since your gran loved eating them fresh from the vine."

"Where's Gran, anyway? She downstairs in her art studio?"

Ash shook his head. "Painting at the section of the creek
that's aboveground. Your play inspired her to paint a kelpie
rising out of the water."

Tempest took a bite of the bramble cobbler and closed her

eyes in ecstasy. She chewed slowly to savor the sweet and tangy flavors.

"Good?" Ash asked.

"How did you get this even more delicious?"

"Magic." Ash grinned and rubbed his hands together. "Let me bring you a second helping."

Tempest followed him into the kitchen. The fragrant scent of the spices melded with the sweetness of the cobbler.

"Something smells different today." She lifted the small glass bowl where he was gathering spices. "Trying a new recipe?"

Ash chuckled. "The spices are the same. Your senses are fooled because the bottle of cider vinegar is open. Once everything comes together, you'll recognize the flavor."

"Until then," Tempest murmured, "it seems like nothing fits together."

"Exactly." Ash lifted the bowl of spices to his nose and gave a contented nod.

"Grandpa, you're a genius." Tempest hadn't slowed down enough to think about what she'd truly experienced last night. How all the disparate pieces fit together. Because their senses had been fooled every step of the way.

They'd *heard* a gun firing, but it was only the faint crack of a fake plastic cap gun, not a real gunshot.

They hadn't *smelled* the accompanying scent of gunpowder that would have been there if a gun had been fired.

They'd *seen* what they guessed was a gunshot hole in Lucas's sweater, but in truth it was simply a hole, and the liquid they could see on the black fabric wasn't flowing and could have been any color.

And finally, they'd all left the living room, so they couldn't see the spot where Lucas lay on floor. Even though it was an open floor plan, the spot was blocked by the love seat. They didn't see where he'd gone, but they didn't hear the front door squeaking as it had every other time it had opened.

In other words: they'd been fooled. But *why?*

Tempest's phone pinged.

"No time for a second helping," she said. And, unfortunately, no time to think about the mystery of what had happened to Lucas Cruz.

Chapter 12

Tempest's dad had called her in to help finish a project in nearby Hayward. A married couple were both professors at the university there, and the job was academic-themed. They wanted to move their home library into an underground crypt, because the husband was a professor of medieval studies who had written a book that had involved extensive research on the catacombs of Paris. His wife was a botanist, so the underground crypt library Secret Staircase Construction conceived of and built was accessed by a new stone courtyard with stone walls that would allow for various flora and fauna to grow in the cracks without jeopardizing the structural integrity. And, of course, a secret entrance to the crypt library, accessed by pushing a stone that resembled a skull.

The job was nearly done, just in time for a big dinner party the clients had planned for later that week, but they'd changed their minds about both the light fixtures and the paint colors of the interior. Tempest didn't want to worry her dad with what she suspected about Lucas, so she donned an old T-shirt and jeans she wouldn't mind getting covered in slate-gray paint and headed to the job site.

Ivy was already there when Tempest arrived. Ivy's schedule these days was working mornings for Secret Staircase Construction and afternoons at the Locked Room Library. Darius had left open a standing offer for Ivy to work full-time for the construction company if she ever wanted the hours, but Ivy wanted to finish her degree and become a librarian, so she split her time.

"Your dad will be back with the new paint in a few." Ivy looked down from where she was hanging an exposed filament string of lights in the garden. "How about dinner at Gray House tonight? That'll give us time to talk before the eight o'clock rescheduled rehearsal. Cameron and I will take care of food, and we can invite Gideon and Sanjay."

"What about Kira and Milton?" Tempest asked.

Ivy hesitated. "The dining room table isn't really that big." Her cheeks turned pink as she spoke, which gave Tempest a clue about what Ivy really meant.

"You want your friends' approval of Cameron."

"I know I don't need you to like him. But it would be—"

"Back with paint and pastries," Darius's voice rang out as a car door closed.

"The pastries are for me," Ivy told Tempest before Darius appeared. "I've already packed up most of my kitchen, and I told him I'd skipped breakfast."

Ivy lived in Hidden Creek in the upper unit of a duplex, above her older sister, Dahlia, and her sister's family. The owners were moving back into the house, so Ivy had been apartment-hunting.

Rents were high everywhere in the Bay Area, and because Ivy had multiple part-time jobs rather than one stable one, she wasn't having any luck finding a rental she could both afford and qualify for. Dahlia and her family were buying a single-family home, but Ivy was still figuring out where she'd go next. She had a standing offer to stay in one of the guest rooms at Fiddler's Folly, but Tempest knew crashing with friends wasn't something Ivy wanted to do. She could see the stress weighing on her friend.

The physical labor of the day's work kept Tempest from spinning with worry over Ivy's predicament and the mystery of what had become of Lucas Cruz. By dinnertime, there was still no sign of Lucas. Whatever was going on, Tempest was certain it wasn't good.

☠☠☠

Tempest arrived at Gray House at 6:33.

Sanjay wasn't free until the eight o'clock rehearsal start time, so dinner would just be Tempest, Ivy, Gideon, and Cameron. Which Ivy had seemed overly excited about. Enid wasn't available to be in the audience that night, so it would be Tempest, Ivy, Cameron, and Gideon watching the interactive play.

Gideon's baby-blue Renault pulled up behind her as she was stepping out of her jeep.

"What are you going to do with your car while you're in France?" Tempest asked. "Need someone to drive it?"

"One of the benefits of having an ancient car," Gideon said, "is that there are no computer chips inside to drain the battery if it sits for a little while. Your dad offered a parking spot at Fiddler's Folly. It'll be fine there until I'm back."

"Too bad it won't get to turn heads for three months." The

French car from the 1960s was an unexpected sight in Hidden Creek.

His lips ticked up into a smile. "I'd be happy to leave you the keys. I could tell how much you liked driving that Impala on your justice-getting getaway."

She grinned at his characterization of her evading the police so she could put the last pieces of the puzzle together to solve a string of murders. "A muscle car isn't quite the same as your classic car that drove right out of an indie film."

"*The Stonemason's Apprentice.*" Gideon ran a calloused hand over the edge of the car. "That's the kind of name my film would have, right?"

"Sounds more like the novelization of your story. The film would be *Ninety Days and Nights in Nantes.*"

"*Quatre-vingt-dix Jours et Nuits à Nantes,*" Gideon translated in perfect French. "I wonder if it'll feel like a long time, or if it'll pass in a heartbeat."

The fire that swept through Notre-Dame Cathedral in Paris had revived the demand for skilled stone carvers in France, and one of the craftspeople who'd helped to restore the cathedral had realized how much he loved teaching the next generation of stonemasons. Gideon would be learning to restore history.

Though the internship was only scheduled for three months, Tempest knew how much could happen in that amount of time. She knew he might not come back at all. His mom was French— thus his near-perfect French—so staying long-term wouldn't be a problem. But the fact that he was leaving his beloved car at her house was a good sign.

She opened her mouth to reply, but the front door flung open.

"Are you two ever coming inside?" Cameron asked. "Ivy and I have prepared a feast, and it's getting cold."

"Meaning," Ivy added from behind him, "that this man knows how to place an amazing restaurant order."

"The trick is asking staff for their favorite dishes." Cameron held up a bowl and popped something into his mouth.

From the cobblestone path, Tempest was too far away to see what it was, but halfway up the path, she could already smell the fragrant food, as well as the smoky scent of a fire in the hearth.

Inside the house, logs were burning in the fireplace, creating a cozy atmosphere that confirmed Tempest's suspicion that Ivy was hoping this would be a double date. In the dining room, a menu from the new vegetarian Himalayan food restaurant was next to boxes of steaming dishes. Tempest recognized momo, jeera basmati rice, and dumplings, but several other, unfamiliar dishes filled the table.

A knock on the door sounded.

Ivy frowned. "You invited someone else, Cam? This was supposed to be—"

"I'm early!" Kira's voice called through the door as she knocked once more.

Ivy's frown became a full-blown scowl. Her hopes of a double date were dashed.

"Um, I'll go let her in," Gideon said when neither Cameron nor Ivy moved. Tempest followed him to the door.

"I'm done closing the library," Kira said as the door squeaked open, "so I thought I could help with anything that needs taking care of before rehearsal." She sniffed, no doubt catching the pungent scent of the takeout. "Oh. I crashed a dinner party. I can go—"

"Don't be silly." Tempest ushered her inside. "There's plenty of food."

"I could sing for my supper." Kira grinned. "It's been a week of clear, starry nights in Hidden Creek, so it feels like a 'When You Wish Upon a Star' kind of evening."

"I love that about Hidden Creek," Ivy said, but her wistful voice held an unmistakable sadness.

Tempest wanted to assure Ivy that she'd find a nice apartment so she could stay in town, but she didn't believe it herself.

"Why do I feel like I've joined a pity party?" Kira asked.

"Because you're letting the food get cold." Cameron handed her a plate, and they all tucked into the food. As they did so, Tempest's phone pinged. So did Cameron's. Then Ivy's.

Gideon's phone didn't make a sound, but when he pulled it from his pocket, he looked confused. "Why would someone text me the letter *E*?"

"I'd say it was a butt dial," said Tempest, "except I got an *L*—and it's *from Lucas*."

"Me, too," Ivy whispered.

"What the—" Tempest took Ivy's and Gideon's phones and set them on the table.

"Let's not get sauce on the phones," Cameron murmured as he pushed the food out of the way, almost knocking over a glass of water in the process. "Sorry. There are too many boxes of food on this table."

"Here." Gideon lifted the phones and put them onto the music stand set up against the wall next to the table.

"L-L-H-E," read Tempest.

"Oh my God," Ivy whispered. "H-E-L-L. He's texting us from hell! So he *is* dead."

"I got a text, too," said Kira. Tempest took it from her hand and set it next to the others. "*O*. He's not texting from hell. He's saying *HELLO*."

As they stared at the message spelled out on their phones on the music stand, a deep voice shouted from above.

"What are you—? No! Help!"

The disturbing words were followed by a horrifying scream.

"Upstairs," Tempest said, the first one to jump to her feet. Normally sure-footed, the scream must have shaken her, because she tripped over someone's foot and had to right herself by bracing the table. In an attempt to help her, Ivy knocked over the music stand holding their phones. Their phones fell to the carpeted floor and bounced under the dining table and bureau.

"No time," said Tempest as Ivy leaned over to right the stand, pulling Ivy along with her. Why had the voice sounded familiar? She was sure she'd heard it before, but she couldn't place it.

"She's right," Cameron said. "Whoever that was needs help."

They sprinted toward the sound and reached the vaulted door leading out of the kitchen at the same time. It was almost comical as they stumbled over one another. Or at least it would have been if not for those frightened words and distressed scream.

As they stumbled out of the kitchen, a banging sounded. But this new sound wasn't coming from upstairs.

"Let me in!" Mrs. Hudson's voice called through the front door. "I heard Harold calling for help. What are you doing in there?" The banging continued.

"We don't have time for this." Tempest yanked open the door. "Come inside already, if you're going to help."

"The voice came from upstairs," Cameron said. Which was rather unnecessary, since he was halfway up the stairs, and Gideon, Kira, and Ivy were already at the top.

Mrs. Hudson gave Tempest a curt nod and headed straight for the stairs. Tempest quickly locked the door before following.

"Where are you going?" Ivy asked as Cameron hesitated and headed *down* the stairs.

Kira and Gideon had already disappeared from sight, and Tempest kept going up the stairs behind Mrs. Hudson.

"Grabbing a weapon," Cameron said. "We don't know what we'll find up there. I'm getting the poker from the fireplace."

It wasn't a bad idea. That scream had sounded tortured.

As Tempest reached the top step, Mrs. Hudson's words sank in. She'd said *Harold*. That it was Harold, *a dead man*, who'd screamed.

Chapter 13

Nobody here," Gideon said as Tempest stepped into the bookcase-lined library being used for the literary escape room game.

"Where is he?" Cameron stepped past them, brandishing the sharp poker above his head. "This stupid game Lucas is playing has gone on long enough."

"You thought he was dead." Kira poked her head out from behind a bookcase. "I don't think anyone is in here, by the way. Unless Lucas can fold himself into a tinier space than the most acrobatic person I've ever met, the room is empty."

"Obviously, I was wrong about him being dead." Cameron lowered the poker. "I've never seen a dead body before, so how was I supposed to know he was acting? If he's not in here, he must be upstairs in the apartment."

Cameron stepped toward the door. Before he got there, it slammed shut. The wooden door banged with such forcefulness that they all jumped.

"Wind?" Ivy whipped her head around, looking for an open window.

"The windows are closed." Gideon turned from where he stood at a window, looking grave. "And there's something you should all see—"

"Later." Cameron rattled the door handle. "We need to catch Lucas first. And this stupid door handle is stuck."

"It didn't sound like Lucas," Tempest said. She hadn't thought it sounded like Harold at first either. But as soon as Mrs. Hudson had said his name, she knew that's who it was. She shook off the idea. Surely it had to be the power of suggestion. She was an expert at it, after all. Had Mrs. Hudson planted the idea in Tempest's mind that made it real?

"Well, who else could it be besides Lucas?" Cameron asked, shaking the door handle once more. It didn't budge. "He's the one playing games with us."

"That voice," said Mrs. Hudson, stepping between Cameron and the locked door. "I don't know who this *Lucas* is, but I recognized that voice. And so did you."

"Don't be ridiculous." Cameron stared at her. "That wasn't Uncle Harold's voice. Mrs. Hudson, will you please step aside so I can get us out of this room and we can catch Lucas?"

Mrs. Hudson raised an eyebrow at him but stepped aside. He knelt at the doorknob and frowned. He gave the knob a twist, but it didn't affect the door. "It's sticking."

"Your hands are probably sweating from nerves." Mrs. Hudson nudged him aside. She shook the door handle gently at first, then more violently. "You built an escape room, so this is what you get."

"Why isn't there a keyhole?" Kira asked, kneeling next to Mrs. Hudson.

"Because it's just a handle," said Tempest. "The escape room door doesn't really lock. We just pretend it's locked when we show players the padlock with the code they need to solve. It's all for show." She tried the door herself. It wasn't possible, but the door wouldn't budge. "This shouldn't be locked. Someone must've locked us in from the outside."

Her gaze fell to Mrs. Hudson, who was looking around slowly, taking in the surroundings. Mrs. Hudson hadn't been inside this room before. At least not since Secret Staircase Construction had begun their renovations. Her expression was difficult to read. She was no longer angry like she had been during their initial confrontation yesterday. Nor was she full of wonder at the magical room they'd created, which was even more bookish than it had been when it had been Harold Gray's private library. Tempest froze when she realized what Mrs. Hudson's strange expression was. *Fear.*

Mrs. Hudson was entirely serious about her accusation. She really believed Harold was here in this house. Or rather, *Harold's ghost.*

Or maybe Tempest was simply projecting her own feelings onto the woman who wore unhappy expressions on her face so well. The one thing she was certain of was that whatever was happening, something was very wrong here. It wasn't only the scream. Something felt *off* about this room, though she couldn't yet place it.

Kira shook the door handle so aggressively that it rattled. *Kira.* Another strange addition to this mix. Did she have an ulterior motive for showing up early?

"Maybe if I try the poker on the door," Cameron said.

"Stop." Gideon said the word so forcefully that everyone instantly froze and looked at him.

Gideon stood in front of the largest window in the room. The window reflected the fairy-tale architecture of the house, tall and narrow with a curved top. With the light of the setting sun behind him, a halo of light surrounded his face. "You all need to see this."

"It's him," Mrs. Hudson said.

Gideon gave her a quizzical look. "I don't know who set this up, but I think we're really trapped."

"Obviously." Kira crossed her arms.

"There's a note," Gideon said, "from the person who trapped us in here."

"The room is filled with notes," Cameron said. "Tempest and Ivy did a great job setting up literary-themed escape room clues."

"This isn't one of their clues," Gideon said.

Cameron gripped the poker with renewed vigor and joined Gideon at the window, where something was taped to the windowsill. It was a small note, written on a four-by-six-inch index card. The note was handwritten in block letters with a black ballpoint pen.

Tempest grabbed Cameron's wrist before he touched the note and read the words without picking up the note card: "*Danger! Poisoned panes of glass. No way out.*"

"Poisoned glass?" Cameron shook free of Tempest's grip but didn't reach out for the card again. "That's nothing like the other literary escape room clues you and Ivy created."

"Because it's *not* one of ours." Tempest stared at the note—the *threat*.

She looked up at the confused faces surrounding her. "Don't touch *anything* around the windows. If the glass is really poisoned so we can't get out, we don't know if it's just the glass, or also the frame and latch."

"If you two are messing with us to test if a scarier version of the escape room works," said Cameron, "then it's in very poor taste. My uncle has only been dead for a couple of months, and to use his voice as part of a game—"

"We didn't do it," Ivy snapped. "When could we even have done it? We weren't here today."

"You weren't?"

"No," Ivy snapped. "We all had other things going on today. That's why we wanted to finish this phase of the interior yesterday."

"Well, how was I supposed to know that?" Cameron asked. "I was at work today, too. You two *really* didn't write that note for the games?"

Tempest shook her head as Ivy continued to look indignant at Cameron's accusation.

"I bet this'll break the glass." Kira hefted a heavy book over her head. It was a glossy, illustrated book of great fictional detectives from history, whose author would surely approve of it being used to get out of a locked room.

"Good point." Cameron picked up the poker he'd brought upstairs for protection. "This is even better."

"Stop." Mrs. Hudson stepped between them and the window. "If the glass is poisoned, we don't know what it's poisoned with—or what it'll do if we break it."

"You mean poisoned gas?" Ivy asked from where she was standing next to the bookcase with a section for classic mysteries featuring poisons. "The library can't be poisoned." She side-eyed the books as if they'd betrayed her and zipped the collar of her pink vest up to her nose.

"Well, we'll just call for help—" Cameron broke off and swore as he dropped the poker and patted his empty pockets. "My phone is still in the dining room."

"Mine, too," Tempest realized.

Everyone's phone was downstairs.

"Lucas!" Kira shouted. "We know you're hiding in this house. You won. We're trapped and at your mercy. You can let us out now."

"I know who's here," said Mrs. Hudson. "And it's not the man you're accusing."

"He's playing *a game*," said Tempest. "I doubt it's real poison, but we can't risk it."

"The poison could very well be real," said Mrs. Hudson.

"The windowpanes are definitely smeared with something clear and gooey," Gideon said softly.

Ivy gasped as Kira leaned closer.

"All of you," said Mrs. Hudson, "get far away from the windows."

"*Poison, poison*," Kira sang. "You're trying awfully hard to convince us there's real poison. Looks more like coconut oil to me."

Mrs. Hudson turned a sour glare toward Kira. "You want to test it?"

"I'm just wondering why you're trying so hard to convince us it's poison. Cameron is right. This is a fun house escape room. Someone wrote a clue in exceedingly bad taste."

"It's a clue," Mrs. Hudson said, "from *Harold*. That scream. That call for help. I've known that voice for more than thirty years. It was Harold Gray."

"But he's is dead," Cameron said. It was the gentlest tone Tempest had ever heard him use with Mrs. Hudson. He led her to the chair at a small rosewood desk.

"I'm not being sentimental!" she roared, breaking free from his guiding arm. "I'm being rational. *That was Harold's voice.* Now we're all trapped in this room by Harold's weapon of choice."

"Agatha Christie loved poison," Tempest whispered.

They stared at the two windows, nobody moving. The only

sound was the faint whisper of wind outside the locked—and possibly poisoned—windows.

"Harold is dead," Cameron said, but his voice cracked on the last word.

"You heard it, too." Tempest's gaze snapped to his. "You recognized his voice."

"You're right that he loved poisons," Cameron whispered. "I mean . . . He never poisoned anyone in real life, but those were his favorite books from the golden age of detective fiction. One of the reasons Agatha Christie was a favorite of his was because of how well she wrote about poisons in her books."

"Agatha Christie was a nurse during the war," Mrs. Hudson added. "She got her poisons right. Harold read every single one of her books, most of them more than once."

"There's no such thing as ghosts," Kira said, but her words were less than convincing since she spoke the sentiment as a whisper.

"Has everyone besides me lost their senses?" Mrs. Hudson stormed toward the locked door.

A vase of fake flowers teetered on the edge of the small desk. The porcelain vase crashed to the floor, cracking in two.

Gideon knelt next to the fallen vase. "No wires."

"There's got to be a rational explanation." Ivy knelt at his side and picked up the bottom half of the vase. "Maybe Mrs. Hudson stomping away shook the desk?"

"Forget about the vase," said Tempest. "We need to let go of the illusion that this was a harmless prank. Whoever is doing this, *it's real*. The thing we have to deal with right now is that we're surrounded by poison and trapped in our own escape room."

Chapter 14

obody touch anything," Tempest commanded. "Look around for more clues, but don't touch anything until we know more." She spun slowly and surveyed the room. "Gideon, take the walls and windows. Ivy, look at the books on the bookcase devoted to Arthur Conan Doyle and Agatha Christie. Kira, take the children's literature bookshelf."

"Kid lit," said Kira. "Got it."

"Cameron, take the bookcase with nonfiction, foreign translations, and short story collections. Mrs. Hudson, please look at the remaining bookcase of general alphabetized classic authors. I'll take the other furniture. I'll see if I can unlock that door."

Everyone got to work on their respective tasks. Everyone, that is, except for Ivy.

"Why are you doing this?" she asked Mrs. Hudson.

"Me? You're the ones who lured me over here!"

"Someone asked you to come over?" Tempest asked.

"Well, no. But you were all coming back over to the house tonight again, after whatever nonsense went on last night that you weren't telling me. Of course I'd be curious. How could I not be?"

"Can we stop arguing?" Gideon said. "Mrs. Hudson, do you have your cell phone?"

For three seconds, everyone simply stared at one another. Then there was a collective round of groans.

Mrs. Hudson reddened. "I should have thought of that."

"You really should have," Cameron muttered.

"I was in shock," she snapped, then looked flustered as she rummaged through her purse. "Where did it go?" Frantic, she dumped the contents onto the rosewood desk. Out poured a hardback notebook, two blue ballpoint pens, a pencil that was nearly a nub, lipstick in the shade she was wearing, a bulging wallet, a jumble of keys with a copper *M* on the keychain, a mini first aid kit, and two rumpled bookmarks.

But no cell phone.

"I swear it was in my purse." She shook the empty bag, growing more frustrated by the moment.

"May I?" Cameron took the purse from her hands and looked inside it himself. He shook his head. "Nothing is hiding in here."

Ivy took it from him and peered inside. "Not even lint. This is the cleanest purse I've ever seen. Like she knew someone would be looking at it."

"What are you saying?" Mrs. Hudson straightened her shoulders as she faced Ivy.

"Obviously," said Cameron, "we're implying that you're the

person who trapped us in here. You've had it in for this library since the start."

"It would have been less suspicious if you'd simply said you didn't bring your phone with you," Ivy added.

Mrs. Hudson narrowed her eyes at Ivy. "I came over to snoop and try to gather information to get more townspeople to see my point of view that you shouldn't be allowed to open a library here. You really think I'd leave my cell phone—*my only camera*—at home?"

"You admit you were snooping to try to ruin the library!" Cameron was nearly shouting now.

"Of course. You lot are up to no good."

"Elderly people often leave their phones at home," said Cameron. "It would have been completely believable."

"Well, it's a good thing there aren't any elderly people here. I'm sixty-three. If you're calling me elderly and questioning my competence, there really will be a dead body here in a minute. It wasn't me, so you're all wasting your time thinking so. We need to figure out how to get out of here. Gideon is the only one paying attention to something sensible."

Gideon gave a start and looked up from the wall where he was kneeling. "This wall has been damaged at the baseboard, like a crowbar was wedged in to pry it up. But it's not an opening we can get out of. Just pointless destruction."

"Another one," Tempest murmured.

"*Another?*" Kira asked.

"There've been a bunch of weird things damaged as we finished this first round of interior renovations," Ivy said.

"That's not important right now," said Tempest. "We need to figure out how to get out—"

"I'd say it's a very important clue," said Mrs. Hudson. "Because this is a game, isn't it? And Harold loves games."

"Tons of people love games," said Cameron. "*Living* people. Harold isn't playing this game."

"Apparently," said Mrs. Hudson, "I was being overly generous in my estimation of your intelligence."

"Generous?" Cameron's face reddened. "How you've treated me these past few months is what you'd consider generous?"

"I was upset at Harold," Mrs. Hudson said. "Not you. I thought you'd have the backbone to make your own decisions about the library."

"We *all* love the idea of a library," said Kira. "So if you're going to be upset at Harold and Cameron, you need to be upset at all of—"

"Fighting is counterproductive," Tempest interrupted. "Let's figure out how to get out of here. Then everyone can go back to arguing about whatever you want to."

She didn't need a mutiny on her hands. It was difficult enough to think while trapped in a room that was possibly filled with poison. She didn't need them all turning on one another.

Kira knelt at the spot on the wall where Gideon had noticed the damage. "You sure there's not a secret passageway through here?"

"There were no secret passageways in these old houses when they were built," Mrs. Hudson said. "But I wonder . . ."

"No secret passageways," Tempest said. She'd seen her dad and Victor, their architect, working on the house plans, so she knew there weren't any secret passageways. But standing inside the fairy-tale house, it certainly felt as if anything was possible. "The walls are solid, but not thick enough for any secret passageways. And before you ask, I know that because we did an inspection when we surveyed the house for the renovation. The spot is a dead end."

She looked around. Something felt different about the room from when she'd been there yesterday, but she couldn't place it.

The room was sensory overload, so it was hard to think. Handmade bookcases both lined this room that had once been the largest bedroom of the house and were also placed to form two rows. Once the library was approved, they'd be knocking down a non-load-bearing wall to make one larger library room, so this room only had a portion of the books that would be there when the library opened.

Agatha Christie had a whole bookcase devoted to her fiction, plus nonfiction written about her. The other bookcase sections were divided into books for kids, English translations of classic mystery fiction from around the world, early detective fiction from Edgar Allan Poe and Wilkie Collins, golden age mysteries of the 1920s and '30s, and nonfiction books about crime fiction and poisons. Once the room was converted, it would also include Sherlock Holmes originals and pastiches, anthologies and mystery magazines, Penguin classics, and the noir and hard-boiled books that were currently downstairs, as well as several other sections they hadn't yet figured out. Downstairs would have popular books for casual browsers, but this floor was for the serious mystery fiction fans.

Tempest scanned the shelves once more, her feeling of unease growing with every passing moment.

"This is ridiculous," Kira said. "Why couldn't I have gone to a café to read before it was time to come over? Oh!"

"You thought of a way out?" Cameron asked.

"Even better," said Kira. "I have no idea what time it is without my phone, but Milton will be arriving in a little while."

"So will Sanjay," Tempest said, "but that doesn't help us."

"Sure it does," Kira insisted. "They'll have their cell phones."

"But we can't risk breaking the window to lean out and ask them to call for help."

Kira's face fell.

"I know what's wrong." Tempest looked around frantically. *She didn't see Ivy.*

"Um, just about everything?" Gideon asked.

"Ivy?" Tempest called.

Her friend had vanished.

"Ivy!" Cameron repeated, whipping his head around.

Ivy poked her head out from behind the Agatha Christie bookcase. "Sorry. Didn't mean to worry you. I got distracted because I found another clue." She held up a folded sheet of paper.

Mrs. Hudson was at her side in a heartbeat, taking the paper from Ivy's hands with a tissue. She carried it to the desk and unfolded it with a tissue in each hand.

"The whole room can't be poisoned," Ivy said with wide eyes. "Can it?"

"Can't be too careful," said Mrs. Hudson.

"*Beware the crooked house,*" Ivy read from the paper. The handwriting was the same block lettering. "*You must get out by 4:50. How will you depart?*"

"This trickster can't decide if they like rhymes or riddles," Kira said.

"And this house isn't actually crooked," Gideon said.

"It sure looks like it is, though," said Kira. "With its fairy-tale wobbly roof. This clue is useless, since the whole house is crooked."

Gideon shook his head. "The architecture is high-quality, and the structure is solid. Even the floors are level after a century. I wonder if the clue means something else besides the house."

"Gideon is right," said Ivy. "*Crooked House* is an Agatha Christie book." She ran to the shelf of Agatha Christie novels.

"Remember not to touch anything!" Cameron called after her. But it was too late.

"Ah!" Ivy cried out, dropping the book as if it were a hot coal. Blood bloomed on her hand.

"Poison," Ivy whispered, her eyes wide with horror. "I've been poisoned."

Even if they'd be able to shout loudly enough for Milton and Sanjay to hear them once they arrived, Tempest was certain of one thing: *they no longer had time.*

Chapter 15

Tempest and Cameron rushed to Ivy's side. So did Mrs. Hudson, with a stack of clean tissues. Ivy accepted it and wrapped it around her sliced palm.

"What hurt you?" Gideon crouched at the side of the fallen copy of Agatha Christie's *Crooked House* but didn't touch it.

"There's a razor b-b-blade inside the pages. It got me as soon as I opened the book." Ivy stared at her bandaged hand. Blood seeped through the handkerchief.

"It'll be okay," Cameron said, taking her hands in his.

"*Crooked House . . . Crooked House . . .*" Ivy repeated. "The poisons in that book are digitalis and a rare one . . . eserine? Is that right?"

"You're shaking," Tempest said. "What are you feeling?"

"Scared to death," said Ivy, but her voice was calmer now. "It just feels like a cut. I don't think I feel like I've been poisoned.

Digitalis in a cut on my hand wouldn't hurt me, and neither would eserine. I think."

"You think Lucas is basing his poisons on these books around us?" Kira asked. "I think that's giving him too much credit. It could be poisoned with anything."

"Come with me," Mrs. Hudson demanded of Ivy, yanking her away from Cameron and sitting Ivy down on the desk chair. Mrs. Hudson grabbed the first aid kit they'd seen in her bag and knelt on the floor as she inspected the injury.

"Were you a nurse?" Kira asked as Mrs. Hudson quickly cleaned the wound, applied an antibacterial salve, and wrapped gauze around it.

"Librarian for thirty years. Libraries are filled with kids, and kids are always having minor accidents." Mrs. Hudson patted Ivy's hand and stood from where she was kneeling. "You might need a stitch or two. I'm sorry the razor blade got you, but I don't think you need to worry about having been poisoned."

"You were a librarian?" Kira asked.

"There are more important things right now," Mrs. Hudson replied curtly, not looking up from Ivy's hand.

Kira had the decency to look embarrassed.

"Please tell me you have a better reason for thinking Ivy's safe than the idea that Harold would look out for her," Tempest said. She didn't say the other thought running through her mind. It was the same one Kira had voiced aloud. Mrs. Hudson *had been a librarian?* Then why was she so opposed to the library?

"There's nothing unusual about this cut," Mrs. Hudson answered. "And there are no signs of anything on the razor aside from blood. But I still don't like this. We should still try to get out of here quickly."

"Page 182," Ivy said.

"Is she hallucinating?" Kira asked.

"I can hear you." Ivy glared at the actress. "And I'm not hallucinating. I don't want to forget the page where the razor blade was glued in place, in case it's a clue that'll get us out of here. Page 182."

Tempest looked to the floor where the book had fallen, but it was no longer there. It was already in Gideon's hands. He'd taken off the thin sweater he was wearing over a T-shirt and was using the fabric to turn the pages, so his skin wouldn't come in contact with the book. He was taking the threat of poison seriously.

Tempest turned back to Ivy. "You still feeling okay?" She wasn't happy that Ivy was sweating.

"I think so?" Uncertainty in Ivy's voice turned the statement into a question. "My heart is thudding, but that could be fear, not poison. Right?"

"I don't think the razor blade was poisoned either." Gideon shut the book and set it next to the note. "No markings were on that page. And even if we take the writer of the notes seriously, look at what this note actually says. It reads, 'Beware the crooked house. You must get out by 4:50. How will you depart?' The window clue said the windows were poisoned, but the crooked house line doesn't."

"It's well past 4:50," said Kira. "Did he set this up when he thought he'd trap us in here earlier?"

"Oh!" Ivy cried. "4:50 from Paddington is a book. 'You must get out by 4:50.' That's where we'll find our next clue."

Gideon extracted three copies of the novel from the Agatha Christie shelf, each with a different cover, again using his sweater to hold them.

"Don't forget What Mrs. McGillicuddy Saw," said Mrs. Hudson. "That's the original US title of the book."

They found four copies with the US title.

"You were really a librarian?" Cameron asked Mrs. Hudson while Gideon turned the pages of each of the books with Ivy looking on.

"Starting when I was twenty-three, for just shy of thirty-one years." As she spoke the words, her voice and demeanor were wistful, but as soon as she remembered her surroundings, her hardened expression was back.

"Why are you fighting against this library?" Cameron asked. "Especially since you clearly love mystery fiction. You knew the different titles of this century-old book."

Mrs. Hudson didn't meet his gaze and instead kept her attention directed at the books. "We have more important matters at hand than the indignities of my own life."

Indignities? Tempest would have pressed further, but Gideon turned a page in one of the books with a UK title that caused Ivy to gasp. A folded note card fluttered to the floor.

"Here we go again," Kira muttered as Gideon unfolded the note and set it on the table on top of the previous one.

"*Inheritance powder isn't your key to freedom*," read Cameron, "*but find monkshood and you'll be free.*"

Gideon groaned. "Another riddle."

"Arsenic and aconitine," said Ivy. "Those are the two poisons in *4:50 from Paddington*."

"The clue says *inheritance powder* and *monkshood*," Kira pointed out.

"Those poisons *are* arsenic and aconitine," Ivy explained. "Arsenic is known as *inheritance powder*. It was commonly used in earlier times in history to kill an older relative without it being suspected that they were poisoned, since the symptoms were the same as other stomach issues that used to be common."

"And monkshood is a plant containing aconitine," Cameron

said. "Uncle Harold pointed it out to me growing wild in the area. Ivy, are you all right? Oh God, you're not feeling worse, are you?"

She shook her head. "I'm trying to remember where I saw a picture of monkshood."

"The poison garden," said Tempest. "One of the framed illustrations on the wall is a poison garden. Where did I see it . . . ?"

"Here," Gideon called from a far wall obscured by the bookcases. "There's a sticky note on the frame."

They all rushed over to Gideon.

"Stand back," he said. "I shouldn't have called you all over here." He caught Tempest's eye. "I'm sorry."

"You didn't touch it, did you?" Tempest felt her heart constrict as she saw the look on his face.

He shook his head and pointed at the note. "I didn't touch it. But look at the text. *'Bye-bye.'*"

"*'Bye-bye'*?" Mrs. Hudson repeated.

Gideon gave a weak smile. "That can't be good."

"Get away from it," Cameron said. "This is ridiculous. Maybe it's dangerous and maybe it's not. But we can't keep playing these twisted games. We need to get Ivy out of here and to a hospital."

"That line *bye-bye* isn't the title of a classic mystery novel, is it?" Tempest asked hopefully.

Ivy and Mrs. Hudson both shook their heads.

"I don't believe so," Mrs. Hudson added. "At least not one that would be in here."

"If it's not a clue, then how do we . . ." Tempest trailed off as she watched Gideon's expression.

"Did anyone else just hear that?" he asked.

"Is he having an auditory hallucination?" Kira whispered. "Does monkshood poisoning cause that?"

Gideon shook his head as he hurried past them and around the bookcases. "I knew I heard squeaking. The door is open."

He was right. He wasn't hallucinating. The door leading out was ajar.

Tempest tentatively peeked outside. "I don't see anyone."

"Let's get Ivy to a doctor." Cameron grabbed the poker, took Ivy's uninjured hand in his, and led the way.

"I feel fine," she insisted. "I don't think there was any poison on that razor blade."

"*Bye-bye . . .*" Mrs. Hudson murmured as she scooped up her purse and followed them out of the escape room.

"Were these games meant to be dangerous or not?" Gideon swept his gaze around the room one last time from the doorway.

"It wasn't meant to be a game at all," said Tempest. "Whoever locked us in here has something else in mind entirely."

"It's like Lucas couldn't commit," Kira said. "When he performs a role, he goes *all in*. But this game wasn't as dangerous as the clues suggested."

But Kira couldn't have been more wrong. When they got downstairs a few moments later, Lucas was waiting for them.

Lucas Cruz once more lay on the floor, unmoving. But this time, his face was bashed in and his clothing rumpled, as if he'd been in a terrible fight. This time, he lay face up, and there was no mistaking the lifeless look in his eyes.

And this time, the bullet hole in his chest was real.

Chapter 16

Mrs. Hudson knelt over Lucas's body and shook her head. "This man is dead."

Tempest pulled Mrs. Hudson away from the body. "There's no way he's faking it this time." She felt ill. Lucas's face was battered. This wasn't a peaceful death. She stumbled away from him, bumping into Sanjay's magic show trunk. "Someone really killed him this time."

"Oh God," Cameron whispered. "He's really dead."

Tempest stared at Lucas's prone form. Something was wrong. Of course it was very wrong in that he was dead. But something beyond that. Something about the way he was splayed out on the floor with his beaten-up body and a bullet hole in his chest.

She took in her surroundings. Something was off. Was anything in a different place? Or had something been removed or added? The furniture was all there, even the twelve folding chairs from Storage Solutions. The fireplace was the same except for the missing poker that they'd taken upstairs. The floor was carpeted, so there weren't any dirty footprints leaving marks on a hardwood floor like a clue in the books that surrounded them in this house. *What was it that was different?*

"His partner must have killed him while we were escaping from that room," Ivy murmured.

But who was his partner?

"I'd like to report a murder," Gideon was saying into his phone. He was the only one who kept his head enough to retrieve his phone from the dining room and call 9-1-1. "We also need an ambulance for someone who might have been poisoned."

Pounding fists sounded at the front door. Both Ivy and Cameron yelped. Tempest didn't balk. She was used to holding in her reactions on stage.

"That's too early for the police to be here," she said.

"Hello?" a familiar voice called through the door.

"We can hear you inside," another voice added from outside. "Are we rehearsing or not?"

"It's Sanjay and Milton," Ivy said, glancing at the grandfather clock. "We were in there so long they're here to start the dress rehearsal."

"Or," said Mrs. Hudson, "one of them arrived early and killed this poor man."

Everyone objected at once, while Tempest opened the door to let the two men inside.

"Is that—" Milton broke off.

Sanjay swore in Punjabi and muttered, "I'm never doing anyone a favor. Ever. Again."

☠☠☠

This time, the police took them seriously.

So did the two medical technicians who arrived in the ambulance and checked out the injury on Ivy's hand. They didn't see obvious signs of poison, but they strongly suggested Ivy let them take her to the hospital.

Ivy struggled to get out of the blanket they'd wrapped around her. "But I have to give a statement."

"That'll keep." Tempest wrapped the blanket back around her. She and Ivy were at the back of the ambulance while the others were gathered on the driveway, speaking to the officer who'd arrived almost as quickly as the ambulance.

"Really," Tempest added as she eyed Ivy's pale face and bandaged hand. "Go get checked out at the hospital."

"But—"

"Ivy. Do you really want to be like one of the characters in your beloved classic mystery novels who does something that makes you throw the book across the room?"

"This is hardly the same thing as following a shadowy figure into a dark basement while a killer is on the loose."

"You're right," said Tempest. "It's worse. A man is dead, his killer wrote notes about *poison*, and you got sliced by one of his traps."

Ivy shivered. Tempest hoped it was only because it was a mildly chilly night. She didn't know what she'd do if anything happened to Ivy.

"Fine," Ivy consented.

Tempest softened her voice. "I can go with you if you—"

They were interrupted by a squeal of tires as a dark sedan pulled up behind the two police cars.

"You're needed here," Ivy said as Detective Blackburn stepped out of the car. "He'll trust what you tell him."

Tempest had known the detective for six years. He was a

good man, and a fair one. He'd been the detective who caught the case when her mom had vanished under mysterious circumstances, and he'd been the one who helped her finally solve the case this past year. His full head of hair had turned white prematurely, and Tempest suspected her mom's unsolved case was responsible. Her mom's case was definitely one of the reasons he retired earlier than he should have, and she was glad he was now reinstated.

"You sure?" Tempest asked Ivy.

"I'm sure." Ivy nodded at the ambulance technician, and he got her inside.

"Was that Ivy?" The detective's gaze followed the ambulance as it pulled away.

Tempest nodded. "Just a precaution. She seems fine, but there's a chance she was poisoned."

"Excuse me," Milton called from the driveway, where he was gathered with Sanjay, Cameron, Kira, Mrs. Hudson, and one of the two officers who'd secured the crime scene inside. "Detective, I have pertinent information."

He did? That was news to Tempest.

Mrs. Hudson frowned at Milton. "We *all* have important information."

Blackburn walked over to them. "I'm going to speak with each of you in turn. As soon as my team clears the scene."

"You heard that it's not only that there might be someone inside," Tempest asked, "but there also might be poison on some of the surfaces in the main library room on the second floor?"

Blackburn nodded, and the officer, whose name Tempest had forgotten, told him, "We're at all possible exits until a hazmat team arrives to clear the interior."

"I'd like to talk to each of you about what happened," Blackburn said. "Separately. What you saw and—"

"I can do better than that," said Mrs. Hudson.

"As can I," Milton said.

"After the funny business last night," Mrs. Hudson said to the detective, ignoring both Milton and the hand Blackburn raised to ask her to stop, "I installed a security camera this morning. It will have captured everything that happened today." She eyed Tempest. "*Everything*."

"A camera on the front of your house?" Detective Blackburn turned and looked across the street.

"It's on my porch, but it captures this whole house as well. It won't tell you what happened *inside* this cursed house I was trapped inside against my will, but it'll show us exactly who came and went all day. Also whatever it picked up through the windows. I'll happily share the footage."

"With the possibility of a suspect at large," said Blackburn, "if you'll willingly share this video footage presently, that could help."

She frowned at him. "I could do so if someone hadn't stolen my phone."

"Convenient," Sanjay said through a cough.

"It's digital footage," she snapped. "Any phone will do." She held out her hand with the palm up. Blackburn handed her his phone.

Mrs. Hudson logged into an online account and handed the phone back to the detective.

"What do you see?" Sanjay asked impatiently.

"Stay here," Blackburn said to the group as a new team arrived. "Lyons, make sure everyone stays here." He jogged over to the new arrivals.

"What did you have to say that was so important?" Tempest asked Milton.

"That's for the detective's ears."

"No way," whispered Kira. "You know who killed Lucas."

"What?" Sanjay was so startled he dropped his hat onto the concrete.

"I knew it," Milton said as he observed Sanjay's fumble. "I hoped I was wrong, but—"

"Knew what?" Tempest didn't like the smug look on Milton's face as he watched Sanjay pick up his beloved bowler hat. "Sanjay didn't kill anyone."

"Yet Sanjay," said Milton, "was coming around the side of the house when I arrived. Like he'd already been inside."

"Thanks for the vote of confidence." Sanjay scowled at Milton before turning to Tempest. "The house was locked when I got here, and nobody answered the door. So I did what any sensible person would do—I tried the back door. I get it that I was off camera, but obviously, I didn't kill him."

But to anyone who didn't know him as well as Tempest did, what would it look like?

☠☠☠

Blackburn and the crime scene crew kept them waiting for half an hour. When he returned, he wore a confounded expression. "We didn't find anyone in the house. We'll need to review this video footage more carefully, but from what we can tell watching at a sped-up pace, it looks like nobody besides all of you approached the house tonight."

"Nobody else?" Tempest said.

"How is that possible?" Kira asked. "Someone got inside and killed Lucas. Or are you telling us he faked his death *again*?"

"I can confirm that Mr. Cruz is dead," Detective Blackburn said. But he left the other half of her question unanswered.

He didn't need to say more. Tempest knew exactly what he'd left unsaid.

"If there's nobody else inside the house," Tempest said, "then he means it was one of us."

"But we were together the whole time," said Gideon. "I'd swear to it."

"He's right," Kira added. "We were all in that tiny, claustrophobic room filled with poison."

The second-floor library was actually quite spacious, but Kira wasn't wrong that it had felt claustrophobic while they were trapped inside.

"Gideon and Kira are right," Tempest said. "What you're saying is impossible."

"Unless," said Mrs. Hudson, stepping away from the group and looking up at a light in the second-floor window, "it was Harold."

Chapter 17

Hidden Creek's police station was in an old Victorian house, like the rest of the buildings in the civic center. Every few years, a new city council member would propose modernizing the buildings, but the whole downtown area was part of the small town's charm, so the plans to modernize were never approved.

Which is how Tempest came to be talking with Detective Blackburn in his office that looked more like the tiny study in a university professor's home.

"I was informed that Ivy got the all clear," he told her as he sat down.

"I heard." But she appreciated him letting her know.

"Tell me exactly what happened at that house," he said.

"Did you look at the video footage more carefully yet?" It seemed safer to start with facts, rather than disputing the reasons why it couldn't be Harold Gray's ghost. Even though she'd sworn it was his voice she'd heard.

"So far, the footage confirms what I saw the first time around."

"Wait, do you mean nobody else—?"

"Tempest. Please just go over what you saw."

She opened her mouth to ask about the video again, but decided against it. "Should I start when we arrived this evening?"

"For now."

For now? She was hoping he'd be less formal, after having gone through so much together, but it was also strangely comforting to go over the horrible events in a more structured way.

"Lucas wasn't on the floor of the living room when we arrived," she began. "We were going to eat before the actors arrived for a rehearsal. Ivy and Cameron were already at the house when Gideon and I got there."

"You came through the front door?"

"The door in the living room. Lucas *wasn't* dead on the floor when we came inside. Kira and Mrs. Hudson both arrived after I did. Neither was supposed to be there. Kira was early for rehearsal, and Mrs. Hudson was just being nosy."

"This was supposed to be a dinner party?"

"Cameron and Ivy got takeout."

"From where?"

She gave him a raised eyebrow. The food was still there. He knew all this. Why was he asking? "The new Himalayan restaurant down the street. I forget the name, but there's a menu stapled to a paper bag in the kitchen—no, the dining room. Food was out on the table when I got there, and after Kira arrived, we were starting to serve ourselves dinner when my cell phone buzzed. I had a text message. But it wasn't just me. As I looked at it, I noticed everyone else had a message as well. Each of us got a single letter—from Lucas. We didn't understand what was happening at first, but we realized that if we lined up the phones, they spelled a word. *HELLO.*"

"Who suggested lining up the phones?"

"You mean if one of them was working with Lucas and already knew it would spell out a message?" She shook her head. "I don't remember, but honestly, it didn't seem like anyone knew. It was a group decision." She thought back on the series of events. Her impression was that it was a group decision, but could it have been *a force*? The technique was used all the time in magic, for a spectator to think they were making a choice of their own free will, but really the magician had forced their hand.

"So you all decided to line up the phones."

"On the music stand, so we could see them. That's when we heard someone calling for help." She swallowed. "And a horrible scream."

"What can you tell me about the voice?"

"Nothing I want to admit is real."

"What does that mean?"

Tempest hesitated before answering. The voice she'd heard earlier tonight was Harold's. She was sure of it. It wasn't only the power of suggestion introduced by Mrs. Hudson. That meant it had to be a recording, didn't it? It couldn't have been his ghost. She refused to believe he was haunting Gray House. There was something else she'd seen that she couldn't quite remember . . .

"The voice we heard was Harold Gray's," she said after twelve seconds of indecision.

Blackburn attempted to keep his face neutral, but Tempest detected a minor twitch in his left eye.

"That's Cameron Gray's great-uncle who used to own the house, who died earlier this year," Tempest continued.

"I know who Harold Gray is. I've been hearing a lot about him tonight."

"You have? Then why aren't you pointing out that a dead man can't call for help?"

"I assume it was a trick. Just like you do. You built games and puzzles into that library."

"Obviously, I didn't have anything to do with—"

He held up a hand. "I'm not saying you did. I'm more interested in *who* would have staged this game. The *how* will fall into place from there."

Tempest nodded. That was one way to approach things. It simply happened to be the opposite of how her own mind worked.

"The call for help came from above us," she said instead, "from the second floor. We were all so flustered by the sound that we knocked over the music stand. Our phones fell behind the table, but we left them so we could rush upstairs."

"Which is why you were trapped without your phones."

She nodded.

"Who knocked over the stand?"

Tempest didn't answer right away. Memory was a funny thing, and she wanted to make sure she wasn't misremembering what had happened. Manipulating both present perception and memory of past events were tools magicians used to create successful illusions. She wasn't wrong about her memory here, but she couldn't believe what that meant.

"Tempest." Blackburn interrupted her thoughts.

"It was Ivy," she admitted, "but Ivy couldn't have been the one who didn't want us to have our phones. She wouldn't—"

"Go on with the series of events."

"It wasn't Ivy who did this to us," Tempest reiterated.

Blackburn simply waited for her to continue. It was an effective technique, because she did.

"Mrs. Hudson was outside spying on us. She heard the scream as well, so she started banging on the front door. We let her in—*I* did. I don't know why, only that I wasn't thinking straight. None of us were. If you'd heard that scream . . . "We knew by then that something dangerous was going on."

"But you didn't find Lucas upstairs."

"No. But that's when he trapped us inside the escape room game. The door slammed shut, and the twisted escape games began." She rubbed her bare arms as goose bumps appeared at the memory of blood on Ivy's hand.

Blackburn's eyes flickered with concern. He already knew the broad strokes of how they'd been trapped, from their frantic words at Gray House, but he hadn't heard the details from Tempest as she relived it.

"It wasn't a game this time. It wasn't the literary escape room puzzles we'd set up, but all about poison. I don't know if they were serious enough to be trying to kill us, but Ivy got sliced by a razor blade, and because of the notes in the room, we were worried it was poison."

"And that's why you thought the window was poisoned so you didn't smash it to get out."

"Exactly. We know the razor blade that cut Ivy doesn't appear to have been poisoned, but what about the windows? There was something coating the glass."

"They're running more tests to be sure, but it looks like that note about poison on the windowpanes was just so you wouldn't smash the windows and get out too soon."

"It worked. It took us nearly an hour to get out of there. Sanjay and Milton were already waiting outside for rehearsal to begin."

"What time were they supposed to arrive?"

"Eight o'clock?" She thought back to make sure that was right. "Yeah, eight."

"Did you know Sanjay arrived early?"

She couldn't read his expression. "You don't seriously think Sanjay killed Lucas. Kira was the one who was suspiciously early. You know you can never predict how long it'll take to drive here from San Francisco. Of course he'd give himself more time than necessary in case traffic was bad. I already know he went around to knock at the back door when nobody answered the front."

Blackburn nodded. "Do you have any idea what someone would want to do in the house during that time?"

She stared at him. "A diversion?"

"You were trapped in there for quite some time. At least an hour?"

"There isn't anything—" Tempest broke off as an idea came to her.

Blackburn straightened. "You know something?"

"Not exactly. But you said *in the house*. That made me think of something. Because it's not simply a house anymore. It's *a library*. Filled with thousands of old books."

"You think this is about a valuable book?"

"Cataloging begins next week." Tempest leaned back and looked at the imperfections in the old ceiling. "As soon as the summer stroll games are over, Cameron will be creating a list of all the books in Harold's collection. If someone wanted to steal a valuable book, this is their last chance before anyone realizes it's gone."

Chapter 18

S *coobies meeting in the turret at my place*, she texted Ivy,
Sanjay, and Gideon on a group text as soon as she left
the station.

The secret turret room was barely large enough for four people
and a rabbit, but it was the best place to gather in private. The
room looked like a circular tower on the outside, but on the inside, it had seven flat walls and an opening for a narrow stairway. Stretching eight feet in diameter, the only seating was
movable beanbags. On the walls, Tempest had hung framed
magic show posters from classics like Houdini and Adelaide
Herrmann and her mom and aunt's popular Selkie Sisters show
they'd staged in Edinburgh.

Abra helped calm her nerves enough that she didn't feel her
heart pounding in her throat, but she hoped the others would
arrive soon. She couldn't believe that Lucas was truly dead.

He'd been a selfish guy in many respects, but also a good man who'd made a lot of people laugh and who'd put his career on hold to care for his sick mom. What had he gotten himself into?

Gideon was the first to arrive. It was a few minutes to midnight when he set a duffel bag on the hardwood floor of the turret.

"I don't even know what to say about what went down tonight, so I'll start with this." He reached into the bag and withdrew a lopsided object, roughly eight inches tall, that was wrapped in a white cloth. "I've had this in the trunk of my car all day. I didn't have time to complete it, so I couldn't decide if I should give it to you."

As the cloth fell away, a sandstone carving was revealed. Calling it a *carving* didn't do justice to the masterpiece. The lop-eared rabbit of stone was poised to leap, its body so lifelike that it was as if it was frozen in time in a photograph. It wasn't exactly Abra, but the creature's eyes had the same hint of mischief as her real-life bunny. The stone was hard, yet Gideon had made the animal look as if it were covered in soft fur. This was exactly why he'd received the prestigious internship opportunity in France. He could work magic with stone.

He placed the carving into Tempest's hands. Further cementing the impression that it wasn't quite a representation of Abra, the animal's hind legs weren't the legs of a rabbit, but where fluffy paws with claws should have been, cloven hooves anchored the carving.

"He's gorgeous," Tempest said.

"As long as you don't mind that its left ear isn't quite right yet, he's yours." He leaned in and examined the unfinished ear more closely. "Maybe I should—"

"Don't you dare take Satan bunny away from me."

Gideon laughed. "I was going for the hooves of a deer, not the devil, but you're right that Abracadabra can be quite devilish."

Abra looked up at the sound of his name.

"Thank you." She set the carving on the floor next to Abra. "You didn't have to make me something . . . but I love my magical devil bunny. I—"

"The detective put a tail on me." Sanjay's head appeared at the top of the steep stairs. "He thinks I'm the killer!"

"He doesn't think that." Tempest was fairly sure she wasn't lying. "Why would he think that?"

"He wasn't arrested yet." Ivy appeared a moment after Sanjay. "So that's a good sign, right?"

Tempest hugged Ivy as Sanjay flung himself down on a beanbag and put his bowler hat over his face. Abra nuzzled his hand, doing a great job of taking on the role of emotional support bunny.

"Thanks, buddy." Sanjay lifted the hat from his face and scratched Abra behind the ears.

"Everything okay at the hospital?" Tempest asked Ivy. "I thought you were going to text me for a ride."

"My sister would have killed me if I didn't call her. She took me to the station to talk with Detective Blackburn. Sanjay was still there, so he gave me a ride."

"I was still there," said Sanjay, "because the detective was grilling me."

Abra grew bored with Sanjay's half-hearted petting and went over to the corner to sniff the devil bunny sculpture.

"Who's the new helper?" Sanjay pointed at the little stone carving from Gideon.

"I'm thinking of calling him *Devil Bunny*." Tempest picked up the little figure. "Or maybe *Devil Rabbit*."

"Are those cloven hooves?" Sanjay leaned closer to see its back haunches.

"Gideon's carvings are always animal mash-ups," Tempest said.

"Usually mythological," Gideon added, "but I didn't know of any mythological rabbits, so I made one up. His hooves are from a deer."

"Looks more like a devil," Sanjay said. "Definitely a devil bunny." He eyed Devil Bunny one last time before putting his hat back over his face. "I can't believe I'm debating the name of a devil bunny when I'm about to spend the rest of my life in prison."

"I keep telling you it's a good sign he didn't arrest you yet," Ivy said.

Sanjay groaned.

"You're not going to be arrested," Tempest assured him. "Because we're going to figure out what's really going on."

Sanjay lifted the hat and smiled at her. "You're right. That's what we do best." A mini bouquet of pressed white flowers appeared in his hand out of thin air. He handed it to her, but a second later, the smile vanished. "You have a plan? Please tell me you have a plan. Because I certainly don't."

"Are those flowers from the bouquet you bought on behalf of Lucas yesterday?" Gideon asked. Tempest hadn't noticed that the tiny white flowers were the same ones that had been placed in between the roses, but he was right.

"Not that it matters," said Sanjay, "but I bought these myself and took out some of these little flowers before I arrived back at the house. I don't know what they're called, but they fit perfectly in one of my hiding spots for pressing flower petals."

"I think there's an app that can tell you," Gideon said.

"Dear God, we've created a monster." Sanjay shook his head.

"This is why you should have eased into having a cell phone before you turned twenty-five. You'd have a healthier relationship to technology."

"Back to the matter at hand." Tempest tucked the pressed flowers into the frame that held a vintage poster of Houdini. "If Blackburn suspects Sanjay, there's got to be a reason."

"It's because I was working with Lucas on that little deception yesterday." Sanjay flipped the hat so forcefully it grazed the high ceiling before falling back into his hands. "And also . . ." He trailed off and flipped the hat into the air once more.

Tempest caught the bowler hat. "I don't like the sound of that."

"I arrived before Milton tonight." Sanjay stood and snatched his beloved hat back from her before collapsing back onto the beanbag. "When nobody answered the front door, I walked around to the back."

"So you were off camera," Gideon said.

"We already know that," Tempest said. "It was perfectly reasonable for you to try the back door if nobody answered in front."

Sanjay squirmed on the beanbag. "The thing is . . . I was back there quite some time. I thought I could slip into the house through the back door."

"Please tell me you didn't," Tempest said. "You *did*?"

"What did he do?" Gideon asked.

"He tried to pick the lock," Tempest answered without taking her eyes off Sanjay.

Sanjay lowered his eyelids as if blaming Tempest for his poor decision. "I was expected at the house. I thought you all went out for dessert and were running late. It didn't seem like a big deal. I almost had the door unlocked when I heard another car pull up. It was Milton. So I abandoned the lock."

"Did you tell Detective Blackburn you were trying to break into Cameron's house?" Ivy asked.

"Of course not," Sanjay snapped. "I couldn't admit to a detective that I had a lock-picking kit with me. I told him I was looking for a way in. Which was true. I did try the windows first, to see if anything was unlocked. Nothing was."

"Blackburn will also be investigating the other suspects," Tempest said.

"He told you that?" Sanjay asked. "He didn't tell me that."

"He didn't exactly tell me that," she admitted. "But he wants to solve the case, not railroad you into a false conviction."

"How does he know who to investigate? According to that damning video, I'm the only one who could have slipped into the house." Sanjay stood and began to pace the length of the narrow space.

"Blackburn is a by-the-book detective," Tempest said. "His strength isn't in solving impossible crimes, but in digging into the victim's life and movements and gathering forensic evidence."

"Lucas was hiding inside my magic trunk for yesterday's prank," Sanjay grumbled, "so my DNA will be all over him. And I'm the one he was scheming with yesterday."

Gideon scooped Abra into his arms. "Let's make sure you don't get squished," he murmured to the bunny.

Sanjay rolled his eyes. "I was nowhere near that rabbit. He knows I was no danger to him. Come on, Abra," he said to the bunny. "I bestow my magical powers to you, Abracadabra, so you can tell us who really killed Lucas Cruz."

Abra stopped nuzzling Gideon's hand and looked directly at Sanjay.

Sanjay blinked at the bunny in stunned silence. "I was joking!"

"He knows his name." Tempest took Abra from Gideon's arms. "Don't you, Abra?" He wriggled his nose a way that looked like a nod, but Tempest knew better. Rabbits were far smarter than people gave them credit for. Especially Abra. But not *that* smart.

Ivy burst out laughing. She tried to stop for a breath of air, but couldn't, which just made her laugh even harder.

"You all right?" Gideon asked.

Sanjay put his hands on Ivy's shoulders. All that did was cause his arms to shake along with her. "We've broken Ivy."

Tempest was simply happy that her BFF seemed to have fully recovered from her fake poisoning ordeal.

Ivy sighed and wiped her eyes. "I'm okay."

"What just happened?" Gideon asked.

"Don't you see?" Ivy grinned at them like a maniacal super-villain. "We all already know we're mystery-solving friends. That's why Tempest called a Scoobies meeting." Ivy started laughing again. This time, so hard she snorted. Which only made her laugh harder.

"Uh, I really think we broke her." Sanjay waved his hand in front of her face. "Do you know what year it is? And that you're not trapped in a Nancy Drew novel? How many fingers am I holding up?"

Ivy batted his arm away. "It's not *just* that we're friends who solve mysteries." She pointed at Abra. "We're two guys, two girls, *and* a supersmart animal mascot."

"Abra did help us solve a couple of murders," Tempest said. The bunny hadn't known he was sniffing out clues, but still.

"As if this week couldn't get any worse," Sanjay grumbled, "now I'm living in a psychedelic cartoon about a talking dog."

"Abra doesn't talk," Tempest pointed out.

"So . . . are we the Abracadabras?" Gideon asked.

The three other Abracadabras groaned in unison.

"Now that that's settled," said Tempest, "are we ready to solve this murder?"

"You have an idea where to start?" Sanjay asked.

"Mrs. Hudson got a security camera this morning, and remember that the only people on the video were us, Kira, Milton, and Mrs. Hudson."

"No Lucas," said Gideon.

"Nobody was watching the house during the night," said Sanjay. "And the security camera wasn't yet installed. Lucas could have slipped out then."

"He could have," said Tempest. "But *how did he get back inside tonight?*"

Ivy gasped. "You mean he was in the house today, before we got there? *Why?*"

"I don't know why he wanted to freak us out last night," said Tempest. "But it was Detective Blackburn who gave me the idea that Lucas wanted to stay in the house for some reason. The detective had seen the video evidence that suggested Lucas was inside the house while we were in the escape room."

"It's a house full of *books*," Gideon said. "And cataloging begins next week after the library games are over."

"Wait," said Sanjay. "Do you mean to tell me that I'm a murder suspect because someone is searching for a stupid book?"

"A *valuable* book," Ivy said.

Sanjay scowled at her.

"Milton," Ivy continued. "He works at the Hidden Bookshop and knows all about rare books. It has to be Milton!"

"What I don't understand," said Gideon, "is why now? Why did Lucas have to plan something so complicated like this, when Harold's library has been here all along?"

Tempest shook her head. "You're forgetting that Lucas and

Milton are brand-new to seeing the library. They weren't working with us on the renovations of Gray House. The three actors
only visited for the first time last week."

"A book," Sanjay growled. "All this for a book?"

"Maybe," said Tempest. "It's just one theory. But one that
Blackburn will be looking into now. So you don't need to worry
that he's only focused on you as the only suspect."

"Omigod!" Ivy shouted so loudly that Sanjay dropped his hat.
"I know what happened!"

"You do?" Sanjay gaped at her.

"It's so obvious in retrospect." Ivy grinned. "Tempest must
be right about the theory of the motive being finding a rare
book—because I know exactly how Milton Silver killed Lucas
Cruz."

Chapter 19

Harumph." Ivy Youngblood stood tall in the tiny secret turret, looking powerful in head-to-toe pink and a bandaged hand on her hip.

Tempest, Gideon, Sanjay, and Abra the rabbit looked on with bated breath.

Technically, Abra was far more interested in the Devil Bunny statuette than Ivy channeling her fictional hero, Dr. Fell, who solved impossible crimes for his creator, John Dickson Carr. But the human occupants of the tiny room above Tempest's bedroom were indeed ready to hang on her every word.

"When one considers a seemingly impossible crime," said Ivy, "it's important to look beyond your assumptions."

"Ivy," Sanjay barked. "If you're attempting to give us a lecture on locked-room mysteries instead of simply telling us how on earth Milton killed Lucas, I swear I'll—"

"Everything I'm about to say is vitally important," Ivy said. "If I don't explain *how* it happened, you'll dismiss what I'm saying. But you shouldn't. So no, I'm not going to give you a whole speech about all the different possibilities that exist for a seemingly impossible crime—you've all already heard my version of that lecture. I'm only going to ask you to think back on what we saw tonight."

"Next you're going to tell us to close our eyes," Sanjay muttered.

"Hey, as long as she has a solution that doesn't involve the ghost of Harold Gray," said Gideon, "I'm more than happy to do whatever she asks."

"If closing your eyes helps you visualize what we say," Ivy said, "then go for it. But I think we can all agree on what we saw tonight. Sanjay, you'll just have to take our word for what Tempest, Gideon, and I saw when we got out of that creepy escape room. Tempest and Gideon, let me know if you disagree with this: Lucas was both beaten up and shot, so we knew that someone—presumably his partner in crime, though that part is just an assumption—was in the living room with him when we were trapped in the escape room, and that this person killed him."

"True," said Gideon as Tempest nodded.

"But even if we leave aside the assumption that it was his partner in crime who killed him," Ivy said, "the rest of what we saw is *also* an assumption. The house was locked up from the inside, so how did the killer get out of the room?"

"Secret passageway?" Sanjay asked.

"There aren't any." Gideon shook his head.

"Just because they're not allowed in Ivy's favorite golden age of detective fiction novels," Sanjay said, "doesn't mean there can't be one in real life."

"You're right," Tempest agreed. "But the fact that we're all working on the renovations of the house *does* mean we know there aren't any secret passageways."

"We made an assumption," Ivy said, "that the killer was inside the room with Lucas. But what if he wasn't? Lucas, having found the valuable book Milton had told him about, would have handed his partner the book through an open window, at which point, the killer punched Lucas in the face, shot him, and then Lucas closed and locked the window before stumbling backward and dying. And we know that the only two people captured outside the house on the security camera footage were Sanjay—who we know is innocent—and Milton!"

Ivy's excitement faded as her three friends didn't respond with anything beyond blank stares.

Tempest was the first to speak. "That was a good idea to challenge our assumptions, but that doesn't seem plausible."

"But the video isn't crisp from that far away," Ivy said. "It wouldn't necessarily show Milton's small movements, like what he was doing when he stood at a window."

"What our dear Tempest is trying to say diplomatically," said Sanjay, "is that it's an idiotic idea on every level."

"Hey." Tempest kicked his foot. "What's the matter with you tonight?"

"Hello. Murder suspect." He pointed at his own chest.

"We've faced far bigger problems before that we've gotten through. Being a jerk to Ivy isn't helping."

"Fine. Sorry." Sanjay shoved his hands into his pockets. "I'm a little on edge."

Ivy scooped Abra into her arms and attempted to hand him to Sanjay.

"Even Abra can't help," he said, keeping his hands firmly in his pockets, so Ivy kept Abra in her own arms.

"There are a few problems with that theory," Tempest said as gently as she could. "First, if Lucas found whatever he was searching for in the house, why wouldn't he simply walk out with it? Unlike us, it's not like he was trapped."

"Because his partner told him the house was under video surveillance?" Ivy suggested.

"So he was going to stay inside the house forever?" Tempest shook her head. "Plus, even if the footage doesn't capture small movements, Lucas would have appeared in the window if it was opened for him to hand Milton the book."

"Maybe," Ivy admitted.

"Most importantly," Tempest continued, "Milton arrived *after* Sanjay. Even if Milton somehow disguised his actions and blocked the window so the camera didn't see anything suspicious, Sanjay was around at the side and came back quickly. How could Sanjay have missed hearing or seeing anything?"

"I wouldn't have," Sanjay agreed. "Thanks for trying, Ivy. But Milton isn't the killer."

"We don't know that he's innocent," Tempest said. "We just know that's not how Lucas was killed. It's still most likely Milton, Kira, or Mrs. Hudson. But we can't rule out Enid or Cameron."

"Of course we can," Ivy said. "Enid wasn't there tonight, and obviously Cameron wouldn't kill anyone."

"I'm only pointing out that Blackburn will both review forensic evidence and be thorough with everyone who's been at the house," said Tempest, not wanting to start a fight about whom they could trust. "Mrs. Hudson is hiding something, so hopefully Blackburn will be able to shake loose her secrets."

Sanjay groaned. "I'm doomed. I don't think that woman would ever reveal something she didn't want to."

"I don't get a murderous vibe from Mrs. Hudson," Tempest

said, "but she's definitely not being straight with us. Why is she so opposed to the library?"

"Some people are simply miserable people and want to take it out on others," Sanjay said. His own frown was so deep that Tempest hoped they'd clear him before he became a permanent Mrs. Hudson himself.

"Did you think she was being honest about suspecting Harold's spirit of screaming?" Gideon asked.

"I don't know." Tempest shrugged. "You weren't there the first night, but Enid was also weirded out about the possibility of it being Harold's ghost messing with us."

Ivy zipped her pink vest to the top, covering half her face. "You're right that they both independently mentioned that. You don't suppose that means it's true, do you?"

"No way." Tempest shook her head. "But it might mean *they're working together.*"

"My head is going to explode." Sanjay stepped to the narrow window and pushed aside the curtain to look out into the blackness of night. "Literally. I'd say I have about three minutes left on earth. That's all I can take. This is all getting *more* confusing, not less."

Tempest's phone buzzed. It was her grandfather, so she picked up.

"Your light is on," Ash said. "Why don't you come over to the tree house for a midnight snack?"

"My friends are over—"

Ash clicked his tongue. "Tempest. There's always enough food for all. Besides, I know what's going on. I baked fresh cookies for the police officer parked outside who said he's keeping an eye on Sanjay. Isn't it time you told your gran and me what's going on?"

Chapter 20

Ash clicked his tongue once more as the four friends and a rabbit walked into the tree house kitchen. "You're all skin and bones! When did you last eat?"

Tempest doubted they'd lost weight after skipping one meal, getting a dreadful escape room trap instead of delicious Himalayan food, but if she looked half as frazzled as her friends, she could understand his concern.

"Our dinner got interrupted earlier, so it's been a while."

"I could eat," Sanjay said, apparently having decided he wasn't going to spontaneously combust. Ivy and Gideon chimed in with their agreement.

"Don't look so solemn," Ash said as he gathered two platters of cookies from the counter. "It's a bit chilly for the deck, so we can gather in the breakfast nook if you don't mind getting cozy."

"Cozy's good right now," Ivy said.

"I invited Officer Kwan inside, but he said he was obligated to wait outside. I hope those police cars have good heat."

"What's this about an actor being killed at Gray House?" Grannie Mor asked as she came into the kitchen.

"Sit," Ash insisted, pushing them toward the banquette in the corner of the kitchen barely big enough for four people to squeeze around.

"I'll put on the kettle for tea," Tempest's grandmother said.

Morag Ferguson-Raj evoked glamour no matter the setting. It was partly effort, visiting her hair salon once a month, and she always had her favorite lipstick on hand. But there was also something inherently graceful about her small, angular frame, currently draped in a white dress dotted with a beautiful palette of colors.

"And you need something more substantial than these cookies." Ash's head disappeared behind the door of the fridge.

As the friends explained what had happened, Morag fixed them tea, and Ash threw together a "simple midnight snack," which, of course, was far from simple.

He began by reheating Rajaloo on the stovetop. Rajaloo was Tempest's grandfather's variation on the British-Indian dish vindaloo. Ash was the self-described *dabawalla* for the Secret Staircase Construction crew. It was well known that one of the perks of working for Tempest's dad, Darius, was that his father-in-law, Ashok Raj, delivered home-cooked lunches to the crew if they were working on a local job site. He'd never lived in Mumbai, but he still called himself a *dabawalla* after the Indian city's complex lunch network, in which skilled bike messengers would pick up home-cooked meals packed in tiffins— the multilayered stainless-steel lunchboxes—and deliver them across the city. Ash was both cook and bike messenger. He loved cooking for others, riding his bike all over the Bay Area was his exercise, and meeting people along the way was a perk. No matter how much the team shrank or grew, one tradition that remained firmly in place was the perk of lunches from Ash. Today, he'd brought tiffins of Rajaloo to three landscapers on a job in Richmond.

Ash also defrosted a frozen stack of homemade chapatis, which he served with a fresh salad of cucumber, tomatoes, and sliced avocados, plus pulled a container of homemade coconut ice cream from the freezer for anyone who wanted something sweet.

"*Ada kadavulae*," Ash whispered when Tempest and her friends were done with their story of Lucas Cruz's strange murder at Gray House. "That's terrible. But I know how we can help."

"You do?" Sanjay looked up from his bite of ice cream with a face full of hope.

Ash locked eyes with Morag, and with only the slightest of nods, Tempest knew that a whole silent conversation had taken place between them. After being married for more than half a century, it was inevitable that they'd be as close to telepathy as humanly possible.

"The book?" Ash said to her.

"Aye," his wife answered. "And your cards."

"Good," Ash agreed with a nod, although nobody else in the tree house kitchen had a clue as to what either reference meant.

"I'll begin," Morag said. "You're all too close to what happened tonight. You *cannae* see the simplest thing you've overlooked." Even though she was admonishing her granddaughter, her Scottish accent gave the words a jovial lilt.

Ash nodded. "Harold Gray's collection has yet to be cataloged."

"Which is why whoever is going to steal a valuable book needs to do so before we realize it's missing," Tempest said.

"Then why would they not simply have taken the book already?" Morag asked.

"They were still searching for it," Tempest explained.

Ash and Morag shared another look before Morag continued, "For your theory to hold up, you *cannae* have it both ways. If an unethical person with expertise in antiquarian books found a valuable book that had not yet been cataloged, *they would simply take the book*. Or, if they're searching for a book, *there must already be a catalog record of it*."

Tempest's gran gave her a kiss on the cheek before walking out of the kitchen. The weight of her grandmother's words crashed over Tempest; she'd been so certain it was a good theory.

Sanjay swore. "Morag and Ash are right. There's no reason Lucas would need to clandestinely hide out in Gray House to look for a book. If he spotted it to know it was there, he'd have already taken it."

"Never fear." Ash clasped him on the shoulder. "There's something else we can help with."

Morag returned to the room carrying Ash's Rolodex of business cards he'd collected over the years from people he met on his bike rides through Hidden Creek and surrounding towns.

"Your grandfather knows more people than all of us combined," Morag said.

"As soon as we've finished this midnight snack," said Ash, "I'll begin seeing who knows something about this unfortunate chap who was killed."

Whoever had killed Lucas Cruz shouldn't have done it in a way that affected people Ashok Raj cared about. Tempest was well aware that while Grandpa Ash might appear to the outside world to be a sweet grandfather, and indeed he was 99 percent of the time, but if you messed with his family, you'd find out just how big a mistake you'd made.

Chapter 21

By morning, news had broken about Lucas Cruz's death.

Tempest's dad should have been at a job site that morning. After the good publicity about the family business earlier in the year, Secret Staircase Construction was booked solid and had started expanding the team to include trusted contractors. But instead of being on-site to manage one of their big jobs, Darius was waiting for Tempest in the kitchen when she came downstairs after getting a few hours of sleep.

"You're lucky I let you sleep past sunrise." He pushed a travel mug of coffee in front of her. "I would have woken you if you'd slept ten more minutes."

Tempest breathed in the fragrant steam. This wasn't the sweet jaggery coffee like her grandfather made. Jaggery coffee didn't have much caffeine, but it was a warm, calming drink you could enjoy at any time of day. This mug, on the other hand, was filled with her papa's strong, rocket-fuel coffee. And it was exactly what she needed.

"Three sips," Darius said. "As soon as the caffeine hits your brain, we start walking up the hill. As we're walking, you're going to tell me everything. And I do mean *everything*. You didn't wake me last night, so your penance is no holding back any detail, no matter how small."

"I don't keep secrets," Tempest said as she took a sip. Not anymore. That hadn't gone well. It was only once she and her family had gotten over keeping secrets from one another that they'd figured out what had happened to her mom and aunt. Tempest had been the one to figure it out, but she'd needed the help of all her friends and family to do it.

That's why she'd told her grandparents everything last night. She was thankful her grandfather insisted on using his magic Rolodex of contacts to look into possible motives.

Tempest was useless when it came to contacts. She'd cut ties with most of the people from her former life and hadn't gone back to social media after her spectacular fall from grace last year, even after her redemption this spring. She didn't feel comfortable with either public persona: hero or supervillain. The online world was so binary, with people screaming at one another that she was either a villain who'd endangered countess lives, or a hero who'd single-handedly solved several baffling crimes without anyone's help. Neither was true.

She tried to ignore the ridiculous stories and memes about her, but she couldn't resist saving one viral video from her exploits at the Whispering Creek Theater that made her look like a badass. Sometimes, she missed her stage persona, the Tempest. But mostly, she was happier living in the real world.

With only a bare-bones cell phone devoid of social media apps, she didn't have feeds of wildly inaccurate information to scroll through that morning. Instead, she picked up one of the newspapers on the kitchen table as she took a second sip of coffee. Her dad subscribed to two old-school print papers. Only the local one included news of Lucas's murder, and it made the front page.

"Shouldn't I read this before we walk?"

"Nah. I want to know what really happened, not what the press is reporting." He set down his own mug of coffee and crossed his tree trunk–size arms. Darius Mendez was a man whom most people swooned over when he wasn't attempting to look menacing, or shrank back from when he was. He'd accidentally scared off more than one guy who was interested in Tempest when she was younger. She didn't mind; if that was all it took for someone to run the other way, she didn't need them in her life.

Tempest's height and propensity for muscles came from her dad. She was a few inches shorter than him, and her biceps were many inches smaller in diameter, though she was trying to keep up the muscle tone she'd developed when she had a rigorous stage routine. She used her mom's surname, Raj, partly because she was carrying on the tradition of the famous Raj family of magicians, and partly because of the added layer of security. It was hard enough for someone who'd been as infamous as she'd been to retain some semblance of privacy, but the Fiddler's Folly property was in her dad's name and not easily connected to her.

She took another sip of coffee. Her grandfather was the chef of the family, but her dad knew how to make the best strong coffee in Hidden Creek.

"That's your third sip," her papa said. "Now we walk."

"Grandpa Ash and Grannie Mor didn't fill you in?" Tempest asked as they walked up the hill in the backyard.

"They did, and Ash told me he's using that magic Rolodex of his to look into people who might know the dead actor or are connected to that library petition, but I want to hear your version. You should have woken me up last night."

"It's not like you could have done anything if I'd woken you." She stepped over a gnarled tree root and thought about where to begin. It had become a tradition for them to climb the hill at sunrise if there were important things that needed to be said. Watching the day begin over rolling hills and the bay was both invigorating and a great way to say difficult things without having to look into each other's eyes.

"Lucas Cruz," said her dad. "His name was familiar. Didn't you and Ivy go to school with him?"

"He was a year younger than us," Tempest said as they left Fiddler's Folly through the back gate. "And you're not going to like hearing about what happened to him."

"Of course I'm not going to like it. A man you went to school with trapped you in your library escape room and then was murdered. I get why you didn't want to wake me, but Blackburn should have called me. I'm in charge of the renovations at Gray House, so I'm involved."

"The day is still young. When they're done gathering evidence from the crime scene, they'll probably ask you about secret passageways."

He flexed his forearms. "Why would they do that? A secret passageway was involved? There aren't any at that house. Why are they looking for secret passageways?"

"You're right. I should start at the beginning." Tempest told him about the game Lucas was playing that he'd roped an unwitting Sanjay into, followed by being trapped in the escape room with Gideon, Ivy, Cameron, Kira, and Mrs. Hudson.

"When we got out," she concluded, "Lucas's body was on the

floor of the living room. Whatever he was up to finally caught up with him, because he was dead this time. And now Blackburn thinks Sanjay is the main suspect, because he's on video as having disappeared around the back of the house during the time Lucas was murdered."

"Sanjay can take care of himself. I'm more concerned that a psycho trapped you in the library's escape room. Sounds like you don't even know if it was Lucas or his killer who did that. I get that you didn't have your phones, but why didn't you just break a window to get out?"

"Um . . ." Her grandparents must have left that part out. Or had she and her friends even told them about the poison last night? She couldn't remember.

"Tempest."

"There may have been poison on the windows and in a few books. I don't think there really was! But the clues left for us made it seem like there was poison. We think it was just so someone could keep us out of the way for a little while."

Darius swore and kicked a pebble. It went surprisingly far and came to a rest at the stone wishing well.

"Does the newspaper say how Lucas was killed?" Tempest reached the well and looked over the edge. They hadn't heard a gunshot last night. Was it because the walls of the century-old house were thick? Or with his battered face, were they wrong about what had killed him?

"The press isn't reporting it." He handed Tempest a penny.

She tossed it over the edge. The mossy stones were cool under her fingertips, and the penny splashing into the pool of water brought her back to her childhood. If only tossing a penny over the edge would magically give her the answers.

They continued the short walk up the rest of the hill in silence, leaves crunching underfoot. The sun had already risen, but the new day was just waking up, filled with so much promise. Tempest took a deep breath and looked out across the bay. There was very little fog today, and she could see clearly for miles.

"So it's not about a rare book?" Darius asked. "I know it's irrational, but since we've been surrounded by books in that house, I feel like anything that happens there has to be connected to those books."

Tempest finished off the last of her coffee and faced her dad. "I get that sense, too, but there's something else going on we're missing. The killer turned the whole thing into *a game*. Why trap us in that room? Why pretend there was poison? We were only trapped for about an hour. Why go to all the effort for such a small amount of time?"

"You're holding something back."

Tempest smiled at her papa, in spite of what she was about to tell him. Last year, she would have found it infuriating that he could tell she wasn't telling him something. But now? She loved that she had people in her life whom she could trust so completely, even if it meant they could read her mind.

"You're *really* not going to like this next bit." She took a breath. "Between the game, the poison, and the voice we heard, Mrs. Hudson is convinced it's Harold Gray's ghost that was messing with us."

Darius barked out a laugh. "I knew there was something off about that woman."

"There's a bigger problem than Mrs. Hudson's imagination." Tempest looked down at her ruby-red sneakers damp from the morning dew. Was she really going to admit this to her dad? "The thing is . . . I'm not entirely certain she was wrong. I could have sworn it was his voice—"

The ring of a phone sounded.

Darius answered, and his expression grew graver with every passing moment. He barely spoke, leaving Tempest to wonder who he was talking with and what it was about.

"City council's tabling the vote about the library," he said after he hung up.

"They can't do that. Can they?"

"Now that there's been a murder at Gray House," Darius said, "we're lucky they didn't scrap the whole library project."

He kissed the top of Tempest's head, causing her to smile in spite of the situation. Her papa was one of the few people tall enough to do that. He gave her a quick squeeze before he looked at his cell phone once more.

"I missed a dozen texts while we were talking." He shook his head. "It's that secret garden job. The landscapers are there, and they need me to get over there. It's a good thing they're such fans of Ash's cooking, or they'd have quit by now."

It was an ambitious project with a walled garden and multiple portions of the stone wall that opened secret entrances. Gideon had been in charge of the stonemasonry for the project, which was now complete. The inside was another story. Curved tracks snaked through the garden, with a small custom train car set up to be a dining car for two. Miraculously, the train tracks and newly constructed train car were relatively easy, though costly, to manufacture and install. It was the landscaping around the train that was proving more difficult. The client's vision to have the landscaping re-create the garden from one of their favorite books was proving challenging in Northern California's climate.

"What's the deal with the landscapers?" Tempest asked.

"The team is great. It's the client who needs an intervention." He paused. "But it can wait. If you need—"

"I'm fine. Go take care of the clients."

Her dad was equally adept at charming people and intimidating them, even though he wasn't aware of either quality. Darius simply thought he was a fair, straightforward guy. When people listened to him, he thought it was because they were being reasonable. It never occurred to him that they were either enamored or intimidated as well.

Darius Mendez also hadn't been interested in another woman in the six years since Tempest's mom had died, which made him all the more attractive to people. Now that they knew what had really happened to Emma Raj, Tempest wondered if he would finally move forward—and how she would react when he did.

"Sure you'll be all right?" he asked.

"Always." She watched him hurry down the hillside. She wasn't worried about him. He'd tackle the problem and have the project neatly wrapped up in a bow in no time. It was time for her to do the same thing.

Chapter 22

Tempest's dad departed for the crisis job site, but only after checking that Ash and Morag were home. Tempest's friends arrived as he was pulling out of the gate—as did the patrol car that was following Sanjay. Darius knew as well as Tempest did that Sanjay wasn't a killer, so he welcomed the police presence since it also meant someone was keeping an eye on them.

Ivy wasn't due to be at work at the Locked Room Library until that afternoon, and neither Tempest nor Gideon was needed on a job site that morning, so the friends had decided to regroup in case a good night's sleep had helped shake loose any ideas.

Grandpa Ash insisted on serving a huge spread of breakfast options on the tree house deck for Tempest, Gideon, Sanjay, and Ivy, before mumbling something vague about a "lead" that he and Morag needed to follow up on. Ash wouldn't say more about it, instead simply distracting them with food—savory dosa pancakes with half a dozen fillings to choose from. It worked—Tempest's grandparents slipped out of the house before she could interrogate them further.

It was now half an hour later. Tempest, her three friends, and Abracadabra had filled up on a big breakfast to fuel their brain cells. Ash never liked Abra to feel left out, so he'd prepared a basket of hay with several leaves of lettuce so the rabbit could join the social breakfast. The bunny was now napping on the deck. Something Tempest wished she had time to do.

"Was everyone so busy stuffing themselves silly that you didn't have time to share any brilliant ideas you had in the night?" Sanjay patted his lips with a handkerchief, which vanished a second later. "Now's the time to speak up."

"Want to head to the turret?" Gideon asked.

"We're fine here on the deck," said Tempest. "The alarm will sound if anyone tries to get through the gate or over the fence." With the fencing around the property that Darius had installed after the danger last year, Tempest wasn't concerned about anyone eavesdropping—or worse.

Her phone buzzed with a text message.

"News about the case?" Sanjay asked. Gideon and Ivy looked at her expectantly as well.

"It's my grandfather," said Tempest. "But not with news about whatever he and Grannie Mor are up to. He wanted to make sure I knew there's enough leftovers in the fridge for all of us for lunch."

"How can he possibly imagine we need more food?" Gideon said. "This blackberry cobbler might be even better than my mom's blackberry tart. But don't tell her I said that."

"Ivy needs another coffee." Sanjay waved his hand in front of her face and made a flower appear from thin air. Tempest recognized it as a snapdragon from the secret garden behind the house. But Ivy didn't even notice.

"Earth to Ivy." Tempest took the empty mug from her hands.

"What? Oh. Sorry." Ivy rubbed her eyes. "I didn't sleep well."

"More coffee coming up." Tempest stepped inside the open sliding door to refresh Ivy's coffee, but she could still hear everything out on the deck.

"It's only natural," said Gideon. "We saw a dead body last night."

"It's not only that." Ivy yawned. "I was following up on some apartment leads after I got home. You all know I have to move out of my apartment by the end of the month, and it's been a nightmare apartment-hunting. Nearly everything is out of my budget, anything decent that's not out of my price range is rented immediately, and a bunch of landlords won't even rent to me because I have two part-time jobs instead of a stable full-time job."

Tempest stepped back outside and handed Ivy a steaming mug. "You know the guest room here is yours for as long as you need it."

Ivy gave her an appreciative smile. "Your dad told me he already built an extra bookcase for all my books. But I can't help feeling like I'm moving backward if I can't figure this out."

Tempest winced. "You do realize you just said that to the person currently residing in her childhood bedroom."

Ivy's cheeks turned pink. "It's not the same. You're working on building your own home. It'll be on the same property, but your own place."

"A luxury I won't have as soon as I'm thrown in jail," Sanjay cut in.

"You're not going to jail," Tempest insisted.

"It's *prison*, anyway," Ivy added. "Murderers go to prison. Not jail."

Sanjay's eyes bulged.

"Who wants the last piece of blackberry cobbler?" Gideon said quickly, holding up the nearly empty platter.

"The peacemaker," Sanjay grumbled. "This might be my last meal, so I'll take it."

Tempest rolled her eyes. "Nobody sitting at this table is going to jail—or prison."

"You and Ivy had some good ideas last night," Gideon said.

"They didn't hold up." Sanjay glared at Gideon. "So what good does that do us? I don't hear anyone sharing brilliant new ideas."

"Hey, at least they're trying to help," Gideon said, "rather than having a pity party for themselves."

"I'm not—" Sanjay began through a mouthful of cobbler.

"You totally are," Tempest cut in. "But I get it. I'd feel weirded out if a police car were following me around."

"Your grandparents are right that I don't think this is about a rare book," Gideon said. "I would have noticed if anyone was rifling through the books at Gray House. Even in that garage with books piled everywhere."

"You're not one of those strange people with a photographic memory, are you?" Sanjay asked.

Gideon shook his head. "I can't recite a list of the thousands of books, or if one book had been removed from a bookcase, but I mentioned the garage because those books aren't on shelves. They're in piles. You can't remove a book in a towering stack of books without disturbing the pile. That, I would notice."

"I don't like it that we still don't know what happened with the break-in at the Locked Room Library last week." Sanjay gestured with his fork, losing a bite of cobbler in the process.

"Enid is involved in both libraries with strange crimes within a week of each other," Tempest said as she handed Sanjay a napkin. With his snippy comments, he was acting so much like a child that he was even eating like one.

"I don't think Enid is involved," Ivy said.

"But we're missing something," said Tempest.

"Clearly," said Sanjay. "We're missing a lot of things."

"Isn't this when you normally pull a dozen classic mystery novels from the shelves of the library and tell us what we can learn from them?" Tempest asked Ivy.

Ivy grinned. "Already planning on doing that later today while I'm at work at the library. I'd be looking through books this morning if Gray House wasn't a crime scene."

"We need to do something more to investigate, like your grandparents are doing," said Sanjay. "I'm the one who's going to be thrown in jail—I mean, *prison*—if we don't find the real killer."

"The fact that you disappeared off camera for a few minutes isn't enough to convict you," Tempest pointed out.

"But I was also the one who was secretly working with Lucas the day before! Phone records will show I was texting with him all day." Sanjay gripped his bowler hat. "Do you think they'll be looking at my phone records?"

"I'm sure they are. Why? Are you worried about them seeing something in there?"

"Well, no." He scowled. "But it just feels so invasive. Especially when I know they're looking for any reason to arrest me."

"This is Detective Blackburn," said Tempest. "I'd be a lot more worried if it was someone else."

"The man put a tail on me, Tempest. He thinks I'm guilty."

"He's careful," Tempest admitted, but she didn't vocalize what else was on her mind. Why *was* Blackburn trailing Sanjay? What else did the detective know that he wasn't telling them? "But we should still do what we can on our end."

"How can we help?" Gideon asked.

"Aren't you leaving for France?" Sanjay asked him.

"I've got three more days. I can't think of a better way to spend them than helping with this."

Tempest smiled at him. It was just like Gideon. She knew that as soon as he got to France, he'd be fully present. But now? Instead of being apprehensive or preparing for a long list of unknowns, he was there for them.

She looked between the two men. They were so different from each other, but had some superficial similarities, both in personality and appearance. Gideon and Sanjay were both incredibly talented and took great care in their creative professions, and they were two of the most loyal friends she'd ever had the good fortune to know. She didn't know if she deserved it, but she knew they'd follow her to the ends of the earth if she needed help.

But it was their physical attributes that she was interested in right now. They both had thick black hair, though Gideon's was a bit longer since he never thought about getting a haircut, whereas Sanjay had a recurring appointment with his barber. Sanjay was clearly of Indian heritage and Gideon was ethnically ambiguous, so you wouldn't necessarily know his mom was French and his dad Filipino. Gideon's frame was smaller and his face more angular. But from a distance . . .

"I've got a job for you," Tempest said to Gideon, before turning to Sanjay. "Give Gideon your bowler hat."

Sanjay clutched the hat close to his chest.

"Just for today," Tempest clarified.

"You can't be serious. You want me to loan Gideon my hat? My *hat*?"

Tempest snatched the bowler hat from his grip. "Do you want to shake your tail or not?"

Chapter 23

Sanjay twirled a coin between his fingers. Without his hat, he didn't quite know what to do with himself. But it was necessary for Gideon to look enough like Sanjay to draw Officer Kwan away when Gideon drove Sanjay's truck from Fiddler's Folly, and the hat was key. Sanjay had no trouble handing over the keys to the expensive truck that he used to transport his magic gear to shows. It was parting with the hat that pained him.

The plan was to learn more about Lucas, which they couldn't do with a tail. Lucas didn't have a significant other or a roommate, so they had to start elsewhere.

"Blaze?" asked Sanjay, looking up from his phone. "What kind of name is Blaze?"

"A hero from a romance novel?" Tempest answered. "Just what are you reading on your phone? We need to focus."

"According to Lucas's social media, that's the name of his landlord."

From the contract for the murder mystery play, Tempest had Lucas's address. He lived in a studio apartment in-law unit behind a larger house in Hidden Creek. It wasn't far from Gray House, so he'd walked to get to the rehearsal and hadn't left his car there.

Ivy had left for work, so Tempest and Sanjay were on their own as they headed out on foot for Lucas's house, only a few minutes' walk away.

"I think we're here." Tempest pointed to an ancient Honda parked in the street with a bumper sticker that read OSCAR-WORTHY DRIVER. Lucas's car. Tempest felt a pang of sadness, knowing he'd never drive the well-loved car again.

The door of the front house was opened by a guy in his forties with sandy-blond hair, an easygoing smile, and a fitted T-shirt that casually showed off a toned physique. He held a fluffy white cat in one of his muscular arms. Yup, he could easily have stepped out of a second-chance romance novel.

After they explained they had known Lucas and wanted to talk with him, he offered his condolences, invited them inside, and told them he had fifteen minutes to spare before a video conference call.

"Can I get you something to drink?" He offered them water or a sports drink from the fridge, which they declined, and they sat down on an oversize couch next to a wall with an assortment of plants that would have looked more at home in a trendy plant store. A desk sat opposite the wall of greenery. The plant wall was positioned to make a good video backdrop.

Blaze—his real name, or at least the name he introduced himself with—asked what he could do for them.

"I know the police have already spoken to you," Tempest

guessed, but luckily, Blaze nodded. "But we're concerned because we think Lucas played a joke shortly before he died that makes Sanjay look guilty."

Blaze turned to Sanjay. "You're surprisingly calm for someone who's being framed for murder."

"Thank you," said Sanjay in all seriousness. "I've learned how to control my outward emotions. I'm a stage performer."

"Like Lucas was," said Blaze.

"And he's not being *framed*," Tempest added. "But we're concerned that the police are overly interested in Sanjay."

"Got it," said Blaze. "Did you do it?"

"I barely knew the man," Sanjay answered.

"That's not a denial. And didn't you say you were friends?"

"I didn't kill him." Sanjay put his hand over his heart. "And we said we *knew* Lucas. That's different."

Blaze nodded. "Maybe I offered you the wrong kind of drink. I've got ten more minutes, but that's enough time for a whiskey."

"We need to keep clear heads," Tempest cut in when it looked like Sanjay was about to accept. "But thank you for the offer. I know you don't have much time, but we were wondering if you noticed Lucas acting strangely in the last week."

"The police asked me the same thing. Honestly, Lucas was always overly dramatic. About everything. He was really into the role he was going to play in the murder mystery play he was part of for the summer stroll and was really excited to be part of saving that new library coming to town."

"He was?" Tempest asked. That was news to her.

Blaze shrugged. "With Lucas, you could never really tell. But even if it was just for show, he still got more signatures on the petition to save the library than anyone else. At least, according to him. He loved being the center of attention."

"I know," Sanjay grumbled.

"I didn't realize he was gathering signatures in support of the new library," Tempest said.

"Lucas made videos about everything in his life, not just his attempt to make it as an actor, so he shared how he was part of saving this important new library for Hidden Creek. He said he had an exciting new video planned to rally support for the library. I guess his library content was getting a lot of views, but I didn't watch many of his videos. I can't be bothered with social media that doesn't involve cats."

Blaze stood up, and Tempest thanked him for his time.

"Any time." He scooped the white cat back into his arms as he saw them out. "Noon will try to escape if I don't hold on to her."

"Noon?" Sanjay asked. "Is that like a philosophy to make the best use of time?"

"I think he means the cat," said Tempest, eyeing the fluffy beast. It eyed her back with disdain, as if it was fully aware she was a rabbit person.

"My ex got Midnight, our scrawny black tabby," said Blaze. "I knew I needed to do things differently after that breakup. I got in shape, learned to take care of plants, and I thought about getting a dog . . . but just couldn't do it."

"So you got a fluffy white cat and named her Noon."

"Hey, good luck finding out what happened to Lucas. He was a lot, but he was a good guy."

☠☠☠

Out on the sidewalk, Sanjay swore in Punjabi. He'd never swear in English. Neither would Tempest. They both knew it was too risky to let yourself swear even when you were upset. If you did, it might accidentally slip out on stage when something went wrong. And things inevitably went wrong when you performed live on stage. Most of the time, mistakes could easily be covered up and the audience would never know something had gone wrong. But they were human. Mistakes happened.

"Why did he have to involve me in this mess?" asked Sanjay. "I don't think I like investigating, even with my own neck on the line. In theory, it's great, and we'd get leads everywhere we went, but in reality, all I'm left with is an inferiority complex that I'll never be a cover model for a romance novel."

"Don't sell yourself short. And didn't you notice what we learned?"

"Nothing. We learned nothing. Aside from the fact that romance-novel guy is a cat dude. So unless you're going to tell me he dresses up in a cat costume at night to creep unnoticed into Gray House—or are you calling that house a library already, even though you're not done with the renovations and opened it to the public? Who names their houses, anyway? I mean, without extenuating circumstances or living in Britain. I know there's a good reason your parents named your house *Fiddler's Folly*, but—"

"Sanjay. Focus. We learned a lot more than that from him. Blaze gave us another good motive for why Lucas could have been killed."

Sanjay stopped abruptly on the sidewalk. "Tempest. What are you talking about? That was a bust."

"Don't you get it?" Tempest waited to see if he did. "If Blaze is right, Lucas was doing more than anyone else to get support for the Gray House Library of Classic Detective Fiction."

"That name is a mouthful. And the acronym is terrible as well. GHLCDF? Maybe if you tried—"

"Sanjay. Truly. I know it's a lot to be a murder suspect, but you need to focus. Lucas had a new video planned that he thought would get support for the library. *What if someone opposed to the library wanted to stop him?*"

Chapter 24

They weren't far from the town square park, so Tempest led Sanjay to a bench on the edge of the grass, under the shade of an oak tree with large drooping branches that would hide them from view if a patrol car drove by.

"You really think gathering signatures for a petition in favor of the library is worth killing over?" Sanjay asked.

"Mrs. Hudson might think so."

"So there are two petitions on opposing sides?" Sanjay typed a search into his phone. "Got it. Oh, I can't sign. Hidden Creek residents add their address to verify they're local, not just random people getting caught up in a cause they saw online."

"Which makes it *less* of a motive, since even if his videos to save the library went viral, the impact would be more symbolic." Tempest stood up from the bench and spun into a pirouette. One spin was enough to clarify her thoughts. "Murder isn't always rational. Plus, I'm still not completely convinced this isn't about a book—maybe not a rare book in the traditional sense, but these are libraries. Doesn't it make sense that a book would be at the center of everything?"

"Misdirection or coincidence is just as possible." Sanjay's face reddened as he scrolled on his phone. "Lucas had nearly as many followers as I do. How is that possible? I'm the Hindi Houdini."

"He posted constantly about every aspect of his life as he tried to make it as an actor. You don't want that level of intrusion into your life."

"Don't I?"

"Stop worrying about your virtual popularity."

Sanjay gave her a sour pout. "We're far too exposed out here, even under this tree. We went to the effort of shaking my tail. I don't want to be surveilled again."

"Veggie Magic is right down the street."

Sanjay turned up his collar as they walked down the block to the café, which only made him look more suspicious.

They found a table in a cozy back corner of the second-floor balcony that overlooked the larger first floor, and ordered coffees and pastries. This was the section that would host the guests for the private meals before this weekend's dinner theater. *If* there was a mystery play this weekend at all.

"Now that you're properly hidden, ready to get back to Lucas?" Tempest asked.

"Already ahead of you. His last post about saving the library was two days ago, not long before he texted me to ask for my help with Kira." Sanjay looked up from his phone. "Where does Kira fit into this?"

"I don't know. It seems like Lucas lied to you about wanting your help to impress her, but I don't know her too well. Most of our conversations have been about libraries. She adores her job at the Hidden Creek Public Library. She loves libraries so much that she stays even though she hates her boss, and she's definitely on the pro–Gray House Library side. She made sure we'd all signed the petition in favor of the new library getting approved."

"I'll grant that you're right that this petition might be a big deal," Sanjay admitted. "But if that makes Mrs. Hudson our main suspect, I don't see how she could have done it, since she was trapped inside with you. Did you see her the whole time? Like, every moment?"

"I did."

Sanjay's face fell. "Which leaves *me* on the hook."

"What happened to your optimism?" Tempest watched her friend's face. She'd known him for so many years that even though he was the consummate performer and knew how to hide his emotions, she could tell when something was off. "You've also been uncharacteristically snippy this week. It started before the murder."

"Pick a card." A deck of cards appeared in his hand, in place of his phone. He fanned the cards in front of her.

"Only after you answer my question."

"How do you know my card trick isn't the answer?" He leaned his elbows on the table, letting her see the deck more closely.

"Fine." She ran her index finger across the fanned-out cards before picking one. He couldn't have forced a certain card upon her.

"Look at your card without showing me what you've got, then slip it back into the deck."

She peeked at the king of hearts and nodded, then pushed the card back into the deck, about a third of the way in, making sure it was even with the other cards.

"Let me tell you a story," Sanjay said as he casually shuffled the deck. "There once was a boy who loved magic. His parents convinced him to have a practical career and go to law school. He was weak and acquiesced. He flunked out."

"Wait." Tempest stared across the table at this man she thought she knew so well. Clearly, she didn't know everything. "You didn't leave of your own free will?"

He shrugged and kept shuffling. "Technically. Only because I was about to be asked to leave. How can anyone focus in law school? Contracts are filled with pages and pages of the most excruciatingly minute details. They're the worst."

"Sanjay. You practice sleight-of-hand tricks and grand illusions that require more concentration and precision than a hundred-page contract. You spend thousands of hours with hyper focus."

"Of course." He cut the deck using a deft move with only his left hand. "But that's only because magic is wondrous and meaningful. Contracts? They're mostly about how to make sure you can eviscerate another person, should you choose to do so. The single lecture we got on the *history* of contracts? Now that was fascinating. Did you know that contracts started as clear, one-sentence agreements long before we reached our current nightmare era of contracts?"

"You're rambling."

He was also still shuffling the cards with a single hand and making it look so effortless that Tempest felt a twinge of envy. She was good at many aspects of illusion, but close-up magic wasn't one of her strengths.

"Really." He slammed his palms together. "How can people be expected to understand contracts?"

"You have to read contracts when you agree to performances."

"Exactly." He laughed bitterly and flipped the cards through the air. They fanned out in a beautiful arc before landing gently at his feet. Only one card remained in his hand.

The king of hearts.

Tempest's card.

Sanjay hadn't seen which card she'd picked; she was sure of it. There were half a dozen ways he could have done it—probably more—but she hadn't noticed which method he'd used, making it look like magic. No, *feel like* magic. That was the whole point.

She smiled—until she saw that the card had been altered. Slicing through the center of the king of hearts was the jagged line of a black Sharpie, making it look as if the king had been ripped in half. In addition to the jagged line, a solitary black teardrop fell from the king's eye.

A server dropped off their coffees, Tempest's chocolate croissant, and Sanjay's slice of pie. He loved the pie here. Normally, his face would have lit up like that of a child and he would have immediately scooped up a bite of pie. But not today. He barely registered its presence.

"No," Tempest murmured. The king of hearts was obviously meant to represent Sanjay. That meant . . . "You didn't. You signed a bad contract?"

"I was distracted! My manager was on vacation, and it seemed like such a small event that wouldn't do any harm . . . I screwed up."

"What did you do?"

"It's what I'm *about* to do." He stabbed the warm peach pie with his fork but still didn't take a bite.

"How bad is it?" Tempest tried not to show the horror in her face. Some of the gigs from her past were so horrid that she'd blocked them out.

"I thought I was signing up to perform magic at a private

event that's local to you, so we'd have time to hang out. I was told it was for the Hidden Bookshop's new wine bar. The bookshop is celebrating the grand opening of their extension."

"I know all about it, and Milton works there. That doesn't sound bad at all."

"What I *really* agreed to do was be a shill for the Hidden Wine Bar's signature line of wine during the summer stroll this weekend. It's not a private function I agreed to do; I'll be at a pop-up on the sidewalk in front of the Hidden Wine Bar on Saturday and Sunday afternoons." He crumpled the playing card in his hand.

Tempest winced inwardly, but she didn't let it show on her face. She understood why he was wary. In their profession, reputation was so important. When it came to private events, Sanjay always said yes to friends, but carefully considered other requests. And public ones? He was far more selective about what he'd agree to.

"Is that really all that bad?" Tempest asked. "This is just Hidden Creek. It's not so different from performing for a friend. The couple who own the Hidden Bookshop are lovely. Alex and Aurora. My grandfather is friends with them."

"Your grandfather is friends with everyone."

This was true.

"I met them before signing the contract," Sanjay said, "and you're right that they're lovely people. They're in their seventies and could easily have retired, but they love the bookshop too much. Aurora started growing wine grapes on the steep, otherwise-unusable part of land behind their house, and they got such a good harvest that they decided it would be fun to add a wine bar to the bookshop and bottle their own wine. Nobody in their right mind does a home renovation."

"You do realize that's what my dad and I do for a living, right?"

Sanjay waved away her comment. "You bring magic into people's homes. But a straightforward renovation? They all cost twice as much and take twice as long. It's better to get something new."

"The storefront next door was already there. It was a small project. All they had to do was knock down part of one wall."

Sanjay blinked at her. "Secret Staircase Construction did their renovation?"

Tempest grinned. "Of course. It's a local bookshop, and didn't you notice it's a sliding bookcase that serves as the secret entrance to the wine bar next door? Anyway, the renovation was *under* budget for once, and they're quite well-off—that's why they can play around with a wine bar that's never going to make much money—and I'm guessing they pay good rates to magicians they hire?"

Sanjay's cheeks flushed. "I should have known there was a catch when they offered to pay me so well. And I know you said it's not so bad, but they requested the Inexhaustible Bottle."

"The kids' trick?"

"Exactly. But in this case, they want me to use it so I can serve adults any type of wine they request from the same wine bottle. Red, white, or rosé, all from the same bottle, to sample their wines."

"I know that trick is a bit beneath what you're capable of, but it's a good one. I've done that one on stage with a teapot. It gets a good audience reaction." She didn't add that it was indeed an audience of kids.

"Don't you see? I'm using magic to publicly endorse their amateur wine! Like a paid spokesperson in a commercial." His face perked up. "Oh. Maybe if I'm arrested, I won't need to perform this weekend. A silver lining."

"That's a bit overdramatic, don't you think?"

"The Hindi Houdini is *my life*, Tempest. I guard that identity carefully. But with this? I'm no longer an independent entity."

"It's really not that bad."

He scowled at her. "I'm a corporate shill."

"Only for one weekend, and it's—"

"Tempest. For someone who's achieved so much, you can be amazingly clueless sometimes."

"I really don't think it's that bad. And maybe—"

"You're not listening to me! Sometimes your friends just want you to be there for them. To commiserate. You don't have to solve my problem. You *can't*. I don't expect you to. Even if I'm wrong about how bad this is—which I'm not—it doesn't matter. I just wanted you to listen." Sanjay shook his head as he tossed more money than was necessary onto the table, then stood and walked off without another word.

"Where are you going?" Tempest called after him, not caring what other diners thought.

"Not that you're listening to what I'm saying," he said without turning back, "but I have things to do that don't involve you."

Tempest sat alone in stunned silence as Sanjay disappeared from view.

She was about to go after him, when a hand grabbed her arm.

Chapter 25

nid?" Tempest looked around and saw the hand belonged to Enid Maddox.

Enid was dressed elegantly as always, in a pencil dress with a black-and-white houndstooth print so delicate that it appeared gray if you didn't look closely.

"I've been there," Enid said. "You should let him be."

Tempest winced. "How much did you hear?"

"Only that he wants a bit of space. I'm sorry to have interrupted, though . . ."

"It's fine. You're right. I need to give him some space. Do you want to join me?"

Tempest looked at Enid more closely now. Even though she was dressed immaculately, her hair was unusually unkempt and she had dark circles under her eyes.

"You heard about Lucas Cruz," Tempest said.

Enid nodded. "I came to find you as soon as I heard what happened last night. You weren't at your house, but your grandmother suggested this as one of the places you might be."

Tempest checked her phone but didn't see any missed messages from Enid.

"I didn't call ahead," Enid said. "I . . . I wanted to tell you this in person."

Tempest was suddenly aware that there were only a couple of other diners around. Enid couldn't be about to admit she had a hand in Lucas's death, could she?

The server arrived, and Enid ordered an iced tea. That put Tempest at ease. She couldn't imagine that Enid would do so if she was about to confess to a nefarious deed.

"What did you want to talk about?" Tempest hid her expression behind her coffee.

"Is it true that Lucas Cruz's death has some strange elements?"

"I don't think I'm supposed to be talking about—"

"I'm not here for gossip. We need to talk about Harold Gray."

"*Harold?*" That wasn't what Tempest was expecting.

"I know it's not possible." Enid twisted a napkin between her fingers. "I mean, the rational part of my brain knows it's not possible. But."

"Enid. Are you trying to tell me Harold's ghost killed Lucas?"

Enid gave Tempest a defiant stare. "You know me, Tempest. I'm not one for flights of fancy. But there are some things and—" She broke off from whatever she had been about to say and instead said, "I still don't know why Harold asked me to oversee the library instead of Mrs. Hudson."

"The two of them had a falling-out, didn't they?"

Enid paused before answering, "But she's a trained librarian, unlike me."

"You love books and classic mysteries so much," said Tempest, "that you figured out how to open a library devoted to your favorite genre. You hired the right people, and within a few years, you made it thrive beyond your wildest dreams. It's no surprise that a friend and fellow classic mystery lover appointed you in charge of setting up his sister library."

Enid gave an awkward shrug. "I got the sense that there was something left unsaid between Harold and Mrs. Hudson."

"Romantically?"

"I don't think so. She's decades younger than he was. I know that doesn't matter, but that wasn't the sense I got from their relationship."

"You mean the fact that she'd grown to hate him."

Enid shook her head. "There was something more complicated going on."

"But you don't know what it was?"

Enid twisted the napkin even more tightly between her fingers. "I was thinking . . . maybe we could ask Harold. If he really is haunting that house, we could contact him to ask what's really going on. That way we'd know for certain if he was involved."

Tempest studied Enid Maddox. She was outwardly well put-together, and she always carried herself confidently, but she was incredibly nervous today. She wasn't joking.

"A séance?" Tempest asked. "Sanjay isn't a real medium, you know. When he does séances, they're performances. And he's sworn never to do one ever again. Not after what happened at Lavinia's house."

"I don't know if that's what I even meant." Enid twisted the napkin so tightly that her knuckles were turning white. "Do you know why I love locked-room mysteries?"

"Because they're pretty damn awesome?"

That got a small smile from Enid. "Because you get a ghost

story with *a rational ending.* The whole premise of an impossible crime story is that it looks as if there could only be a supernatural explanation, but then you get a perfectly rational and satisfying explanation at the end."

"You're not in it for the fun of a page-turning mystery?"

Enid shrugged. "I like the puzzle, but that wasn't the main appeal for me when I started reading mysteries. I was drawn to impossible crime mysteries *because of what happened.*"

Enid's hands shook. As soon as she noticed, she abandoned her mangled napkin and hid her hands beneath the table.

The server dropped off Enid's iced tea, giving Enid a moment to compose herself. She stirred a sugar packet into the tea and watched the liquid spiral.

"When I was a girl, just ten years old, the elderly woman living next to us died. It was a full week before anyone found her body."

"How awful."

"What's even worse," said Enid, "is that for that entire week, *I saw her.*"

"Oh, I'm so sorry, Enid. You saw her body from your bedroom window?"

Enid shook her head. "No. I mean I saw her walking around. At least that's what I *thought* at the time. But when I learned what had happened, I knew it was her ghost I'd seen."

Tempest blinked at Enid.

"I know you don't believe me," Enid said.

"You were a kid—"

"I was. And nobody believed me. They said it was my imagination. *It wasn't.* But as soon as I discovered Ellery Queen, John Dickson Carr, and Agatha Christie as a preteen, they gave me the answers I desperately needed. I learned, then, that there were all sorts of ways that the impossible situation I saw could have happened. I was told that the house was locked up, but maybe a squatter had figured out how to get inside to take advantage of a warm house in the wintertime. Or maybe the police got the time of death wrong because of some trick with the temperature of the room. Or maybe she didn't die of natural causes but was murdered and the killer was back to cover up their tracks. I was relieved."

"Relieved that she could have been murdered?"

Enid laughed. "No. Relieved there were so many possible rational explanations to something that appeared impossible. But now?" Enid's smile fell away. "Being inside that house, *seeing* a truly impossible crime in front of my eyes that first night when there was some sort of twisted game set in motion. And the next night another impossibility that ended in murder? It's something Harold would have loved."

"You think Harold Gray is a murderer?"

Enid gave a hopeless shrug. "You were there. I need to know . . . was it really impossible? Or can you give me the rational explanation?"

"We'll figure out what happened," Tempest assured her.

"So you *can't* give me a rational explanation."

"Not yet. But it can't be impossible. It can't be Harold Gray's ghost."

"Can't it? Ivy told me you heard Harold's voice."

That's why she was here. Ivy had shown up to work and already told Enid everything.

"We heard something that sounded like him. Maybe Cameron knows how to imitate his great-uncle's voice. Maybe—"

Enid gasped. "You think *Cameron*—"

"I didn't say that." Tempest really needed to think before she spoke. Especially to someone thinking irrationally because of a childhood trauma. "I was just pointing out that there are numerous possibilities."

"Such as?"

Tempest took a sip of the coffee from her warm mug, hoping it would give her time to figure out what to say. It didn't.

"The police are working on it," she said instead. "Detective Blackburn won't let this murder go unsolved. There's going to be a rational explanation."

"I hope so," said Enid. "I hope you're right, but I don't think you are. I should have trusted my gut all those years ago. I don't know what happened to my neighbor who lived next to my childhood home, or in Harold Gray's house, so be careful, Tempest."

Enid was right about one thing. Whatever was going on in Gray House wasn't a straightforward murder.

Chapter 26

After admitting her lingering fears after that traumatic childhood experience, Enid was spent. She asked for her drink to go, leaving Tempest alone in the café.

Tempest glanced at her phone. She'd missed a text message:

Time to cancel the mystery play and escape room game.

The message from Cameron Gray wasn't surprising, but it was still like a punch in the gut. They'd put so much effort into Gray House and this weekend . . . She wrapped up her croissant that she hadn't had time to eat. Sanjay had driven, so she'd have to walk home. She called Cameron from the sidewalk as she began walking.

"Don't cancel yet," Tempest said as soon as Cameron picked up. She couldn't help glaring at the phone, even though nobody besides a dog-walker on the sidewalk, who looked disturbingly similar to his dog, could see her.

"It's not like I have a choice. Detective Blackburn asked me to call off everything happening this weekend. Both the escape room game and mystery play. I guess we don't get to be part of the summer stroll after all."

"Did he *ask* you or *tell* you?"

"He told me he couldn't guarantee when the house would be released," Cameron said. "I was about to email everyone who booked a ticket that it's canceled."

"Where are you?"

"At my apartment."

"Not at Gray House?"

"It's *a crime scene*, Tempest. I'd already planned to take this week off from my job to be there, but obviously I can't be now. Nobody's allowed in."

She kicked a pebble on the sidewalk. Right. A crime scene. "We have one more day. Tomorrow is just preview night for a few guests. Cancel tomorrow night. But give it one more day before you call off the opening on Friday night."

He didn't answer right away.

"Cameron? Did I lose you?" Sometimes reception cut out in the hills, but she hadn't gotten far beyond the main square.

"No. I didn't know what to say. I still don't. You think you can do the impossible? You think you can solve Lucas's murder in one more day?"

"I'm going to make sure we get your library approved to open as well. But you need to tell me everything you know about Mrs. Hudson and your uncle's relationship."

"Um, that was random." Cameron lowered his voice to a whisper. "Wait. Does that mean . . . You think *Mrs. Hudson* is the killer?"

"Why are you whispering?"

"One of my roommates is in the other room."

"He doesn't know about the murder?"

"We're not close."

Which is why, Tempest remembered, he was very much looking forward to moving into the little apartment Harold had
built for him on the top floor of Gray House. He lived with two
other guys, one of whom was an old college acquaintance, but
they shared the apartment for economic reasons rather than
friendship.

"What can I tell you about Mrs. Hudson and Uncle Harold?"
Cameron asked, his voice back to normal now that he wasn't
speaking of murder.

"There's something more going on with Mrs. Hudson than
we understand."

"Whoa. Are you *investigating?*"

"I assumed Ivy told you," she said. Because she did. She wasn't
crossing Cameron off her suspect list, but it didn't hurt to tell
him something he already knew.

"She mentioned it. But I assumed she meant she'd use her
knowledge of classic mysteries to think about motives and
weird solutions to seemingly impossible crimes. Is that safe
to—"

"It's less safe to carry on before we know if Mrs. Hudson is a
murderer. Lucas might have been killed because he was helping
get the library approved."

When Tempest had first learned of the idea of Harold Gray's
vision for his library to be a neighborhood gathering spot as
well as a library where anyone was free to borrow books, she
thought it sounded very much like something that would happen in a movie from the 1980s. Her dad loved those cheesy
movies where the little guy wins against all odds. All it lacked

166 ※ Gigi Pandian

was a rec center and an evil real estate developer—though she supposed Mrs. Hudson played an equivalent role.

Cameron swore. "Lucas said he wanted to help, but I didn't know it was more than talk. You think Mrs. Hudson wanted to stop him? I don't know if she's capable of something like that."

"We never know what someone else is capable of," Tempest pointed out. "What can you tell me about her relationship to Harold and the library?"

"She envied my uncle."

"Why?" When Tempest thought about Harold, she imagined the lonely old man with failing health who only had his grand-nephew checking in on him. But that was only the man as he'd been in the last few months of his life.

"Harold filled his house with books and people."

"He wasn't a people person."

"He wasn't," Cameron agreed. "You've met him, so you understand. But long before you met him, he used to throw literary-themed events at that house. He never participated, but he was the puppet master. That way, he could see other people enjoying books, but he didn't have to make small talk or associate with people he didn't like, both of which would have killed him."

Tempest scowled at the phone, even though they weren't on a video call. "Why didn't he ever tell me this when I interviewed him? Why did he make it sound like only the start of an idea, so Ivy and I had to create everything from scratch?"

"How am I supposed to know why Harold did anything?" Cameron was nearly yelling. "Sorry. I didn't mean to snap at you. This whole week. It's been a lot. And anyway, I never attended those parties. I was just a kid when he threw them. I probably wasn't even born when he started them. He stopped a while ago."

Which explained why Ash wouldn't have known about the book-themed parties. He and Morag had only moved from Scotland into the tree house in-law unit at Fiddler's Folly six years ago. Otherwise, Tempest was sure he would have known all about them.

"Did Mrs. Hudson wish Harold had left his book collection to her?" Tempest asked.

"I don't think so. They aren't worth much, and what would she have done with them? You've seen what the house looked like before you started renovations, stacked full of books. When I got the call that he'd died, my first thought was to wonder whether he'd been crushed by one of his towering stacks of books and died with an Agatha Christie novel in his hand and a smile on his face." Cameron gave a sad laugh.

"Anyway," he continued, "Mrs. Hudson loves Sherlock Holmes, but Harold didn't have any rare Arthur Conan Doyle novels. Enid's Locked Room Library inspired him and showed him how a small private library in Hidden Creek would be perfect, and then he was able to convince Enid to help him set up his own."

"But then he passed away before it was completed."

"You worked with him, so you know he put in a lot of the work up front."

"We only came in after he'd done the initial planning. What did you do before Secret Staircase Construction came on board? Was Mrs. Hudson involved at all?"

"She wasn't. Uncle Harold got the blessing of the local public library shortly before you were hired for the renovation. Harold asked them what they thought, since he never wanted to upset a local public library. They all supported the idea of a private library down the street as long as it would be open to the community free of charge—which was always the idea.

Uncle Harold got advice from the staff of the library and from Enid. He also got a lawyer to set up a trust. That way, I'll be able to live in the apartment at the top of the house and get both a salary and library expenses paid well into the future. The trust also pays the salary of a permanent library assistant, as well as Enid's salary for two years, to compensate her for getting everything set up properly. She'll make sure everything goes well, like it did with her library. But you already know all this, Tempest. The trust pays Secret Staircase Construction. I don't know what else I can tell you that you don't already know."

"I just don't see where Mrs. Hudson fits. Why she's so angry. By the time I met her, after you and Harold hired Secret Staircase Construction, she was already opposed to the library. You really don't know why?"

"When Harold knew he was dying, all he told me was that she was against it but that we didn't need to worry about her. He said that he knew her past, and she'd come around."

"Her past?" Tempest asked.

"Harold didn't tell me what it was. I got the strongest sense from him that he and Mrs. Hudson used to be friends. Before something happened. He wouldn't talk about it. But whenever I came to visit Harold, I'd see Mrs. Hudson watching us from across the street. It was creepy. Not saying hello. Just *staring*."

Creepy, indeed. What were Harold and Mrs. Hudson hiding?

Chapter 27

Tempest was hoping for some time alone to have space to think about the related elements that were swirling through her mind but not yet coalescing into anything coherent. But as she stepped through the front gate of Fiddler's Folly, the only thing she detected was a sweet, buttery scent. One she couldn't resist. She hadn't eaten a proper lunch, and the steep walk through the winding hillside streets on her way home left her tired and hungry. She made her way up the sloping incline of Fiddler's Folly and knocked on the door of the tree house, using the gargoyle that served as both a knocker and a lock.

The small home in the midst of two oak trees hadn't always locked securely. All you had to do was solve a simple puzzle: if you twisted a pencil in the gargoyle's mouth, the door would click open. That was back when Tempest's parents were experimenting with whimsical architectural elements, before anyone lived in the tree house. Now that Ash and Morag lived there full-time, and murders affecting the family had taken place, a proper lock had been installed. Unfortunate, but necessary. Tempest was glad that the gargoyle itself was still in place.

Grandpa Ash opened the door wearing an apron around his waist and a fedora on his bald head. He grinned at her and stepped aside, letting her climb the stairs ahead of him.

"I thought you were out sleuthing." She breathed in the comforting scent that wasn't only sweet but also tart. "But the house smells amazing."

"I'm baking more cardamom shortbread cookies for my next set of rounds." He still thought of visits as the rounds he did as a doctor. "I already ran out of cookies."

"And store-bought wouldn't do."

He clicked his tongue, and they headed up the stairs. "Of course not. I'm trying to get people to open up to me."

"Any news?"

"Perhaps." They reached the cozy kitchen, and Ash pointed to a computer tablet on the breakfast nook. "I learned two things so far that might be of interest. I found the list of people who signed the petition to prevent the library from opening."

"You sweet-talked someone into giving it to you?"

"It's public record. Don't sign a petition if you don't want your name known."

Huh. She hadn't thought about that before. "Anyone interesting?"

A timer dinged and he pulled two baking sheets from the oven, making the kitchen even more fragrant. Tempest wished she could curl up in the breakfast nook and take a nap in a bed of cardamom cookies.

"What's more interesting," said Ash, "is who *didn't* sign. Martha Hudson didn't sign her own petition."

Tempest blinked at her grandfather. She didn't know what was more surprising. That he knew Mrs. Hudson's first name—Martha!—or that she hadn't signed her own petition.

She told him as much and added, "It had to have been an oversight. Like she thought that she as the organizer was a given."

He chuckled. "I don't believe so. I think that as angry as she was about the library across the street from her home, and whatever had happened between her and Harold, she couldn't bring herself to personally condemn a library."

"Because she'd been a librarian for her whole career."

Ash touched his finger to the tip of her nose. "She retired young, in her early fifties, to take care of her husband when he was battling cancer. He didn't make it."

"That's why she's so bitter."

Ash shook his head. "I wouldn't necessarily jump to that conclusion. But she's more complex than simply someone you're thinking of as the enemy."

"You don't think she's Lucas's killer?"

"Not enough information." He pointed at the cookies. "I have more work to do. I should tell you one more thing before you go see your guest. I—"

"My guest?"

Ash frowned. "He didn't text you?"

"Who?"

"Well, maybe it's a surprise."

Tempest raised an eyebrow. "I hate surprises."

Ash picked up a bowl of cookie dough and spun on his heel. When he came to a stop, the bowl of dough was a small platter of baked cookies. He handed it to her.

Tempest couldn't resist grinning as she accepted the platter. "Fine. You're right. I love being surprised."

Even in his eighties, he really was better at sleight of hand than both her and Sanjay. Not that his reflexes were as good, but he'd been a magician since he was a kid. Even though Ash left India after a family tragedy and switched careers, Tempest knew he still practiced in private. Magic is something that's a part of you. Tempest didn't practice as much as she would if she were expecting to be on stage, but she found herself unconsciously practicing the movements she'd done thousands of times. It was second nature.

"Your guest is with Abra in the Secret Fort," Ash said. "At least that's where I last saw him heading."

Tempest paused before starting down the stairs. "Didn't you say you'd learned one more thing of interest?"

"That petition against the library," said Ash. "It has less than a hundred signatures. It was going to fail. The new Gray House Library has tremendous public support. There's no way for it to fail."

"At least there was no way for the library to fail," said Tempest, "until a murder happened at Gray House."

Chapter 28

Tempest left her grandfather in search of her mystery guest.

The paved path that wended across the steep hillside between the main buildings of Fiddler's Folly didn't stretch to the Secret Fort. The unfinished stone structure didn't yet have a full roof either, but it now had a door.

This was the small stone building that Tempest was making into her own home. For now, the unfinished structure held both Abra's hutch and a big table for Tempest to think through the architectural plans to expand it into a house. The hutch was bigger than the six-foot worktable, fashioned in the shape of a sprawling castle, and Abra preferred lording over his dominion more than being inside the house with Tempest, even though he was house-trained. She could tell because the curmudgeonly lop-eared rabbit had no qualms about nipping at her heels or scratching on doors when he wanted to go somewhere else.

Tempest opened the door and found Abra happily resting in the arms of her visitor—a sight that made her do a double take.

Sanjay's bowler hat rested on his head, but this *wasn't* Sanjay. Gideon looked up from Abra and smiled at her.

She lifted the hat off Gideon's head. It looked good on him, but it was jarring to see the hat on anyone besides Sanjay.

"Thanks," he said. "This retro hat is surprisingly heavy."

"You didn't mess with anything inside, did you?" She flipped the black hat in her hands, which was more difficult than it looked from how casually Sanjay spun and flipped it.

"I tried not to touch it more than necessary, in case I accidentally dislodged a secret compartment. That's why I left it on my head. Seemed the safest place for it."

"You came by to bring back the sacred hat?"

"I wish I could say I was being so altruistic. I finished cleaning out my rental and did my walk-through with my landlord."

"You've moved out already?" Tempest knew he was leaving in a few days, but it hit her that this was the end of an era. Even though he was renting, he'd made the small house in Oakland his own, especially the backyard, where he displayed his sculpture works in progress. He'd strung fairy lights throughout the yard that made it look as if the stone creatures, imbued with such personality from Gideon's skill with stone, had come to life.

"In an attempt to get my security deposit back, I was being overly flexible. I shouldn't have done it. I failed anyway."

"What was your offense?" Tempest couldn't imagine careful Gideon doing anything to damage a rental.

"I fixed the fireplace. How was I supposed to know he didn't want a functioning fireplace? He said now he has to pay to seal it up again before someone else moves in."

"Please tell me you didn't leave that gorgeous dragon mantelpiece sculpture behind."

Gideon had carved a sculpture in the shape of a dragon's open mouth as the mantelpiece around the fireplace. When you lit a fire, it looked as if the dragon's open mouth was breathing fire.

"Nope." Gideon grinned. "The fireplace in the rental is now functional but stripped bare. My dragon is in the barn now until I figure out where it's going. My boxes and suitcases are there as well."

"Our workshop barn here at Fiddler's Folly?"

"Your dad came to get the mantelpiece so I wouldn't lose it, and he saw my car filled with all my stuff, so he asked what my plan was. I, uh, hadn't thought that far ahead."

"You're leaving in three days, and you hadn't figured out where your stuff was going?"

He shrugged. "My mind's been on other things. Aside from my sculptures, most of which have already been delivered to galleries, I don't have that much stuff, so Darius insisted on keeping it here. He knows my parents aren't close by, so he insisted I stay in one of your guest rooms." He scratched under Abra's chin and smiled at Tempest. "I'll earn my keep by feeding Abra."

"Three days," murmured Tempest. "I can't believe you're really leaving."

"I know."

Tempest didn't want to think about it, so instead, she said, "Were you seriously just standing here holding a bunny, not listening to music or a podcast, not reading anything on your phone, when you had no idea when I'd be back?"

He shrugged. "Abra and the stones are good company."

"I'm glad to see the rumors of your cell phone addiction were exaggerated."

Gideon set Abra back in his extravagant castle-shaped hutch. "Fighting my demons is still a work in progress. It *is* addictive."

"You still have it, though, right?"

He nodded. "I know it comes in handy. I borrowed three historical fiction books from the library to remind me I don't need a phone to entertain myself. If I don't have time to get back to my local library before I leave, I might need to leave them with you to return for me."

Tempest laughed. "Only you would check out physical library books with historical settings to get over cell phone addiction instead of internet articles on how to get over it."

"It's working so far."

"Staying off your phone is working so well you didn't text me you were here."

"I figure we'll be seeing a lot of each other for a few days. I thought . . . Actually, I don't know what I thought. Or rather, I guess I didn't know if you'd like it that I was crashing at your house."

"Why wouldn't I?"

"I know it's been fine when it's a bigger group . . . but I wondered if you were mad at me."

"Why would I be mad at you?" Her words came out more defensively than she'd meant them to. She wished she could take back the childish tone.

"Because I'm leaving for France."

"You think I'm mad at you for accepting the internship?" Now her defensive tone had crossed the line into anger. She hadn't been mad at him before, but now she was. "I never said anything like that."

She set Sanjay's hat on the table where she thought about plans for building out this partial structure into a house. She didn't want to accidentally snap it in two.

Gideon ran a hand over the rough stone wall beside him before looking back at Tempest. "Exactly. You never said anything. You never acknowledged it *at all*."

"Of course I did." Didn't she? "I totally did. We wrapped up all your skill-specific projects because we knew you were leaving."

"Tempest. That's Secret Staircase Construction. Not *you*. You never said anything. You never *asked me to stay*."

She stared at him for five seconds. He was right. But she couldn't tell him why. That she wanted, more than anything, to ask him to stay.

"We haven't spent time on our own since I found out I got the internship," Gideon said. "Not just the two of us. So I thought—"

Tempest threw her arms around him and stopped his words with a crushing hug. The warmth of his body and strength of his embrace felt more amazing than she wanted to admit. Both comforting and exciting.

She leaned back and looked at him. The man who saw things nobody else did. Who carved the most magical creatures in stone she'd ever seen. Who didn't realize he'd forgotten to eat for sixteen hours while working on a carving. Whose shoes were perpetually covered in stone dust.

"Silly man," she said. "I'm not mad at you. I'm sad that you're leaving, but happy for you that you got this fantastic opportunity. I didn't want to say anything, because *you're right*. I would have asked you to stay."

"And I would have," he said softly.

She shook her head. "I know. Which isn't fair to you. This is a great opportunity. That's why I couldn't say anything. Or even suggest spending time just the two of us. Luckily, it's been so busy that there wasn't time anyway. I'm sorry. I should have told you I'm sad and happy and proud and frustrated. All the things simultaneously."

The edges of his lips ticked up into a smile. "Let's make the most of my last few days in town and solve this murder. My last three days as an Abracadabra."

Abra perked up at the sound of his name.

"How about we solve the murder by tomorrow," said Tempest, "so you can attend the mystery play and try your hand escaping from a fun, non-poisoned escape room before you leave."

"Sounds good. And you know this internship is only for three months."

"I know . . ." Tempest knelt at Abra's hutch before finishing her thought. She looked up from Abra's mini turret and met Gideon's intense gaze. "But what if you decide to stay?"

He looked at her even more intensely. Which, for Gideon, was saying a lot. "I'm not staying in France."

"But you could. You never expected to be solving murders either."

He drummed his calloused fingertips together. "Turns out, I'm pretty good at helping with that, aren't I?"

Tempest raised an eyebrow. "You didn't finagle your way into the guest room to keep an eye on me, did you?"

Gideon held his hands over his heart. "You think I'm that clever and deceitful?"

He was certainly that clever, but she doubted he had a deceitful bone in his body. He took a step closer to her and tucked a lock of windblown hair behind her ear.

Tempest expected him to step back after he'd fixed her errant lock of hair, but he didn't. His hand lingered on her cheek, and he leaned forward—

The door slammed shut, plunging them into darkness in the unfinished stone tower.

Chapter 29

Tempest and Gideon sprang apart as the door slammed shut.

In the darkness, Tempest ran forward and flung open the door. She poked her head outside. A strong wind blew leaves across the ground into swirls, but she didn't see anyone.

"Wind?" Gideon asked. "Or is Sanjay back?"

"*Pae-kaathu.*" She shivered. Not because the summer wind was cold, but because of the phrase from her grandfather that had popped into her head as the wind curled around her.

"Um . . ."

"*Pae-kaathu,*" Tempest repeated. "That's what my grandfather calls this type of wind that comes out of nowhere and leads to destruction. It means 'devil wind' in Tamil." The wind swept her hair around her face. She kicked a stone in front of the door, using it as a door stopper.

"Great," said Gideon. "That's all we need. Devil wind."

Tempest shook her head at the foolishness of being disturbed by a strong breeze. "It's just the wind. I'm not expecting Sanjay for a while. He said he had something to do." She didn't feel the need to tell him she'd spectacularly offended one of her few friends. "Besides, he wouldn't be playing a joke on us. Not right now."

"You're lucky you didn't twist your ankle. With the door shut, I couldn't see anything in the dark. There wasn't time for my eyes to adjust."

"Yeah, I'll be adding more windows now that the purpose of this building is to be a home. And I need to figure out electricity in addition to windows and a proper roof." She stood next to the open door, wondering when she'd have time for this project of her own.

With the smooth knob in her hand, she was reminded of their first rehearsal at Gray House. The living room door that hadn't opened, the darkness they'd been plunged into, Lucas's dead eyes that had stared up at her when she thought he was Sanjay and flipped him over.

"I wasn't wrong," she whispered.

"I believe you about the wind."

She shook her head with frustration. There was something she was missing about Lucas's game and his murder. *Many* things, but one that was just beyond her grasp, so close she could sense it yet not quite grab hold of it.

She kicked the stone away and swung the door shut again, leaving them enveloped in near darkness.

"Tempest? Um, Tempest? Why are we in the dark again?"

"The darkness," she whispered, the realization hitting her with a force that made her shake.

"You okay?"

"We've been looking at this all wrong, Gideon."

Abra thumped his foot. He didn't mind darkness, but he sensed the anxiety in Tempest's voice. She heard the thumping, but she could barely see Abra's fluffy form.

"It was so dark that night," said Tempest. "For the ten seconds when the lights were out during the rehearsal, we could only see shadows."

"You've remembered something."

Tempest swung open the door and let the daylight in. "Sanjay and Lucas were the only two people who knew Lucas was hiding in the magic trunk, waiting to switch places with Sanjay when the lights went out. The two of them are roughly the same height and build."

"Sure," said Gideon, "but why does that matter?"

"Nobody else knew Lucas was there besides Sanjay." She'd been wrong about everything. They all had.

"Um, are you trying to say that now you think Sanjay was involved in Lucas Cruz's death? Where is he anyway?"

Her heart thudded in her chest. Sanjay had stormed off. *Alone.*

"Tempest? What's the matter? What aren't you saying?"

"Detective Blackburn didn't put a tail on Sanjay because he thinks he's guilty." She closed her eyes and tried to steady her breathing. Blackburn hadn't said those words, and neither had the officer for whom her grandfather had brought cookies.

"You think the patrol car was watching someone else?"

"The officer said he was *keeping an eye on Sanjay*, Gideon." This was bad. The truth had been in front of them the whole time, but they hadn't seen it. "Don't you see? Blackburn isn't worried about Sanjay running away. He's worried about Sanjay *being in danger.*"

"You mean . . ."

"My first instinct that night was right." Tempest thought back to that terrible moment two nights ago when her gut told her she was looking at a dead man. "Lucas Cruz has been dead since that first dress rehearsal, when the lights went out. *Sanjay was the intended victim.*"

Chapter 30

"Am I right?" Tempest stood in front of Detective Blackburn in his office, her hands balled into fists. "You're not tailing Sanjay because you think he's a killer, but because you're worried he's the intended victim?"

"Why did you all think otherwise?" Blackburn shook his head. "Were you part of helping him disappear this morning? If you know where he is—"

"I have no idea where he is. Truly. He's angry at me, so he's not returning my texts." She sank into a chair and put her head in her hands. "We were right that first night when we thought Lucas was dead?"

Blackburn gave a curt nod. "I didn't know for certain last night, which is why I admit I might have been a little bit vague with Sanjay. Last night, what I knew was that if Mr. Cruz was killed while you were trapped inside that escape room, Sanjay was looking like my main suspect—yes, in spite of his connection with you. But if the ME's initial assessment that he was killed the day before was correct . . . The two men do look very much alike."

"Especially in the dark," she whispered.

"Exactly. If the killer failed in their first attempt, it was prudent to keep an eye on Sanjay. He was either the prime suspect or the intended victim. A good person to keep an eye on."

Tempest gripped the edge of the desk. Where was Sanjay now? Gideon had gone in search of him while Tempest talked with Blackburn.

"I got confirmation just a few minutes ago," he continued. "Mr. Cruz was indeed dead long before you were all trapped in the escape room. That's why I'm back at the station. I need to take new statements. Mr. Cruz was killed the previous day, like you and your friends initially thought. I need statements about *that* night."

"So it couldn't have been Lucas who trapped us in that escape room before his partner turned on him." She'd been hoping she was wrong, because it would mean Sanjay wasn't in grave danger. "But that prop gun couldn't have—"

"Why do you think he was shot?"

"Because of the bullet hole." She blinked at him. She'd seen Lucas's dead eyes and the bullet hole in his chest.

"That wasn't a bullet hole, Tempest. Lucas Cruz wasn't shot. He was stabbed."

Chapter 31

Normally, Tempest Raj processed large amounts of information in a short space of time. She had to. On stage, with thousands of people giving their full attention to you, it was essential to make calculations so a routine would go off down to the fraction of a second. Live on stage, there were no do-overs. A hiccup in the stage lighting had to be accounted for. A distraction from the audience had to be ignored. Landing on the stage a few inches out of alignment after spinning into a tempest had to be rectified invisibly.

But this? Lucas was truly dead long before a trickster trapped them in the escape room. Sanjay was really in danger. *And* a bullet hole wasn't really a bullet hole?

None of this made any sense. It couldn't really have been Harold's ghost, could it?

"We saw a bullet hole. Lucas—" She broke off with a gasp.

"He was stabbed by something that made a round hole that looked like a bullet hole?"

Blackburn perked up. "You have an idea what that could have been?"

"I know exactly what it was. An *ice pick*."

"You saw an ice pick? Our team didn't find it."

"It's a prop for a block of ice. Our mystery play is set in the 1930s, so we sprinkled in bits of authenticity, including a block of ice for drinks." She pressed her fingertips to her temples. "We're supposed to have an ice pick . . . but I didn't actually see it before we started our rehearsal that night."

She wanted to think it was because they didn't have an ice block in place either, but realistically, that meant the murder was premeditated. *Someone had already pocketed the ice pick.* To kill Sanjay. She felt ill.

"Let's go over the events of that night."

Tempest shook her head. "I need to find Sanjay—"

"Our team is already looking. I don't really think he's in immediate danger. The patrol car was just a precaution. We all enjoyed your grandfather's shortbread, by the way. He gave Kwan enough cookies for everyone in HCPD, as well as the county's forensics team."

Tempest relaxed for the first time since she'd arrived at the station. He was right. It would be stupid for the killer to try again when there was so much attention. Even though Sanjay had shaken his tail—thanks to her stupid-yet-successful idea for Gideon to take his bowler hat—and had gone off on his own, he was most likely fine.

"I need to let Sanjay, Gideon, and Ivy know about this," Tempest said as she reached for her phone. "Then I'll give my statement about that first night."

"Put that thing away. Ivy's already on her way in to give a

statement, but we haven't reached Sanjay, and Gideon wasn't there the night of your dress rehearsal. You ready?" Blackburn started a recording and said the date and their names.

"Ivy and I wrote a short murder mystery game," Tempest began. "One of those dinner theater plays, with a few actors. It's supposed to have a preview night tomorrow, and we have a full opening two nights from now."

"As part of the Hidden Creek summer stroll."

"It's sold out all weekend. Two shows a night Friday, Saturday, and Sunday. We hired three actors from the Creekside Players. They're all amateur actors having fun."

"Tell me more about them."

"You already know—"

"You know how this works, Tempest. Details matter."

"Sanjay was never supposed to be there that night, so none of us knew until that afternoon that he would be there."

"Mr. Cruz canceled that day?"

"Lucas called him earlier that day, saying he couldn't make it to the dress rehearsal and asking if Sanjay could fill in for him. Nobody was suspicious at the time. It's not like Lucas was a professional actor, so we thought maybe life got in the way or maybe he was just a flake. But then we learned otherwise."

She took a deep breath to make sure she'd recount the information correctly. She was a terrible eyewitness in the sense that *everyone* was. Her own preconceived notions shaped what she experienced and what she remembered, but the truth was in there somewhere. She'd been there when Lucas was killed. She simply had to put the pieces together of what had really happened.

"Lucas told Sanjay he wanted to pull off a stunning magic trick to impress Kira, who he had a crush on. You met Kira last night, since she was with us in the escape room."

"Ms. Kendrick," Blackburn acknowledged.

"So Sanjay brought over his magic trunk, which has two false bottoms and plenty of air holes for someone to hide in. They arranged for Sanjay to play Lucas's character for the first few minutes, then when the lights went out for just a moment, the two of them would miraculously swap places. Lucas would appear, and then Sanjay would appear a few minutes later at the front door, carrying a bouquet of flowers for Kira, courtesy of Lucas."

Blackburn looked skeptical.

"It's an impressive trick on stage," Tempest said. "And Kira is a performer—both a singer and actor—who likes theatrics, so it was a plausible story for Lucas to tell Sanjay to get his help."

"What happened during the performance itself?"

"I was sitting in the back of the room in one of the folding chairs we rented to have room for the audience. We rented furniture to have enough seats for attendees. Ivy, Cameron, and Enid were sitting in the larger pieces of furniture in the front. The four of us were the audience for the dress rehearsal. Kira and Milton were performing in front of the fireplace, and Sanjay came into the room through the archway leading to the kitchen and dining room. Then the lights went out."

"The power went out?"

Tempest shook her head. "No. Milton turned off the lights, like he was supposed to in the script. He fired a cap gun—the one the officer took to humor us, even though it was just a toy. When the lights came back on a second later, Sanjay was lying on the floor like he was supposed to be—only it wasn't Sanjay. It was Lucas."

"Where was everyone in relation to one another?"

"The furniture was set up in a U shape, facing the fireplace, where there was room for the actors to perform and address the audience. After Sanjay walked on stage, he took center stage in front of the hearth, right behind the trunk. Milton and Kira moved to the two sides of the fireplace to give him room for his speech, and also for Milton to cut the lights at the planned time."

"Mr. Silver, who was outside with Sanjay last night. Everyone knew he'd be the one turning out the lights?"

"Yes. And everyone knew exactly when the lights would go out."

"But only Sanjay was close to the trunk where Lucas was hiding?"

"He was the closest. Sanjay opened the trunk for Lucas, then slipped out through the back door in the kitchen—except we didn't know that at the time. What we saw at the time was that a man we thought to be Sanjay was lying on his stomach. We thought he'd forgotten his lines, since he was supposed to be on his back to point at a clue on a bookshelf. When I turned him over, it was Lucas." She pressed her eyes shut. "And he looked dead. Because he *was*."

She should have listened to her gut at the time, but she hadn't, because it had seemed impossible for her to believe her eyes.

Someone involved in their murder mystery play had killed Lucas Cruz right in front of her *two* nights ago, and then the body had simply vanished. She'd convinced herself to believe the only rational explanation—that Lucas had walked away. But Lucas hadn't walked away. How did he vanish? What else was she wrong about?

Chapter 32

L et me get you some water," Detective Blackburn said.

"I'm fine," Tempest insisted. She was as fine as it was humanly possible to be right now. "Let's get this over with so I can go find Sanjay. So, Sanjay had vanished, and we thought Lucas was dead—which he was, but things got all confused when he vanished—so we started freaking out. And we all ran to the kitchen to get our phones to call 9-1-1—staying together the whole time."

"Your phones were in the kitchen?"

"Phones get locked up to make the games more fun. It's the 1930s, so you're not supposed to have phones for help with clues."

Blackburn looked as if he was rolling his eyes on the inside, but he didn't say anything.

"We were all within sight of one another, but when we got back to the living room, Lucas was gone. And yes, we searched. Everywhere. He'd simply vanished."

Blackburn let her words sink in. "Tell me more about everyone who was there."

She nodded. "Kira Kendrick, the librarian around my age. You already talked with her, so do I need to—"

"What else can you tell me about her from that first night?"

"That's when I learned she's a fantastic singer. She has both talent and stage presence. And she's the best actor of all of them. I don't know her well. She's close to Milton, who you already spoke to. So you know he's the rare books expert who works for the Hidden Bookshop—" Tempest broke off and winced. She'd been the one to suggest the rare book motive to Blackburn, then hadn't followed up when her grandparents pointed out how illogical that was.

"We already know Mr. Cruz wasn't searching for a book," Blackburn said, "since he died that first night. What else do you remember about Mr. Silver from that night?"

"He was acting stiffly, but I can't attribute that to being about to stab the person he thought was Sanjay. Can't we do this later?" She looked at her phone. "Sanjay isn't texting me back, and we really need to find him."

"The best way to help him is to find out who did this. You were talking about Mr. Silver."

"Milton takes himself too seriously, so I wonder if he got into acting in an attempt to loosen up. Even though he's around my dad's age, he only got into acting a couple of years ago and has taken Kira under his wing."

"I thought you said Ms. Kendrick was the talented one."

Tempest gave him a wry smile. "You've never been an attractive woman in your twenties in a performance-oriented profession. It can be helpful to have people in perceived positions of authority watching your back."

"Understood."

"Kira also knows Milton isn't going to hit on her. I've heard him talking about his husband, who he adores and who'll be coming to the play this weekend—if it happens."

"We already spoke with his husband," Blackburn said, ignoring the implied question about releasing the crime scene. "Don't look so surprised, Tempest. I've been doing my job. Like I am now. What else can you remember about Ms. Kendrick's and Mr. Silver's movements that night?"

Tempest shook her head. "It was just a normal play rehearsal, except with Sanjay filling in for Lucas."

"What happened right before the lights went out?"

"I really don't know. Can't we finish this later? I need to—"

"Just one more question. Who else was there that night? I want to make sure I've got everyone I need to talk with."

"Ivy and I were both there, since we wrote the play and wanted to see the rehearsal. Cameron Gray was also in the audience, since it's his house that'll soon be a library."

"Mr. Gray was trapped in the escape room with you, so we already talked with him, but what about his movements during the rehearsal?"

"That's more than one question. But fine. I don't remember anything about his movements that night. There was nothing weird about Cameron. Secret Staircase Construction has been working with him for months—and he and Ivy have just started dating. Or are at least at a point where we know they'll be dating as soon as this is solved."

"Good to know."

"And before you ask, there are two more people to mention. Mrs. Hudson, whose security footage you're using from the escape room ordeal, was spying on us from across the street and arrived later. She'll be happy to tell you exactly what she and her sister saw from her front porch. And Enid Maddox was in our audience. She wasn't there last night when we got trapped, so you wouldn't have spoken to her already."

He shook his head. "I've heard the name. Is she another neighbor?"

"She was a friend of Cameron's great-uncle, Harold Gray. You've probably heard me mention her. She's the woman who opened the Locked Room Library a few years ago. Harold got the idea for his Library of Classic Detective Fiction from Enid, for what to do with his collection of more than ten thousand mystery novels."

A knock sounded on the door. Blackburn excused himself and asked Tempest to stay put.

"But—"

"I'll only be a minute. While I'm gone, I want you to think about one thing. That moment before the lights went out. Who was close enough to stab Lucas Cruz?"

"What, you mean besides Sanjay?" Tempest regretted the words as soon as they'd left her mouth. "You don't really think he—"

"We don't know what to think yet."

"But you just admitted I was right that he's the intended victim!"

"Tempest. You know how this works. It's early days." Blackburn slipped out and the door clicked firmly shut behind him.

Tempest wanted to run after him, but forced herself to sit still and think. She pressed her eyes shut. When they thought Lucas had been shot, it could have been any of them who'd done it. But if Sanjay wasn't the intended victim, *he was the closest to Lucas to stab him.* She didn't believe it for a second, but the police might.

Chapter 33

Detective Blackburn returned five minutes later, his lips pressed together and a strange expression on his face that she couldn't read.

"Sanjay?" Tempest could barely get out any words with how constricted her throat felt. "Is he—"

"No word on your friend's whereabouts. Sorry to worry you. We've reviewed Mrs. Hudson's security video from last night much more carefully. To see if we missed anything."

"When we were trapped in the escape room?"

"Not just when you were trapped inside. Nobody else went into or out of that house *all day and night*. Even if someone had a grappling hook for that back wall and went in from the back or sides of the house, the camera would have seen and picked up that movement. Nobody."

"But that's impossible," said Tempest. "I know we thought

it seemed impossible at the time, but I really thought a closer look at the footage would reveal more."

"So did I."

"Someone had to have placed Lucas's body in the living room. We were all with one another the whole time while trapped in the escape game, and Sanjay and Milton were together the whole time. What about Lucas's cell phone?"

Blackburn pressed his hands to his eyes. "Dead end. It never left that house."

"Neither did Lucas's body." Lucas's body had been in the house the whole time. "How did he get onto the floor last night?" Tempest asked. "Why the deception?"

"Tempest." The detective crossed his arms and gave her a stern, fatherly look. "I know you think this type of impossibility is your line of work, but you need to leave this to us. When we're done here in a minute, don't go off investigating—"

"You can't just reveal that you know Sanjay is either in danger or the killer and expect me to do nothing." She crossed the small room, but Blackburn stepped in front of her.

"We don't know what's going on yet." He was so close to her that she could smell the coffee on his breath. His tone was firm, but not unkind. "Someone, or multiple someones, is purposefully muddying the investigation. There's a chance Sanjay is still in danger. If he's not involved in the deception himself."

"You can't really think—"

"And you're too close to this to see all the possibilities."

"Are we done?" Tempest headed for the door.

"Don't you want to hear about the magic trunk?" He stepped aside, giving Tempest a wide berth to leave.

Blackburn's words had the intended effect. Tempest froze with her hand on the doorknob. She didn't open the interrogation room's door.

196 ※ Gigi Pandian

"Sanjay's magic trunk?" she asked without turning around.

"The very one."

"No." Tempest shook her head as she turned to face Blackburn. "We looked inside already."

"Like you said, it has false bottoms."

"Don't you think we already checked inside?" she snarled. "Lucas Cruz's body wasn't hiding inside the trunk."

"Well then. It looks like your friend's steamer trunk really is magic. Because that's exactly where his body was hidden."

Chapter 34

I t was supposed to be me." Sanjay gulped so audibly that it would have been comical if it hadn't been for the situation.

It was two hours later, already midafternoon, and Tempest and her three best friends had gathered in the turret above her bedroom after Sanjay was done giving another statement to Detective Blackburn and Ivy had wrapped up a few hours of work at the Locked Room Library. Sanjay had only believed Tempest's text messages after he'd listened to the voicemail messages from the detective. Until the police got involved, Sanjay thought Tempest was simply trying to provoke him.

"I don't know how I missed it," Ivy said. "But it's so obvious. It's like I've been training my whole life to solve a mystery like this, and I failed completely."

"You're not filling me with confidence that we'll solve this."

Sanjay tugged at the brim of his hat, causing an errant flower petal to escape. He gasped in horror when he spotted it.

"Then let's figure it out," Tempest said. "Nobody besides Sanjay knew that Lucas would be switching places with him at that moment. Right?"

She thought back to that devastating moment when she thought Sanjay was dead. When the body was lying unmoving on the floor and it was clear something was wrong. She shook off the feeling.

"I didn't tell anyone," Sanjay confirmed. "What's the point of putting in the work to create an illusion if it's not going to surprise people?"

"Before the lights went back on and we found Lucas lying on the floor," Ivy said, "it was dark, like we wanted it to be for the drama, but it couldn't have been completely dark. We didn't have blackout curtains."

"It only seemed so dark because our eyes hadn't yet adjusted," Tempest said. "But the darkness affected everyone. Nobody had night vision goggles."

"That you know of," Gideon pointed out.

"We would have spotted that," Ivy said.

"So it *was* me they were after." Sanjay paced back and forth. "Why didn't Blackburn simply tell me that in the first place? Why did he let me think I was going to jail?"

"Isn't being stalked by a murderer worse than jail?" Gideon asked.

"Why did I agree to help Lucas in the first place?" Sanjay wailed. "This is what being a nice guy gets me. Your dad's home security system is still in place, right?"

"It is," said Tempest. "But I don't think you're especially in more danger now. If you were the intended victim and the killer screwed up, it would be risky to kill again so soon."

"Unless it's time-sensitive," said Ivy. "If that's the case, they'll try again."

Sanjay's eyes bulged.

"Good point," said Tempest, and Sanjay's eyes bulged even more. "Seriously, Sanjay. We need to think about who'd want to harm you."

He groaned. "Why can't we just have a normal summer like normal people? Going to the summer stroll together, indulging in food and drink specials at the local restaurants and bars, buying gifts from local crafts shops, and taking our photo in the vintage photo booth at the town square information desk."

"That's never been your life," Tempest pointed out. "And you wouldn't have it any other way."

Sanjay smiled. "It's true. Who wants normal? Give me a curmudgeonly animal mascot any day. Where's Abra, anyway?"

"He's happy in his castle," said Tempest. "But I'll go get him if you need an emotional support bunny for cuddles."

"Bunny cuddles sound good to me," Ivy said, "but I'm supposed to have dinner with my sister and her family tonight. It's one of the last family dinners we'll have at the house, so let's just hurry up and finish figuring out who wants to kill Sanjay. I brought a bag of books from the library, but we should start with facts from Sanjay."

"I'm famous," said the man in question. "Lots of people resent that. Or they're upset I won't be their best friend or their boyfriend."

"You're *semi*-famous," Tempest corrected. "Just because your stage name includes the name *Houdini* doesn't mean online searches for Houdini are people looking you up."

Sanjay ignored her and flipped his bowler hat in the air. It touched the high, pointed tip of the ceiling and landed back on his head. "Two guys in particular are jealous and bad-mouth me online any chance they get, and one woman from my Hindi Houdini Heartbreakers fan club had to be kicked out because she had an unhealthy obsession with me, but luckily, she lives in Germany. None of the problematic people I know of live in California, and none of them would have paid someone to stab me with an ice pick that night."

"What about anyone who'd benefit monetarily from your death?" Ivy asked. "That's the most common motive."

Sanjay frowned at her. "You're really creepy when you say that so matter-of-factly. But no. My manager made me set up a will before I performed my illusion escaping from a coffin in the Ganges River, but it's incredibly boring. My money goes to my parents, with a request that my mom set up a fund for young magicians struggling financially. Even if you don't believe my parents love me, they're very well off already. No motive there. And are we really entertaining the notion that someone there that night is a contract killer?"

"You're right," said Tempest. "It's far more likely it's someone who was there. Who have you offended among our suspects?"

"I've helped Enid in the past," Sanjay said, "so there's no way she'd want to kill me. I barely know Cameron or the actors. And I'll take it on faith that none of you want to kill me. That leaves the most likely possibility being that Mrs. Hudson found a way into the house that we don't know about."

"You know her?" asked Gideon.

"I met her for the first time that night," said Sanjay, "but she was awful to me. I wouldn't put it past her to want to get away with a murder—of anyone—just to do it."

"Oh!" Tempest cried.

"I was mostly joking," said Sanjay.

Tempest shook her head. "So much has been going on today that I totally forgot my grandfather got some helpful information about Mrs. Hudson. She didn't sign her own petition against the library, and it looks like she wasn't even trying to gather signatures. Hardly anyone has signed it."

"That could just mean the community loves the idea of a new library," Ivy pointed out.

"Mrs. Hudson is hiding something," Tempest insisted. "I don't think she's really trying to kill the library, but what if someone else was? If someone wanted to prevent the library from opening, a murder there would hurt its chances. So even if they *thought* they were killing Sanjay, the fact that it was accidentally Lucas wouldn't make a difference."

"You mean no reason to kill again?" Sanjay perked up.

"Only if that theory is right that it's about the library," said Ivy, "not a specific person they wanted to kill."

"And that theory makes less sense," Tempest added, "when we think about the fact that the body disappeared."

"It was your theory," Sanjay grumbled.

She glared at him. "I'm brainstorming. Why would you think solving a murder would be easy?"

"I'll have you know that I've solved—"

"Um, I don't know that murder is the easiest way to get a library project shut down," Gideon cut in.

"Finally," said Sanjay. "A voice of reason."

"They did try minor sabotage first," said Tempest. "Remember the water damage, and the sliding bookcase was also wrecked."

"When was this?" Sanjay asked. "Nobody tells me anything around here."

"We've got to be overlooking something important," said Gideon. "Do we even know for sure that nobody else knew Lucas would be there that night? Sanjay, how do you know who else Lucas told?"

"He wouldn't have . . ." Sanjay trailed off. "Oh. You mean if he was lying about trying to impress Kira and had another motive, we don't know what he was up to."

"Without knowing that," Gideon said, "we don't know who Lucas would have told his plan."

Sanjay groaned yet again. He really was having a terrible day. "So was I the intended victim or not?"

"You should lie low for now," said Tempest. "Just in case."

"I can't. I signed that stupid contract to perform at the summer stroll this weekend."

"But these are extenuating circumstances," said Ivy.

Sanjay gasped. "I can't believe I forgot to tell you all what I learned after I left you at Veggie Magic. Tempest, I forgive you for forgetting what your grandfather told you. You're right that today is a hot mess. When you and Detective Blackburn told me I was the one who was supposed to be dead, everything else slipped from my mind."

Tempest raised an eyebrow. "You were investigating? I thought you had something personal to take care of."

"I *was* fulfilling a personal obligation. I did a full rehearsal for the Hidden Bookshop's staff, showing them the Inexhaustible Bottle act, and how they could choose one of three wines from the same wine bottle. They wanted four, but I pointed out that it's mostly a visual act, so red, white, and rosé do the trick. Nobody is impressed if you have a burgundy and a merlot pour out, since they look nearly identical. They—"

"Sanjay," said Tempest. "Focus."

"Right! Right. Milton was there."

"That's not suspicious," said Ivy. "We know he's a rare book guy who works at the Hidden Bookshop. Is there a name for a rare book expert?"

"I think it's 'antiquarian' something-or-other," said Sanjay.

"But he's *not*. That's the thing I learned. He lied to us. He's not their rare books expert. He's their *accountant*."

"Why would he have lied about that?" Ivy asked.

"I don't know. Maybe he's embezzling and thought I was onto him and was there that night to catch him? Or maybe he's even the person who suggested me to Lucas."

"But you don't know him," Ivy said, "do you?"

"Not personally, but I've occasionally visited that bookshop when I've got time to kill in Hidden Creek before traffic lets up back to the city. I've bought a couple of really old and rare magic books from Aurora, which is how they know me. Do you think this means I won't have to perform at their booth after all?" Sanjay looked hopeful for the first time all evening. "I never thought I'd utter these words, but I hope Milton wants to kill me. I'm pretty sure that would get me out of my contract with the Hidden Bookshop."

Chapter 35

What's the plan?" Gideon asked as a ray of afternoon sunlight shone through the window of Tempest's secret turret. "Please don't tell me you want to confront Milton directly."

"Of course we do," said Sanjay. "The element of surprise is effective."

"Hang on," said Tempest. "Gideon is right that we can't simply rush into confronting a possible murderer."

Sanjay scowled at her. "When have you shied away from that in the past? This is my neck—"

"One I care about very much." She put her hands on his shoulders. He was understandably tense, and her touch did little to relax him. "We need to think this through first. Didn't Blackburn tell you the other thing he'd confirmed with forensics?"

"You mean how even if I'm not the intended victim, the detective is going to pin this on me?" Sanjay asked.

Tempest let go of him. "About your steamer trunk."

"He suggested that Lucas's body was hidden inside my magic trunk." Sanjay shrugged. "But he was just trying to get me to confess. Wait . . . you don't really think—"

"Lucas was in a secret hiding spot inside the trunk the whole time?" Ivy shivered. "Detective Blackburn didn't tell me that."

"Blackburn doesn't really think that." Sanjay gaped at them. "Does he? He can't possibly—"

"He has to be wrong," said Tempest, "because it's impossible. We looked in the trunk's false bottoms."

"Exactly. He was just playing mind games."

Tempest hated to break the news to him, but it wouldn't help to keep it from him. "It sounds like he has forensic evidence."

Sanjay flung himself down on the beanbag. "His body was really inside my trunk? You see what that means, don't you?"

"That your steamer trunk really is magic?" Ivy asked.

"I was going to go with the fact that it would be creepy to use it ever again," Gideon added.

Sanjay didn't dignify either comment with a response. "Lucas was hiding in the trunk when he was alive, so of course they'd find his DNA."

"Blood," said Tempest. "So he was put back into the trunk after he was killed."

Sanjay took two deep breaths. "Since Lucas was stabbed rather than shot, I'm the only person who was close enough to him to have stabbed him when we changed places."

"I can't tell which you dread most," Ivy said. "Being the intended victim or being the main suspect."

"I don't want to be either one!" Sanjay screamed. "This is what I get for my generosity of loaning out my trunk for the murder mystery game."

"We looked in that trunk," said Ivy. "Lucas wasn't there, either living or dead. How did we miss him?"

"Presumably Sanjay knows all the secrets of that trunk," said Gideon.

Sanjay lowered his hat to his chest and scowled at Gideon. "He *wasn't* in there."

"You think the police planted evidence?" Gideon asked, and it didn't look as if he was being sarcastic.

"If Blackburn says they found Lucas's blood or other evidence in the trunk," said Tempest, "then I'm sure they did. But that doesn't mean his body was in the trunk the whole time."

Sanjay groaned. "So we've got the joker who trapped you in the escape room moving bodies around the house and using my trunk after we looked inside? I can't imagine ever climbing inside my dead-body trunk again."

"You made that custom trunk to your specifications," said Tempest. "You can build another one."

"But I can only build a new one if I'm not in prison."

"That magic trunk can't possibly have a third fake-out hiding spot, can it?" Ivy asked.

"Actually," said Sanjay, "it does."

Ivy gasped.

"But not one that can hide a person!" he added hastily. "The fake-out is that the false bottom opens up into a shallow secret compartment to hold something like a small stack of papers. It's only two inches high. No room for a body. But big enough that it fools the eye into thinking that if you found the first secret hiding spot that it fills the rest of the space. But if you . . ." He trailed off.

"You thought of something," Tempest said.

Sanjay eyed Ivy and Gideon. "No. I can't reveal any secrets in front of the non-magicians in the room, even if we're the Abracadabras or whatever we are. I'm not going to reveal my secrets and risk having my fingers cut off."

That was one of the challenges stage magicians faced. If you didn't patent your original creations, anyone else could use the same gimmick—if they knew how to create it. But if you did patent your invention, it was public record.

Gideon frowned. "There's not really a council of illusionists who'd cut your fingers off, is there?"

"How have you survived into adulthood without understanding sarcasm?" Sanjay retorted.

"Ignore him," Tempest said to Gideon. "He's got more problems right now than being a murder suspect."

"Oh!" Sanjay perked up and twirled his hat in his hands. "That's right. Let's get back to Milton. If he's trying to kill me, that'll get me out of my performances this weekend."

"Don't change the subject," said Ivy, transfixed on the precision with which Sanjay was maneuvering the hat. "Isn't being suspected of killing someone more important than keeping a magician's secret?"

"Knowing the secret won't help us." Tempest snatched Sanjay's bowler hat from his hands. "Your hat is distracting everyone. Back to the magic steamer trunk. I can back Sanjay up here that Lucas wasn't hiding in a two-inch spot."

Without his hat to fiddle with, Sanjay twirled a coin between his fingers. "Can we get back to Milton already? He was the one in charge of the lights, so it's yet another reason he's looking guilty."

"The lights were out for the ten seconds we agreed on," Tempest said. "But everyone knew that was the agreed staging."

Sanjay snatched his hat back from Tempest and headed for the steep stairs leading down. She could have resisted, but let him have his security blanket back.

"It's time to get me out of my contract." Sanjay grinned as he started his descent.

"Isn't catching a killer who's after you more important?" Ivy asked.

"And why'd you agree to something you're dreading so much?" Gideon asked.

Sanjay's face darkened. "I accidentally agreed to perform."

"How does one accidentally agree to that?"

"Don't ask," Tempest said as Sanjay disappeared from view. "Come on. We need to follow him."

☠☠☠

"Hey, where did my patrol car go?" Sanjay asked as they stepped out of the house. He jogged a few paces ahead.

Tempest texted her grandfather, who was bound to know. Sure enough, Grandpa Ash appeared through the gargoyle-knocker door of the tree house twenty-five seconds later, while Sanjay was at the front gate frowning at his lack of protection.

"I'm glad you caught me." Ash held a lidded wicker basket in his arms. "I'm about to leave to follow up on one more lead."

"I don't think you should be investigating on your own," Tempest said.

"I promise it's not a dangerous visit. But I'm worried about you. Officer Kwan was called away on an urgent matter."

"How do you know that?" Ivy asked as Sanjay ran back up the sloping drive.

"Morag and I were chatting with him when he got the call." Ash handed the basket to Tempest.

"I'm a sitting duck now." Sanjay scowled at the gate.

Tempest hated to agree with the disturbing thought, but what was the "urgent matter" that the officer had been called away on? Had someone created a distraction so Sanjay would be left exposed—for the killer to strike again?

Chapter 36

Sanjay insisted on driving, claiming to be the one on highest alert. Tempest ensured they'd all buckled their seat belts as they peeled out of the driveway.

Now, she opened the picnic basket her grandfather had thrust upon her. He'd long since learned that there was no controlling his granddaughter and her friends. "I assume you're off to investigate," Ash had said simply. "You'll be at your sharpest if you're well nourished, and I know you skipped lunch, so I've got an assortment of sandwiches for everyone."

"Who wants the spicy hummus baguette sandwich?" Tempest asked.

"Not me," said Sanjay. "I'll take something mild."

"Isn't it only like a five-minute drive to downtown and the Hidden Bookshop?" Ivy asked. "I'm sure Ash's sandwiches will keep until we're done. Or are we going to Milton's house first?"

"We should try the bookshop first," Sanjay said, "since that's where I last saw him. Convincing a murderer to confess can take a bit of time. I want to be sure to get a confession this afternoon, so I can get out of that contract. Hand me anything that doesn't smell spicy."

"I still don't see why you're so eager to get out of performing this weekend," Gideon said. "It doesn't seem that bad. You perform magic for all sorts of people. Even kids' birthday parties."

"First of all," said Sanjay, "at this point in my career, I do kids' parties only as favors. I don't accept money for them. And besides, kids are fun."

"As long as they're old enough to have fun with magic," Tempest added.

There's a certain age below which magic falls flat on kids. When they're really little, *everything* in the world is magic to them, because they're seeing it for the first time. Water comes out of a tap? And you can make it start or stop? *Amazing!* Your shoes leave a mark in the dirt that you can identify later? *Fun!* A man in a bowler hat pulls a flower from behind your ear? No reaction. Because *I've seen a flower before. They're everywhere.*

But by around five, kids have a basic understanding of how the world works. Faucets and footprints are only fun if they're part of a game. There's an opening in their imagination for things they know aren't supposed to fit into how the world works. That's when magic becomes truly magical.

"True," said Sanjay. "So true. Always ask the age of the kids if you're going to do a party. Five to nine is the sweet spot. And willing adults who've bought tickets. Not people wandering down Main Street on the summer stroll who don't care about a good but dated trick."

"Still doesn't seem that bad," Gideon insisted.

"It's because he feels like a shill," Tempest explained. "He doesn't want to do magic on behalf of a company, even one that's a bookshop and wine bar."

"A private event is totally different from a public one," Sanjay explained. "This is like I'm a spokesperson endorsing their product. How do I even know if I like their product?"

"You said you liked their wine." Tempest caught his eye in her rearview mirror.

"I do. It's really good for a passion project of an amateur winemaker. But that's not the point."

He only had time for two bites of a cucumber sandwich before pulling into a parking spot in the lot a block away from the bookshop.

"Shouldn't we have a plan before walking through the door?" asked Gideon.

"This is the plan." Sanjay turned off the engine and took another bite of the cucumber sandwich. "This cumin spread is delicious. I'm definitely saving the rest of this sandwich to celebrate catching Milton." He turned in the seat to address Gideon, who was behind Tempest. "Tempest will ask Aurora about an arcane magic book, Erdnase's *Artifice, Ruse, and Subterfuge at the Card Table*, to get her into another section."

"I will?" Tempest asked.

"I didn't call out Milton's lie about his job in front of his co-workers today," Sanjay said, "but I want to know the truth, so that's my cover story for coming back to talk with him alone."

"I'm pretty sure it's not a crime to lie about your job title," Tempest said. "And how do you know they have that book?"

"I saw it behind glass when I was there earlier." Sanjay took one last bite before wrapping up the remains of the sandwich. "And even though it's not a crime to lie, you agree with me that it's suspicious."

"I do," Tempest said. "One of our main suspects lying about

anything is suspicious right now. Since you've thought this through so well, what will Ivy and Gideon be doing?"

"Watching from across the street, in case he tries to flee."

Ivy wrinkled her nose. "I'm supposed to tackle him?"

"I thought it would probably be Gideon who did it," Sanjay answered.

"I'll do my best," Gideon said, "but my money's on Ivy."

"Nobody's tackling anyone." Tempest grabbed the sandwich from Sanjay and tossed it into the picnic basket sitting between Gideon and Ivy. "Let's go figure out why he lied."

The Hidden Bookshop storefront was technically on the town square, but the actual entrance was set back a few yards, making it feel as if you were already entering a secret world as you stepped through the wrought iron gate and walked over black limestone paving stones to get to the front door.

If you looked closely at the top of the gate slightly above eye level, you'd see that the caps weren't a plain spike or the common decorative fleur-de-lis, but each cap was a tiny open book made of iron.

Tempest breathed in the scent of old books as they reached the door of the Hidden Bookshop. A faint bell jingled as they stepped through the door, alerting the staff that a customer had entered, though Tempest didn't see a soul.

Her gaze fell to the cherrywood bookcase against the wall that her dad had built. The one that would slide open and lead to the new wine bar next door. The shelves had live edges—the type of edge that looked like natural driftwood and gave a bookcase a rustic appearance. The grain pattern of the cherrywood Darius had selected was filled with swirls that gave it a beautiful, distinct character. A good choice for the bookcase that would be used more as a door than simple shelving for books.

"Milton?" Sanjay called out when a full minute passed without anyone greeting them.

A slight woman with white curly hair that included several pops of bright purple stepped out from a section in the back.

"It's good to see you, Tempest," Aurora said, greeting her warmly before turning to Sanjay. "That magic bottle trick is going to delight customers this weekend! Not that I'm unhappy to see you so soon, but did you forget something?"

"I forgot to ask Milton about something." Sanjay's eyes darted behind Aurora, even though there was no movement from the back room. The bookstore didn't even have a cat.

Aurora shook her head. "He left shortly after you. But I'm glad you came back with Tempest. I have something I think her dad would like. A gift."

"There's no need—" Tempest began.

"Nonsense. Darius undercharged us for his beautiful work on the bookshop." She disappeared in back, and less than a minute later, she returned and pressed a small leather-bound book of old carpentry techniques into Tempest's hands.

She opened the cover and saw it was from the nineteenth century. "He'll love it."

☠☠☠

"If you tell me you spotted any clues in the five minutes we were in there," said Sanjay as they went to collect Ivy and Gideon, "I'll eat my hat."

"As much as I'd like to see that," said Tempest, "I didn't learn anything except for the fact that Aurora and Alex are lovely people, so there's no way they're working with Milton to try to kill you."

The four friends piled back into Sanjay's truck and followed his GPS to Milton's house, less than a mile away.

"We're here." Tempest pointed to a single-story bungalow in a similar style to the original house at Fiddler's Folly.

"I don't think he's home." Gideon pointed at the windows. "The house is dark, and there's no car in the driveway."

"He has a garage," Sanjay said.

Tempest shook her head. "With a house this small, no way he's using that garage for his car."

They walked up to the front door and rang the doorbell, then knocked twice, but nobody answered.

"Looks like we have a visitor," Gideon said.

"Milton is back?" Sanjay whipped around.

Tempest turned as well. It wasn't Milton who'd arrived. It was a police cruiser. It came to a stop in front of the house, blocking Sanjay's truck.

Officer Kwan, who'd been following Sanjay before, stepped out of the patrol car. "Detective Blackburn thought I might find you here. He requests your presence back at the station."

"Have you arrested someone?" Tempest asked.

"Or are you arresting me?" Sanjay stepped behind Tempest.

"Neither. But it would be in your best interest."

Tempest hooked her arm through Sanjay's elbow and coaxed him back to his truck.

"I'm never helping someone ever again," Sanjay muttered under his breath.

Tempest waved at Officer Kwan. "We'll meet you at the station."

Chapter 37

You know I don't think this weekend is a good idea," Detective Blackburn said to the four of them once he'd closed the door in the larger of the interrogation rooms.

"You mean the library play and escape room?" Tempest asked. "Cameron already told me you couldn't say when the crime scene would be released."

He nodded. "I told him that. However, I'm getting pressure to release the crime scene as quickly as I can. I've told Mr. Gray as well. Tickets to both the play and escape room are sold out, and people are even coming in from out of town for the summer stroll events, which is great for the local economy."

"You have new information about whoever is trying to kill me?" Sanjay asked.

"I should ask you the same thing." Blackburn crossed his arms. "I wanted to think I was wrong that you'd be interviewing my suspects—"

"Milton Silver lied about his occupation." Sanjay crossed his arms to match Blackburn's posture.

"What makes you think he's not an accountant for small businesses?" Blackburn asked.

Sanjay's shoulders slumped. "You knew that?"

"What did you think he did?"

"He makes himself sound like a rare books expert," Tempest said.

Blackburn shrugged. "One of his clients is the Hidden Bookshop, so he probably knows more than all of us combined about rare books. Mr. Silver's occupation isn't your concern. You'll do the most good for this investigation by leaving things to us."

"So we can get back to work on rehearsing the play and getting the escape room set up again?" Tempest gave him her best attempt at an innocent smile. "We can move forward?"

"*If* I determine it's safe," Blackburn said. "We're done with forensics, but it depends on toxicology. If there's no trace of poison from our tests in the escape room game, and if I can confirm one more thing, then I can release it."

"What's the other thing besides testing for poison?" Tempest asked.

"I can't speak to that, aside from cautioning you to stop attempting to interrogate my witnesses and suspects."

"Who are your suspects?" Sanjay asked.

"Your time would be better spent preparing for this weekend, not slowing down my investigation."

"So you think it's likely that forensics testing will be completed in time?" Ivy asked. "I didn't know Hidden Creek had a lab that could get tests done so quickly."

"We don't have a lab at all," Blackburn said. "It went to the county. Normally, it would be slow to get results—since test results aren't as quick as they are on TV. But there's an eager young guy who has dual MD/PhD degrees and wrote his dissertation on poisons, so he's testing for all sorts of things."

"Above and beyond his normal workload?" Tempest asked.

"Bingo. He's fascinated with old poisons, so he's the one who reached out to me. He heard about the case details, and they fascinated him. We did a video call early this morning, before he went into his office. He was at his house, and I saw a bookshelf that included books like *A Is for Arsenic: The Poisons of Agatha Christie.* Said he'd work all night tonight if it could give us some answers."

"And you'll release the house if he says it's clean?" Gideon asked.

Blackburn sighed. "We'll have to see what we've found by the time the test results come in."

"Meaning that you're closing in on the person trying to frame me or kill me?" Sanjay asked.

"Nobody is trying to frame you," Blackburn said, "but until we've made an arrest, we can't be entirely certain who the intended victim was, so I do advise you to be careful. Stop harassing suspects and let me get back to work."

Sanjay stood up so hastily that the chair nearly toppled. "Happily."

Tempest pushed him back down. "There's something more Blackburn isn't telling us."

Detective Blackburn's mouth ticked up into the hint of a smile. "About a hundred things. There's a lot that goes into an investigation. I wish we'd known about the murder two nights ago, not just last night. We'd be in a much better position now."

He opened the door for them, then paused. "One last thing. There's a lot going on with the summer stroll coming up this weekend, so we can't leave an officer watching Sanjay. Until we know what's going on, you three are sticking with him, right?"

Tempest assured him they were.

Sanjay grumbled something under his breath that sounded like a complaint against "babysitters," but Tempest noticed he was careful to walk in between them when they left the building.

"What do you all think?" Tempest asked as soon as they'd piled into Sanjay's truck.

"That we should have searched the back before we got in," Ivy said. "I've seen horror movies. I know how this works."

"I'll look." Gideon hopped out and looked under the tarp. "Unless the killer is curled up where the spare tire should be, he's not here."

Sanjay's eyes grew wide.

"I shouldn't have said that," muttered Gideon, but he checked for anyone rolled up like a spare tire. "All clear."

"Now that we've got that out of the way," Tempest said, "how about we finally eat this feast from my grandfather and make a real plan?"

Chapter 38

Tempest led the way as they took their picnic lunch to the edge of the town square park.

"Where do you want to begin?" Ivy asked.

"With the rest of that cucumber-cumin sandwich." Sanjay reached into the basket and found his baguette.

"You seem surprisingly blasé for someone who was almost murdered two days ago," Gideon said.

Sanjay blinked at him. "The three of you are protecting me."

"Gideon is right," Tempest said. "I should have insisted we go back to Fiddler's Folly."

"It's such a beautiful sunny day out here," said Ivy. "And we're far apart from everyone else. We'll see if anyone comes near us."

Tempest raised an eyebrow. "You hate the sun. You'd much rather be curled up inside with a book with it pouring rain outside."

Ivy pursed her lips. "That was before I thought we might have a ghost on our hands."

"Not you, too."

"What? Both Enid and Mrs. Hudson believe it's Harold," Ivy said. "They're perfectly sensible people."

"I don't know about Mrs. Hudson," Sanjay said. "But, Ivy . . . Truly, it's a trick. Not a ghost. I don't know how they did it yet, but I promise you it's a trick. Hey, did Ash include dessert in the picnic basket?"

Tempest tossed him a chocolate chip brownie. "We're missing something, and we just have to figure out what it is. Let's go over everything we know one more time."

"This brownie is heavenly," Sanjay said. "What kind of chocolate chips are these? How are they still gooey?"

Tempest rolled her eyes. "Probably because it's summer and they were in the truck." She would have said *magic* if she'd been in a better mood, but she was itching to figure out the last bits of missing information that would make everything make sense.

Ivy moved her heavy tote bag into the center of the picnic blanket. The canvas bag was designed to look like an oversize library card. She reached inside and drew out half a dozen books.

Sanjay peeked over the edge. "It's like a reverse magic trick. You only pulled out six books, but there are at least a dozen more inside here."

"We start with these," Ivy said. "These six mystery novels are all impossible crimes with specific parallels to our situation this week. I checked them out from the Locked Room Library while I was there earlier today. I thought they might help us shake loose some ideas."

"*And Then There Were None.*" Tempest held up the paperback book. It was so well loved that the edges of the cover were frayed, and a chunk of the lower-right corner was missing. "You usually make selections that are obscurer."

"It's true it's Agatha Christie's most famous novel," Ivy said, "but that's not why I picked it. It's at the top of my list because it's both a locked-room mystery and a closed-circle mystery—a combination we're dealing with. Not only is it impossible for Lucas to have vanished like he did—especially once we learned he was killed the first night—but the house was being watched. That means one of the people there had a hand in what happened to Lucas."

"Meaning it could have been one of the people inside the house," said Gideon, "or Mrs. Hudson herself if she was lying about what happened the first night."

"But the video recording of the following night didn't lie," said Tempest. "Whoever moved Lucas's body from its hiding spot onto the living room floor was either inside or directly outside of the house. Besides the four of us, that's Mrs. Hudson, Cameron, Kira, and Milton."

They all stared at the book cover of *And Then There Were None*, as if it would give them answers. It must have been at least the hundredth book cover design of Christie's famous book about ten strangers who all receive an invitation to a secluded island cut off from the mainland. Once there, the strangers realize their pasts are catching up with them. But who among them is a killer seeking vengeance? And how is the culprit getting away with it?

"I've got nothin'," said Sanjay. "I've only seen the movie, but I'm pretty sure the plot of that book isn't what's going on here. It's been two days, and only Lucas is dead."

"*Harumph.*" Ivy held up the next book cover. "Moving on, *The Man Who Could Not Shudder*. A Dr. Fell novel by John Dickson Carr."

"Dr. Fell is a detective who likes to say *Harumph*," Tempest stage-whispered to Sanjay.

"I got it," he stage-whispered back.

"It takes place at a supposedly haunted house," Ivy said, "where—"

"Next," said Sanjay. "None of us are seriously entertaining the notion that Harold Gray's ghost is haunting his old house, are we? Good. Then we can move on to—"

"Hold up," said Gideon. "Just because we agree a ghost didn't kill Lucas or turn the fun escape room into a horror chamber, *someone* is trying to make it seem like there's a ghost. Ivy, there's not a *real* ghost in that novel, is there?"

"No," Ivy said. "The book has a rational explanation, just like I know we'll find here. But Enid and Mrs. Hudson believe it's Harold's ghost we're dealing with."

"Unless they're faking their fear," Gideon said.

"Enid's not faking it," said Tempest. "I could be wrong, but I don't think I am. Also, she wasn't there the second night. I know, I know, she could be working with Mrs. Hudson or anyone else." Tempest twisted her hair around her fingertips and tugged, frustrated that she could feel they were so close to answers, but every step of the way seemed to bring only more confusion.

"I'll keep going," Ivy said. "Before we see if it's worth going deeper into any of them, I first want to explain the general idea of why I picked each of them. They all offer insights into our lives right now. Next up is *Through a Glass, Darkly* by Helen McCloy. I selected it because it involves a doppelgänger, which is what Lucas and Sanjay effectively were."

"If we didn't look so similar," Sanjay said, "I'd be dead right now. So I'm in favor of doppelgängers."

"We still don't know why Lucas wanted to trade places with

you that night," Tempest pointed out. "For all we know, maybe there could be a sinister reason he wanted someone who looked so much like him."

Sanjay made a choking sound.

"Moving right along," said Ivy. "*The Crimson Fog* by Paul Halter, because it includes an impossible crime that takes place behind a curtain during a magic show performance, which is what Sanjay and Lucas were up to during the murder mystery play. The book also involves a section about Jack the Ripper . . . So maybe for now let's just finish up the last two books with different types of impossibilities. I've got *Death from a Top Hat* by Clayton Rawson, because our resident magician Sanjay is the intended victim. Two magicians are killed—"

"Next!" Sanjay croaked.

"She's trying to help." Tempest jabbed his side with her finger.

"It won't help if I've had a heart attack from comparing my predicament to the horrible circumstances of the poor characters in these classic mysteries."

"I'm sorry." Ivy bit her lip. "But I really do think this will help. Especially this last one. Hear me out about the summary of this last book, and then I can stop. It's another John Dickson Carr novel, since he was the master of the locked-room mystery. *The Nine Wrong Answers*. I selected it because there are so many false clues that Carr adds footnotes to the reader about how they've been led astray—and yet they *haven't*."

Before continuing, Ivy paused and looked at each of them in turn, making sure they were all giving her their full attention. "We're on a similar path here. There's so much going on. We've got Enid's invisible intruder last week, a body vanishing before mysteriously reappearing, being wrong about when Lucas was killed, Cam's new library being under threat, being trapped in our own escape room after a dead man lured us there, an angry neighbor spying on us, and not even knowing who the intended victim was. These things are related and can't be mere coincidences. Assumptions are made because they were the logical things to presume, but you need to look more closely to see the truth."

"You're not kidding," said Tempest. "We've all made so many assumptions, which is why we missed the truth about Sanjay being the intended victim for so long." She turned to him. "Maybe you saw something you weren't supposed to. When you were working with Lucas to plan your deception, where did you two meet up?"

"What? No. We never met up in person. We were texting."

Tempest felt her breath catch. "Did you even *talk* with him?"

"Of course," he said. "I just said we were . . . Oooooh. You mean *talking* like actually speaking verbally on the phone. Who even does that anymore?"

Tempest stared at her brilliant yet clueless friend. "People who want to make sure the person they're talking to is actually who they say they are."

Multiple gasps sounded around the picnic blanket.

"You don't mean . . ." Sanjay scrambled backward on the blanket as if running away from the implication of her words. "I was helping *his killer?*"

"When you let Lucas out of the trunk," said Tempest, feeling her whole body buzzing, "are you *certain* he was alive?"

Ivy's hands flew to her mouth.

"But my trunk has plenty of air holes," Sanjay insisted.

"I know," said Tempest. "I'm not saying your trunk suffocated him. But air holes wouldn't help someone *who was already dead.*"

Sanjay's face contorted with disbelief.

"How exactly did you let Lucas out of the trunk during that first rehearsal?" Tempest asked.

"I tilted it onto its side." Sanjay clutched his bowler hat and looked imploringly at each of them. "That's the easiest way out! I didn't do anything wrong. I had to tip it . . . otherwise, the person inside would have to scramble out awkwardly. I mean, I can do it, but it's not like there's a lot of extra space for a full-grown man, and Lucas wasn't practiced at stagecraft. So I dumped him . . . Oh God . . ."

"Lucas didn't die that night during our rehearsal," said Tempest. "He was already dead before *someone else* texted Sanjay earlier that afternoon."

Chapter 39

have to say," Sanjay said after they'd talked with Blackburn about Sanjay's correspondence with an unknown killer, "I really hate being used like a pawn."

"Isn't it better than being the intended victim?" Gideon asked.

Time of death wasn't an exact science, like TV shows would have you believe. Since Lucas's body hadn't been discovered right away, they might never know the exact time when he was killed, but Blackburn agreed that Lucas could very well have been dead a few hours before their dress rehearsal that first night.

This changed everything.

If Lucas was already dead by the time someone was texting Sanjay, the killer could have put him into the trunk at any time. The house wasn't under surveillance. The killer didn't need to be present when they found the body—at least not the *first* time. But someone had staged the twisted escape room and made Lucas's body reappear last night. *Why?*

Detective Blackburn was adjusting his investigation accordingly, but had walked them out of the station. Hint taken. Tempest, Sanjay, and Gideon now stood aimlessly in front of the station. Ivy had left to have dinner with her sister, Dahlia, and her family, having done her duty to open their minds with her curated selection of classic mystery novels.

"Maybe," Sanjay consented. "I guess I'm glad nobody is trying to kill me, but being used is disturbing."

"That explains how forensic evidence suggested Lucas was in your trunk after he was dead," said Tempest. "Because he *was*. But only that first afternoon before you dumped him out of the trunk."

"That wasn't my fault. I didn't know he was dead," Sanjay insisted. "I simply thought he wasn't great at maneuvering out of a tight space." He typed out a message on his phone.

"Who are you texting?" Tempest asked. "We should leave Ivy in peace for the next few hours. She's at dinner with her family. They're packing up to move from their house at the end of the month, so it's an important meal for her."

"I'm not bugging Ivy," Sanjay said. "I'm texting Milton."

"Please tell me you're not accusing him of murder because he lied about his job. Detective Blackburn already knows Milton's occupation."

"We couldn't find him earlier, and we still don't know why he lied. I'm telling him that tonight's rehearsal is back on." Sanjay grinned at his phone as three little moving dots appeared. "Nobody's trying to kill me! So we might as well see this through and catch our killer. Come on, Milton . . . Be free."

"Gray House is still a crime scene," Tempest pointed out. "And Milton is only one of a bunch of suspects."

Sanjay looked as if he had a rebuttal, but paused. His face fell. "I'll tell him we're moving locations for tonight. How about the barn workshop at Fiddler's Folly?"

"That could work," Tempest said. "I think we've got enough random furniture and plywood that we can re-create the living room at Gray House."

Sanjay looked at his phone and swore. "It's Milton. He texted me back that Kira didn't know about rehearsal being back on. He's already texting with her."

"You didn't think this through at all, did you?" asked Gideon. "And is it just me, or is it weird for us to be plotting to gather all the suspects together when we're literally standing in the shadow of the police station?"

"Is it so wrong to move us forward when everyone else is stuck?" Sanjay replied. "I don't know how much longer I can go on as a murder suspect."

Tempest took Sanjay's phone and made it vanish. "You're not texting him back until we figure out what we're doing."

"I know it's in your back pocket." Sanjay pointed at her hip.

She turned around, palming the phone as she did so. Sanjay knew her well enough that he was able to guess that's what she was doing, but he didn't attempt to snatch the phone back.

"If you two are done fighting over the phone," said Gideon, "I have an idea."

Tempest handed Gideon the phone. He was a good arbiter. She felt a pang of regret, knowing these would be the last couple of days she'd get to spend with him in months and that she'd been running around trying to catch a killer.

"Sanjay didn't mean to set things in motion," said Gideon. "But he did. We can't make the perfect plan—but we can make the plan that exists in reality now. Which seems to me would mean getting *everyone* together for a dress rehearsal tonight."

"I'm not prepared to gather all the suspects together," said Sanjay. "Milton is the only one we have a lie to confront him about. Can't I just tell him I was wrong about rehearsal?" He held out his hand to take his phone back.

Gideon shook his head. "Milton will be suspicious now. So will Kira, since he's already in touch with her. It's not a perfect plan, but the best one we've got."

"He's right," Tempest said. "The sooner we can figure this out, the better. Just because someone wasn't trying to kill Sanjay doesn't mean they weren't trying to frame him now that he's the main suspect."

Sanjay swore.

"If Milton doesn't hear back from us soon," Gideon said, "he'll probably reach out to Cameron to ask what's up with the rehearsal being back on."

Sanjay reached for the phone. Gideon handed it to Tempest, who made it disappear again. This time, not in her back pocket.

"First," she said, "we agree exactly what we're doing. We're gathering everyone together at the Fiddler's Folly barn for a rehearsal of the murder mystery play at nine o'clock."

"Who's 'everyone'?" Gideon asked.

"Everyone involved," said Tempest. "That means Enid and Mrs. Hudson. And nine o'clock is late enough that Ivy should be done with dinner at her sister's house. Milton and Kira are the ones waiting for a reply, so Sanjay should text them." She handed his phone back to him. "And I'll text Ivy so that she can make sure Enid and Cameron are there as well."

"Who's inviting Mrs. Hudson?" Gideon asked.

"Good point," said Tempest. "Anyone have her phone number or email address?"

Nobody did.

"Maybe I'll ask my grandfather to make her cookies that we

can bring her to entice her. Once she smells his cardamom shortbread through the door, she won't be able to resist."

"You're bringing your family into this?" Sanjay asked.

She shrugged. "We're meeting at my house. There's no way to avoid them knowing. I also want to ask my grandfather what else he's learned from his magic Rolodex."

"I can't believe I'm saying this in response to inviting a murderer to your house," said Gideon, "but that sounds good."

"Now let's get planning," said Tempest.

Chapter 40

'm guessing we're not telling that detective we're doing this," said Gideon.

"The fewer the people who know, the better," said Tempest. "If I could avoid telling my dad, I would."

Tempest called her dad and grandparents to get them on board for that night's dress rehearsal at Fiddler's Folly. Darius insisted on being present, as she knew he would. He said he'd make sure that all the sharp equipment was locked away, plus he was setting up a camera high in the eaves so the whole thing would be recorded, and he would be on hand as muscle.

Ash was happy to have an excuse to bake more cookies. He was continuing his stealthy sleuthing under the guise of gossiping with people he knew, but so far, he hadn't learned anything else of interest, so stress-baking was a welcome task. He was home alone, since Morag was talking with an artist friend who worked on set design for some of the Creekside Players shows, in case she knew anything of interest.

When Tempest got off the phone, Gideon was taking a beaten-up sketchbook from his messenger bag and opening it on the tail of Sanjay's truck.

"I thought this might be helpful." He flipped through the pages, stopping at a spread that showed a graphite sketch of the two rooms at Gray House—the living room on the left side of the page, and the second-floor library on the right.

It wasn't a technical drawing, but was exactly the type of artist sketch he did when thinking about his next stone creation. It showed both the "manor house" drawing room as it was set up for the play rehearsal, and the library escape room they'd been trapped in.

"When did you draw this?" Tempest asked.

"When we were waiting at the station last night, I looked at the plans to the house that Secret Staircase Construction mocked up for the upcoming renovation project. My phone screen wasn't ideal, but it was good enough. Then I added what I remembered of where the furniture was. I wanted to get my thoughts down on paper about what I'd seen, since I didn't take photos. Did you two?"

They shook their heads.

"I think you should all look at this sketch and see if I got the details you remember right," Gideon continued. "Then we can head over to the barn workshop to build a basic reproduction."

As Tempest watched him tap nervously at the page, she was certain there was something wrong. Something left unsaid. "What aren't you telling us?"

His calloused finger stopped tapping at the edge of the page, and he smiled as he held her gaze. "It's what I'm hoping one of you will see. Something I'm missing."

"I doubt you missed anything," Tempest said. "You're the one who sees the details we all miss." She fought the urge to squeal as she realized exactly what Gideon was doing with his sketch. "It's not the accuracy of the rooms and furniture. You're looking for the *trick* that the setup makes possible."

He nodded as Tempest continued, "Because we know there's a trick to Lucas's killer leaving his body on display."

Sanjay swore in Punjabi. "Of course. I would have thought of it myself if I hadn't been so worried about staying alive."

"I didn't think of it until I said it aloud," Tempest admitted. "But it makes sense, doesn't it? Either Mrs. Hudson's camera doesn't really cover all the entry points to the house, there's a secret passageway, or there was something mechanical rigged to get the trunk to dump his body out while we were upstairs. Detective Blackburn will find it if there's something rigged in the trunk to make it pop open."

"I'd know if someone messed with my trunk," said Sanjay.

"But it's locked up as evidence," Tempest pointed out, "so that's not happening anytime soon. Let's get back to what we *can* do. First, we can look at Gideon's sketch to make sure he captured everything accurately." She picked up the notebook.

"I made the sketches as accurate as I could from my memory," Gideon said.

The sketch wasn't as magical as renderings of his stone carvings, but even in these simple pencil strokes, you could see that he was a true artist. The details in the mantelpiece from above captured the charm of the real thing.

"And second?" Sanjay asked.

Tempest ran her index finger over the lines of the sketch. "Assuming there's not a secret passageway in the house for a random serial killer to come and go, we face the truth that one of the people who was there last night is our killer."

"What about Enid?" said Gideon. "She was there the first night."

"I don't think it was Enid," Tempest said, "but something is going on with her. She—"

"There's something wrong here." Sanjay took Gideon's notebook from Tempest's hands. "That's not where my trunk was."

"Yes, it was." Tempest thought back to the setup of Gray House. "I know how much you hate being wrong, but you're wrong here."

Sanjay gave her a withering gaze. "I was performing. I had to know *exactly* where that trunk was. I'm not wrong."

"Hang on." She snatched the notebook back from him. "It's not just the trunk that's in a different spot. The love seat and futon are swapped."

"Wait, what?" Gideon shook his head. "I'm sure I didn't mess that up."

"You two were at the rehearsal on *different nights*," Tempest said. "Sanjay was there two nights ago, and Gideon was there last night. Between the two nights, *the furniture was moved*."

There was no mistaking it. Between the time Mrs. Hudson had been spying on them and gotten a security camera set up, the furniture had been rearranged.

"We need to go," Tempest said.

"Where?" Gideon asked.

"We're going to re-create a murder scene—and the solution."

Chapter 41

Aside from birds chirping, Fiddler's Folly was silent as they came through the front gate.

"Aren't we building the set in here?" Sanjay stopped and pointed to the barn workshop as Tempest walked past it.

"Not yet." She kept walking up the hillside toward the tree house.

A sticky note from Grandpa Ash was taped to the front door of the tree house. *Platter of cookies is ready for you to take to Mrs. Hudson. Extra for you and your friends. Back soon.*

"Guess I'll be the one delivering cookies." She crumpled up the note, then texted her gran to ask about borrowing a few art supplies.

Of course, Grannie Mor texted back immediately. *Take anything you need. Home with Ash in an hour.*

Tempest unlocked the tree house door, but instead of going

upstairs as usual, she walked straight into her grandmother's art studio.

"Um, we're making art?" Gideon asked.

"We're getting the scene right before we build it."

Tempest didn't spend much time on the ground floor of her grandparents' tree house. The single room was Morag Ferguson-Raj's art studio. The stairway leading up to the main level of the house cut through the center of the single room, creating additional wall space and making the room feel extra cozy. Drawers filled with loose watercolor paper and stretched canvas and cabinets filled with paint and other supplies lined the interior walls. Easels and worktables lined the outer walls, with picture windows above giving Grannie Mor an ever-changing view of the trees on their hidden hillside.

But Tempest barely noticed the light. They were here for the building blocks and anatomical figures Morag posed to stage scenes for her artwork.

"The question," said Tempest as she cleared space on a rosewood worktable, "is why did the killer need to move the furniture?"

"Because bodies are heavy," Sanjay said. "They accidentally knocked into something on their way back to the trunk."

Tempest shook her head and pointed to Gideon's sketch that he'd just laid on the table. "*Everything* is moved around. Well, not the bookshelves against the wall, but the couches."

Sanjay frowned at Gideon's sketch. "To make room to get Lucas out of my trunk."

Tempest shook her head. "He wasn't necessarily in the trunk. Forensics placed his dead body in the trunk at some point, but he wasn't there when we looked inside it . . ."

"What are you thinking?" Gideon asked.

"That the steamer trunk needed to be in a certain spot for a trick to work," said Tempest. "Nobody was in the living room when Lucas Cruz's body reappeared, meaning there had to be something rigged for the body to reappear. *Something that required the furniture to be moved.*"

Sanjay swore. Gideon's eyes widened as he turned to a side table and grabbed three anatomical sketch study figures made of wood and wires. There were two twelve-inch posable wooden people and one six-inch figure.

"Let's get testing." Tempest took the six-inch wooden figure from Gideon and placed it on the table, positioned like Lucas had been. "Gideon, can you make two sketches of the furniture arrangements on each night?"

"Definitely."

"Then can you approximate the furniture with the wooden blocks from that storage bin in the corner?"

"On it."

"Sanjay, you're on set design. Use cardboard and card stock paper to create the house surrounding the furniture. We need to make sure we get the doors, windows, bookcases, and fireplace."

"What's the scale?" Sanjay asked.

"The figure is six inches, and Lucas was about six feet tall, so we go with one inch to represent each foot. I've got the dimensions of the rooms from our assessment for the renovation. Those notes will show door and window placements as well, but not the furniture, so Gideon's attention to detail of the furniture placements is key for the interior." Tempest searched on her phone while the others gathered materials, then jotted down a sketch with the measurements on a sheet of paper.

"What part are you doing?" Sanjay asked.

"While you two build this diorama, I'm delivering cookies to Mrs. Hudson."

Chapter 42

S anjay and Gideon didn't want her to go alone, but they knew they were short on time, so when she promised not to go into the house, they grudgingly agreed.

They had to stay on schedule, because Milton and Kira confirmed they were on board. They'd never gotten their full rehearsal, and if the crime scene was released in time and Blackburn either solved the murder or gave in to pressure from the city council, they'd be performing the play tomorrow night—unless one of them was the killer.

Enid was the only one to outright decline the invitation, because she was busy with an event at her own library. Tempest was inclined to believe Enid wasn't guilty. Not only because she knew her, but because Enid had been truly frightened that it might have been Harold's ghost. Although, Tempest had to admit, perhaps Enid's fear stemmed from guilt that Harold's ghost had seen what she'd done. Until they knew what had happened, everyone was a suspect.

So Tempest headed to see Mrs. Hudson, the last person they needed present.

"A peace offering." She held up the platter of cardamom shortbread cookies as the door opened.

Mrs. Hudson pursed her lips but didn't slam the door in her face. Tempest caught a glimpse of binoculars on a side table next to the front windows.

"You know my grandfather, Ashok Raj," said Tempest. "He's been baking up a storm the last couple of days, staying busy with the stress of everything that's happening. He wanted you to have these."

Mrs. Hudson narrowed her eyes but still didn't shut the door.

Tempest sighed. "Fine. He really does want you to have the cookies—which are phenomenal, by the way—but I'm the one delivering them because I wanted to invite you to our dress rehearsal tonight. Not at Gray House, of course. But we're doing a full run-through at my house. We'd like you to be in the audience."

Mrs. Hudson's face lit up with a smile.

That wasn't the outcome Tempest was expecting. She thought she'd have to try much harder to convince her.

"You're gathering all the suspects together?" Mrs. Hudson chuckled. "It's rather precious how naive you are, thinking that'll work. However misguided you are in that regard, I know you're not foolish enough to come inside if I invited you in right now— Oh, don't look so surprised! I know I'm one of your suspects. How could I not be? Come on. I'll join you on the porch."

Mrs. Hudson grabbed her binoculars before stepping outside. She popped one of Grandpa Ash's cookies in her mouth, shut the front door behind her, then walked around Tempest and sat down on the porch swing. She gave a contented sigh as she finished chewing the cookie.

"You're welcome to join me here on the swing where we can see the house," she said, "but you might be more comfortable on the corner bench so you're not worried that I'll secretly stab you with a knitting needle—not that I have one."

Tempest looked from Mrs. Hudson to her house behind her. She hadn't been talking about seeing her *own* house. Mrs. Hudson was watching Gray House.

Tempest set the platter of cookies on the bench but remained standing. "You're still watching the house across the street?"

"Of course. Whatever is happening there isn't over yet."

"You really believe it's Harold Gray's ghost?"

Mrs. Hudson laughed once more. This time, it was whole-hearted laughter that shook her entire body. "Oh, dear. *That's* what you thought when we were trapped in that horrible room?"

"*I* didn't think it was his ghost," said Tempest. "It was you who said—"

"I said no such thing. What I said was that it was *Harold*."

As Tempest stared across the street at the crime scene tape blocking the entrance to Gray House, the full force of Mrs. Hudson's words hit her. The house filled with mysteries Harold Gray had read since he was a boy. The vision for a library that would begin with a murder mystery play and a game. All conceived of by a man who loved mysteries and games . . .

The answer was right in front of them. And it *did* come from one of the six books Ivy had selected. The solution that explained everything.

Tempest groaned. "You don't believe it's Harold's *ghost*."

"Of course not." Mrs. Hudson picked up another cookie. "There's no such thing as ghosts."

"There's a reason you've been watching the house this whole time. You've been watching to prove that Harold Gray is alive."

"What else would I have been doing?" Mrs. Hudson popped the cookie into her mouth, a look of satisfaction on her face.

"You mean," said Tempest, feeling as if her brain was about to explode, "Harold Gray faked his death."

rs. Hudson told you yesterday that Harold Gray faked his death?" Tempest paced back and forth in front of Detective Blackburn, so full of nervous energy that she thought she might pop. "How did you not think it relevant to tell us?"

"If you'd stop crawling the walls and let me get a word in," Blackburn said, "I'd tell you."

She sat.

Sanjay and Gideon were already seated, watching the exchange. Tempest had called them as soon as she'd left Mrs. Hudson's house, and they insisted on coming with her to the police station.

"Mrs. Hudson did indeed tell me of her suspicions when I interviewed her last night," Detective Blackburn said. "I looked into it. We have every reason to believe that Harold Gray died three months ago."

"Was he poisoned?" Sanjay asked.

Blackburn pinched the bridge of his nose. "Cardiac arrest. Nothing suspicious. He was in his nineties, had heart disease, and knew he didn't have long to live. That's why he got his affairs in order to renovate his house and turn it into a library."

"A library devoted to classic mysteries," said Tempest. "Books about clever crimes, by devious minds like that of Agatha Christie. Books that filled him with ideas about faking his own death."

"I didn't take it for granted that he was dead." Blackburn's voice was more clipped than usual. He was losing patience with her. "There's a death certificate."

"Signed by someone you know?"

"I don't know every doctor in this town. This isn't *Murder, She Wrote*'s Cabot Cove."

"But if Harold Gray is alive, it explains everything. Or at least a lot of things."

"Tempest." His voice softened as he said her name. "We've known each other a long time. You know I explore all the angles. I follow the evidence. When Mrs. Hudson told me of her suspicions, because you'd all heard his voice last night, I looked into it. That's one of the things I've been tracking down today. Not just speaking with the doctor who signed his death certificate, but looking at other signs that he might be alive and hiding."

"Oh . . . So, nothing suspicious?"

"Nothing so far," Blackburn confirmed.

"You said it was cardiac arrest that killed Harold?" said Gideon.

Blackburn nodded.

"Did you consider the oleander in his backyard?" Gideon asked.

Poison.

Blackburn tried not to react, but Tempest heard a sharp intake of breath. He hadn't considered that.

"We're investigating the strange death of Mr. Cruz," Blackburn said. "One of the possibilities is that Mr. Gray had faked his death and killed Mr. Cruz, for reasons unknown. It's not our main theory. But I thank you for bringing it to my attention that a plant containing toxins that can cause cardiac arrest is growing in the backyard of that house."

"So you'll investigate it?" Sanjay asked.

"Go home," said Blackburn. "All of you. I'm *trying* to do my job, and the more I get interrupted with wild-goose chases, the harder it is to do."

"We're going," said Tempest, scooping up Sanjay and Gideon by the elbow.

"Mr. Gray did love games and mysteries," said Blackburn, "so it was a good idea to explore. It's most likely a dead end, like most leads are. I'm following the evidence of Lucas Cruz's whereabouts leading to his death. We'll get there."

Blackburn saw them out.

"So Harold Gray might still be alive," Tempest said to her friends. "Or he might have been murdered by poison. Whatever is going on, it's time we figured it out."

Chapter 44

When Tempest, Gideon, and Sanjay got back to Fiddler's Folly, the guys showed Tempest the diorama of the living room scene from the first night at Gray House.

Gideon had cut paper to cover the blocks to represent the furniture placement of the first night. Sanjay had cut the cardboard for the exterior walls with door and window openings to scale. Their attention to detail with the architectural details brought the room to life.

They'd each brought their skills to the task—but Tempest was keenly aware that Ivy's perspective was missing. Ivy would know the details of the furniture itself.

"Sanjay, do you agree this is what you saw the first night?" Tempest asked.

"I do."

Bookcases and a low cabinet serving as a bar lined the walls.

The central furniture was arranged in a U shape around the fireplace performance area. Harold's armchair and the love seat were on the right and left side, respectively, with Sanjay's trunk in the center, and the rental futon and folding chairs behind it. The wooden figure lay on the floor between the trunk and the futon. It was a large room, so there was plenty of room to walk around the trunk—and to put a body inside it. Why was it necessary to move the furniture?

"Nicely done with the paper cutout folding chairs made of a continuous sheet of paper." Sanjay tipped his hat to Gideon. "Our furniture needs just one more thing."

Sanjay rummaged through a drawer of gouache paints before settling on tubes of burnt sienna, black, and metallic gray, which he used to paint the paper rectangle representing his magic trunk. "Now it's perfect."

Tempest raised an eyebrow. The trunk really did look perfect, down to its steel bolts, but it hadn't been necessary. "My grandmother will kill you if you don't clean that brush. There's brush-cleaning soap over there."

"We have more important things to worry about right now than a sacrificed paintbrush."

"I'll do it." Gideon took the brush and wiped the excess paint on a rag before cleaning it in the farmhouse sink. "You realize that now we have to wait for that paint to dry."

"We're not playing with a dollhouse." Sanjay pointed at the wooden figure dead body. "We're simply looking at this to remember what we saw."

Tempest snapped two photos of the scene from above. "Let's move things to how they were when we found Lucas the second night."

None of the shelving against the walls had been moved. The trunk was much closer to the fireplace and sliding bookcase, and the love seat and futon had switched places. The wooden figure representing Lucas Cruz was no longer behind the trunk, but now to its left.

"Look right?" Tempest asked Gideon.

He nodded as he pulled a graphite pencil from his pocket, then leaned over the sketch he'd made of the room's second night.

"I didn't think about this until seeing our 3D model," he said, "but look." He drew two straight lines away from the body. The first line reached the bookcase without bumping into anything. The second was a straight shot to the front door. Next, he drew two more lines, this time from the trunk. The same was true.

"You're looking at where people could see the trunk unobstructed?" Sanjay asked.

"No," said Tempest. She understood why Sanjay had asked: stage magicians needed to be conscious of what the audience could see. But that's not what Gideon had drawn. "Those lines Gideon drew represent where the body could have been dragged in a straight line."

"Someone small could have moved his body," Gideon said. "But the front door was under observation the whole time."

Tempest shook her head. "It was recorded last night when we were trapped in the library upstairs. But the house wasn't under observation the *whole time* since Lucas was killed. Mrs. Hudson and her sister were watching it the first night, but she didn't get a security camera until the next morning. She and her sister weren't keeping vigil all night."

"I wish she had been." Sanjay knelt in front of the diorama and looked in through the window with a crisscross detail he'd created. "Then it would be proven I didn't sneak back into the house with a body I'd stolen for some unknown reason. So . . .

we thinking Kira? Gideon, you won me over with your theory that someone small needed room to drag the body. My money's on Kira at this point. How do we catch her?"

"That wasn't my theory," Gideon pointed out. "It was only an observation about space."

"A person dragging a body can also change direction." Tempest took two paintbrushes and set the first one on the diorama between the wooden figure and the sliding bookcase, and the second one between the trunk and the same bookcase. "But it's a straight shot for a trick wire hidden in the sliding bookcase to have pulled the trunk and dumped his body out. It's a piece of furniture that already has tricks up its sleeve."

"I'll call the detective and tell him to look for a mechanical device in the bookcase." Sanjay was already dialing.

Tempest swiped his phone and hung up the call before anyone at the police station answered. "You do realize that if there *is* a trick mechanism anywhere in this room, you'll be even more of a suspect."

Sanjay groaned. "I can't be even more of a suspect. I'm most likely their number one suspect now that you figured out I wasn't the intended victim!"

Tempest raised an eyebrow. "Are you seriously blaming me for figuring out the truth of when Lucas was really killed?"

"Someone's got to be framing me." He gripped the brim of his hat.

"Nobody's framing you."

"Why did you even have us make this diorama if it was only going to implicate me even more?"

"The best way we can help you is to figure out who really—" Tempest broke off as she spotted a movement at the base of the stairs. A *fluffy* movement. She walked over and scooped Abra into her arms. "Did you want to help us solve the case, Abra?"

She turned back to Sanjay as Abra nuzzled her hand. "Our diorama experiment doesn't implicate you. So far, it only shows that we're a great team. Isn't that right, Abra?"

"If you say it's because we're the incarnations of a 1970s TV show, I'm out," said Sanjay as he eyed the bunny.

"I was just pointing out that by working together, we figured out something important."

"We don't actually know for certain that it was a trick," said Sanjay. "And if it was, it points a finger at me. Since I no longer need a babysitter, I'm going to take a walk to clear my head before we set up for this evening."

"We don't have much time," Tempest called after him. Abra squirmed in her arms, sensing her discomfort. "We meet up in the barn in half an hour."

Sanjay waved without turning around as he left through the tree house front door.

Tempest locked it behind him and leaned against it. She closed her eyes and scratched behind Abra's ears.

"Abra knows something is wrong," Gideon said. "What aren't you saying?"

"I don't like the fact that Enid isn't available to come tonight. We still don't know what happened at her library last week. We have two impossible crimes. An invisible burglar and an invisible killer."

Gideon took Abra from her and set him on the floor. He took her hands in his. "I don't think that's the only thing bothering you."

His hands were calloused from his work with stone, but felt so *right*. Their faces were inches apart, so Tempest could see more clearly how thin his face had gotten.

"When you're in France," she said, "who's going to remind you to stop working with stone to *eat*?"

He grinned. "You're worried about me eating enough in *France?*"

"No. I'm worried that you'll be more than five thousand miles away."

"Maybe I need to give you something to remember me by."

"You already gave me Devil Bunny."

"I was thinking of something even better." Gideon leaned in and kissed her.

He slipped one of his hands out of hers and wrapped it around her waist. His body was strong and warm and delicious.

Tempest Raj, the queen of knowing how to keep time, had no idea if ten seconds or ten minutes had passed. All she knew was that she wished she could stay there in the tree house with Gideon indefinitely. But they had a killer to catch.

Chapter 45

At eight o'clock, Tempest, Sanjay, and Gideon were gathered at the Fiddler's Folly workshop. Tempest's dad had insisted on attending, and for now, he was hovering at the barn door of the workshop, keeping an eye on arrivals.

The high-ceilinged barn had been transformed into the theatrical drawing room of Gray House. Using Gideon's sketch of the crime scene furniture's placement on the first night when the murder had occurred, and the diorama they'd made to be sure they got it right, they'd re-created the staging with other furniture on hand.

A desk chair served as Harold's armchair, the couch from the corner of the workshop was carried over to represent the love seat, a wooden bench for the futon, Tempest's own steamer trunk was used in place of Sanjay's, which was being used as evidence, and four folding chairs represented the dozen they had for the audience at Gray House. It wasn't perfect, but the items were placed with precision, so hopefully it was close enough.

The furniture re-created the scene from Gray House, but without Ivy and her trusty nail gun to build prop walls out of plywood, the walls here were only indicated by lines of blue painters' tape on the concrete floor. Since the barn served as a workshop for large construction projects on a regular basis, they had plenty of room to map out the first floor's main room, stairway, bathroom, kitchen, and dining room with the blue tape, leaving gaps for doorways and green tape to indicate the stairway and window openings.

It wasn't only Enid who wasn't available. Mrs. Hudson had declined the invitation, continuing her stakeout of Gray House, convinced that Harold was alive and up to something. Tempest was reserving judgment until she had all the facts, but so far, she didn't see how a ninety-four-year-old man in poor health could be hiding out of sight. She couldn't imagine what his motive could be either, but then again, the man had loved baffling puzzles.

The rest of the group would be arriving by nine o'clock, but there was one guest they'd invited with an earlier start time.

Milton arrived at 8:35. They'd called him back and asked him to come half an hour early, under the pretext of giving him some feedback on Kira's role, which they hoped he could deliver to her in a more constructive way. It was a weak justification, and certainly not one that required a whole half hour, but Milton had a fatherly mentor relationship with Kira, so he accepted it.

Milton stepped through the barn door already dressed in costume in a tweed jacket with elbow patches and tweed trousers. In the bright lighting of the barn that Darius had insisted on, in contrast to the cozy, dim country-house lighting of Gray House, the costume looked like the cheap reproduction that it was.

"Sorry I'm late," Milton said. "I drove past the gate twice before finding it. You're on a dark stretch of road in the hills."

"Glad you found us." Tempest offered him a glass of water, which he accepted.

"I was surprised to hear this was happening after all, but I suppose the show must go on." Milton took a sip and looked around the barn. "This is where the magic of your home renovation business happens?"

"It gives us space to try things out before implementing them."

Milton walked over to the re-creation of the Gray House living room. "I hope you won't be too hard on Kira about her overacting. We're all amateurs, after all."

"This isn't about Kira," said Tempest.

Milton frowned. "It's not? Well, if you have notes about my own role as Dr. Locke, I'm happy to hear them."

"We know you lied about what you do for a living," Sanjay said.

Milton straightened his back and held on to the lapels of the cheap jacket. "I work for the Hidden Bookshop. You saw me there just this afternoon."

"You told us you were their rare books expert," Tempest said. "But you're not. You're their accountant—a guy who manages the money."

Milton's shoulder's fell. "Please . . . I don't want them to know."

"Them?" Tempest asked.

"Both Kira and my daughter."

"Your daughter?" Tempest blinked at him. "I think we're missing something."

"Accounting is a boring profession," said Milton. "I thought it was honorable to have a stable job to support my family, just like I thought I could be straight if I just tried hard enough. So I married my high school sweetheart—a wonderful woman who deserved better—and got a job that made me that boring guy who nobody wants to talk to at parties. I finally stopped lying to both myself and my wife after I met the love of my life, but . . . With a new social circle and a new job in a new town . . . it was easy to keep up with a white lie about what I did for a living."

"So you're not lying because you're embezzling money?" Sanjay asked.

Milton choked on his water. "Embezzling? God, no. I get nightmares about a single cent being out of place at the end of the month. My daughter already thought I was the most boring dad in the world, and she was a teenager when her mom and I divorced, so she still barely speaks to me. I wanted to sound like a cool guy she'd want to spend time with. Do people even say 'cool' anymore? I have no idea—and that's the problem! I'm a fifty-two-year-old accountant for several small businesses who acts in amateur productions in my free time. I never would have lied if I hadn't been trying to impress her."

"So you made up a harmless lie to win your daughter back?" Gideon asked.

"I knew it wouldn't get her back, exactly," Milton said, "but Ellie majored in English in college and works at a small publishing house now. When I told her I'd started working for an antiquarian bookshop, I saw the first spark of interest I'd seen from her in years. She assumed I had a role involving the rare books themselves, not boring spreadsheets." Milton's face lit up with a sad smile.

"Without thinking," he continued, "I said I was trying something new and had learned about books—even though the Hidden

Bookshop is just one of the small businesses I do accounting for. When she came to see me acting in a show shortly after that, it was the first one I was in with Kira. Ellie went out with us afterward, and my profession came up when people ordered drinks . . . I didn't mean for the lie to get out of hand."

"Lies have a way of doing that," said Tempest.

"You brought me here early because you thought I killed Lucas over that lie?" Milton tugged nervously at his beard.

Tempest shrugged. "Lies have a way of getting out of hand, like you said. We didn't know what was going on, so when Sanjay found out about your lie this afternoon, we had to see how it fit."

"I'm just an accountant." Milton shook his head. "I thought it was a noble profession."

"It is," said Gideon. "I wouldn't have a clue how to manage my taxes with the income I make with my sculptures without my CPA."

"Do you like yours?" Sanjay asked him. "Mine is retiring, and I need to find—"

"Can we focus, please?" Tempest cut in, pinching the bridge of her nose. "Milton—"

"Kira's at the gate," Darius said as he slid open the barn door, causing Milton to jump. "I'm buzzing her in, so you've got less than a minute to wrap up whatever you want to say without her here."

"Is it too much to ask for you to keep it from her that I embellished my job?" Milton asked. "I'd hate to go from being cool dad to cringe dad."

"As long as you didn't lie to us about why you lied," said Tempest, "we won't tell anyone."

"Knock, knock." Kira's voice sounded from outside the sliding barn door.

"Thanks for coming," Tempest said. "We're pretty sure the

show will be on this weekend, so we thought it would be a good idea to finally get a full rehearsal."

Kira looked around the room with wonder. "The kids I read to would *love* this place! Maybe I could take the kids from the library on a field trip here?" She plopped an oversize purse down on one of the empty worktables.

"Normally, it's filled with dangerous equipment," Tempest said. "It's packed up right now, but that's probably not a good idea."

"Good point. Who else are we waiting for before we get started?"

"Cameron and Ivy should be here soon," Tempest said.

"This barn is truly lit." Kira stepped farther into the workshop. "And you even re-created the living room so we can practice our blocking, too!"

"Is that the original trunk?" Milton squatted in front of it. "It looks smaller, but maybe that's because we're in this big barn?"

"Different trunk," said Sanjay. "This one is Tempest's. The detective confiscated my bigger one."

"I could fit inside this," Kira joked, but her smile fell away halfway through the sentence. "Sorry. I didn't mean . . . It's just so weird, what happened."

"If another dead body falls out of this one," said Sanjay, "I'm going to scream."

Tempest stared at him. It wasn't possible . . . was it?

He staggered backward under her sharp gaze. "Dear God, Tempest. You don't really think another dead body is going to fall out of another trunk, do you?"

"Of course not." Tempest couldn't resist peeking inside, though. "No body."

"We re-created the set as closely as we could," said Gideon, steering them back on track. "We—"

"This set looks amazing," said Ivy as she stepped through the barn door. "Sorry I'm late. Family dinner ran long."

"You're not the last one here," Tempest said. "Cameron should be here soon. But Mrs. Hudson opted out. So did Enid. She has an event at the Locked Room Library tonight."

"What event?" Ivy frowned.

"She said there was a literary event happening tonight."

"There aren't any events happening tonight at the library," said Ivy. "I'd know. I keep our events calendar."

"Enid lied?" Tempest hadn't even considered that.

"Why would she lie about something like that?" Gideon asked.

"She's been behaving oddly," Ivy said. "I don't know how to describe it except that she's looked frazzled lately."

"We're trying to solve a murder," said Sanjay, "and you didn't think to mention Enid has been acting strangely?"

"Wait," said Kira. "You're trying to solve the murder? You gathered us here tonight like we're in an Agatha Christie novel and you're going to reveal the killer? There's no way I'm going to be a part of—"

"Hang on," Tempest said as she knelt at a line of blue tape. That blue tape represented walls because Ivy wasn't there when they were building the set. There was something about the lines that was bugging her.

Her phone buzzed in her pocket as she was tracing the tape. It was a message from her grandfather. Her breath caught as she read it.

Enid is the executor and trustee appointed in Harold's will, his message said.

That was it. The information she needed to solve one of the biggest puzzles that confused things this week. It gave her the answer to *why*.

"Rehearsal is canceled," she said.

"Uh, Tempest needs a moment." Sanjay knelt at her side and lowered his voice. "Since when do you back down? You're *the Tempest*, for God's sake."

"I'm not backing down," she said. "I figured it out. Well, *almost*. I know where we really need to be tonight to get answers."

Sanjay grinned at her. "We're going after the last piece of the puzzle? I'm in."

Chapter 46

Enid's break-in at the Locked Room Library in San Francisco really was connected to this murder all along as I suspected," Tempest said as they drove across the Bay Bridge. "Those items moved around in the library were a distraction."

"But from what?" Ivy asked.

Tempest yanked the steering wheel more strongly than was needed as she switched lanes, and she had to right the jeep before crashing into the bridge's guardrail. Clearly, she needed to calm down. But how could she? They were so close to seeing through the tricks.

"Misdirection was staring me in the face," she said. "It was leading our attention away from the real purpose of the break-in. I just didn't see it until we were gathered in the workshop. I figured out the tool that was needed for the trick the invisible intruder used at the Locked Room Library, and then my grandfather's contacts turned up an interesting fact today:

Enid is the trustee overseeing Harold's estate. Not Cameron. And Enid lied to us about whatever she was up to tonight."

"You don't really think she's the killer, do you?" Ivy gripped her seat. "Did she help Harold fake his death?"

"I don't know what to think anymore," Tempest said. "But no. I don't believe Enid is a murderer. And we haven't seen any evidence that Harold is alive. But Enid is involved, either knowingly or not. I'm certain now that the break-in is related to the murder."

"Don't tell me you've solved the trick of the invisible intruder," Sanjay said. "I was there with you. It was impossible."

"Nothing," said Gideon, "is truly impossible. Especially when it comes to Tempest."

She caught his eye in the rearview mirror. The edges of his eyes crinkled with a smile, and the flutter in her stomach had nothing to do with how fast she was driving.

She wished they weren't speeding across the bridge to solve a break-in connected to a murder. But right then, more than anything, she wished she and Gideon had more time. Why did she always take things for granted until they were gone?

"You've really solved it?" Ivy asked.

"Part of it." Tempest grounded herself in the present and swerved to go around a slow-moving car. "I know *how* the intruder was invisible. We never saw someone on the library's interior video camera—because the burglar never went inside the library at all."

"Of course he did," said Sanjay. "We both saw the video—"

"Enid showed the video to me as well," Ivy said. "You mean the recording was manipulated?"

"Not at all," said Tempest. "They really did break into the building. But they weren't in the main library during the ten minutes they were inside."

"We saw that fake raven cawing at them," Sanjay snapped.

"We saw Valdemar cawing at *motion*," said Tempest.

"The foyer is too far away to set off his motion sensors," Ivy insisted. "Even if someone were waving their arms around, it's too far. If the raven was that sensitive, it would have driven everyone crazy."

"But the raven's motion sensor did detect the downed lamps."

"*Downed?*" Gideon said. "That's a strange word to use to talk about the lamps that were knocked over."

"I'm being precise by using that word," Tempest said. "The lamps that toppled were caught on camera, but the books that were moved were in hidden places *that aren't visible to the camera*. The burglar moved the books around *earlier*, during opening hours, when they wouldn't be noticed. Then the intruder came back that night and made sure to be caught on the outer camera. Before the burglar went in search of what they were really after, they stood in the foyer, outside the range of any video cameras, and *fired a projectile* at the lamps."

"A projectile?" Ivy repeated. "What does that even mean?"

"A *nail gun*," said Tempest. "You mentioned that you couldn't find your nail gun one day last week."

Ivy gasped. "You're right. I thought I'd misplaced it . . . that could have been the day before or after the break-in."

"It's so obvious," Sanjay sighed. "If only I hadn't been distracted by this stupid contract . . . Does a nail gun even fire that far?"

"They do," Gideon and Ivy said simultaneously.

"But you have to hold down the safety mechanism as you shoot," Ivy added. "Tricky, but doable."

"That's why the brass lampshades were damaged," said Tempest. "Not from their fall, but because they were each knocked over by a speeding nail."

"Why didn't we see the nails?" Sanjay asked.

"Those lamps were made when things were built to last," said Tempest. "The nails didn't stick inside the metal frame, but would have gone elsewhere. I'm guessing it never occurred to Enid that a couple of stray nails would be relevant. She must sweep up all sorts of odd junk from the library floor."

"If the burglar didn't go inside the library when he got inside," said Ivy, "then where did he go?"

"Upstairs," said Tempest, "to Enid's apartment."

Everyone was silent as that sank in.

"Remember how I said my grandfather found the person who drew up Harold's will and trust?" said Tempest. "Enid is responsible for Harold's trust. She's the one who has all the paperwork about Gray House Library and all the details of Harold's finances. She knows how the trust was set up. I think that's what the intruder was after. *Information.* That's why we need to talk with her."

"It's all so awful." Ivy shivered. "They were in her *home*. Not just the library."

"I don't think they meant to hurt Enid," Tempest assured her. "Remember, the burglar went to the house when she was out at the theater."

"But the burglar didn't know that," Sanjay pointed out. "What time was the break-in?"

"Pretty late," Tempest admitted, "but she'd told people that she was going to a musical that night."

Ivy gasped from the back seat. "You mean it's someone Enid knows personally?"

"It has to be," Gideon said softly. "If Tempest is right that your nail gun was used, it has to be someone we *all* know."

"I don't know," Sanjay said. Tempest could see in the rearview mirror that he was sulking. He wanted to be the one to see through the misdirection. "Isn't it common knowledge that Enid is in charge of Gray House as it gets set up? Why would someone need to see her paperwork? Do you think Cameron thinks she's embezzling?"

"Harold deemed Enid the responsible one," Tempest said, "which is why she's in charge instead of Cameron."

"Only at first," Ivy corrected. "It'll be Cameron's soon. It makes sense for Enid to be—"

"I'm not criticizing Cameron's sense of responsibility," Tempest said. "He doesn't have experience setting up a library, so Harold's friendship with Enid and her knowledge from setting up the Locked Room Library makes sense."

Mollified, Ivy nodded.

"My point," said Tempest, "was merely that Enid had all the library paperwork, and we have no idea what was in it. Presumably, it's confidential. And it was probably easier to look through her paper files than break into electronic files. With the misdirection at the library downstairs, as long as nothing was taken from her apartment upstairs, she wouldn't notice if a few papers were moved around."

"That's why the intruder didn't need to take anything," said Gideon. "They only needed to take photos of the information they were after."

Sanjay swore. "I admit defeat. It's a good theory."

"It all fits." Ivy zipped up her pink vest so it covered half her face. "It's so creepy that someone crept upstairs into her private space above the library."

"Honestly," said Sanjay, "I had no idea there could be so much drama in a library."

Tempest turned off at the exit that would lead them to the Locked Room Library. "Now it's time to see what Enid knows—and what she's hiding."

Chapter 47

wo waterspout gargoyles adding ambiance to the façade looked down at them as Tempest, Ivy, Gideon, and Sanjay climbed the steps to the Locked Room Library. The stone creatures had been added as part of the renovation that turned the Victorian house into a library on the first floor, though the Gothic pair looked as if they'd existed for centuries.

"You've got to be kidding me," Enid said as she opened the door. The sleeves of modern pajamas peeked out beneath the stylish vintage robe she wore.

"I'm sorry we woke you," said Tempest, "but I know the secret of your invisible burglar—and why they did it."

Stunned, Enid let them inside. Instead of turning on the lights of the library, she turned to the hidden stairs that led the way up to her apartment.

Before following, Tempest paused in the foyer that overlooked the library but was out of range of its security cameras.

The sleek faux train car her dad had built was visible in the dim light. Secret Staircase Construction had modeled the train car based on Agatha Christie's *Murder on the Orient Express* dining car. Members of the public could book the cozy space that held a dozen people for things like book club meetings.

"Coming?" Gideon asked, and she realized she was the last person not on the stairs.

She nodded, but before following, she waved her arms. The motion sensor raven, named Valdemar after a character in an Edgar Allan Poe story, didn't caw. It was too far away from her. But Tempest had a clear line of sight to the raven perched on a high shelf. She knew she was right about what had happened. She hurried after the others.

"A nail gun?" Enid repeated after Tempest had explained what had happened with her break-in. "That explains why I found a couple of nails with the other trash that day. I'm sorry I didn't make the connection to mention it."

They were now sitting in the living room of Enid's upstairs apartment, which was disappointingly modern compared to the classic décor of the library below.

"The more important question," said Tempest, "is what the thief was after. I believe the library was a misdirection, and the thief went to the part of the house that doesn't have security cameras: your apartment."

"But I don't have anything of value!" Enid insisted. "I don't need the invasiveness of cameras up here. I inherited enough money to open this library in this old Victorian, but on top of all the unexpected costs of the library, maintaining an old house is a lot more expensive than I imagined. I don't have much money left, so they certainly weren't after my banking information. I do love shopping for vintage clothes, so I might have accidentally stumbled across a designer outfit that's worth more than I think. That's the only thing of value that might be here."

"You're Harold's trustee," said Tempest.

Enid crossed her arms. "I'm not stealing from his estate. A bank is the true manager of the estate, since Harold's will was *very* specific about everything, but I'm the named person to oversee the estate being settled."

"I don't think you're stealing," Tempest said. "But you have all that paperwork related to his will and trust. Which could be of interest to someone else."

"It's on my password-protected computer, with the originals in a safe-deposit box." She whirled around to where Sanjay was typing on her computer keyboard. "What are you doing?"

"Seeing how easy your password is to guess."

"Ha. Have at it. You'll never guess it."

"Hmm," said Sanjay. "You're probably right. Ivy? What would she use that someone she works with knows?"

Enid laughed again. "Oh, I do love your enthusiasm. If you had your rabbit with you, I'd almost think you were like that fictional group—"

"Please don't say it," said Sanjay.

"If you type in the wrong password too many times," said Enid, "you'll probably lock me out, so please don't keep guessing. I promise my password isn't anything silly like Agatha1920, HerculeForever, or Sherlocked."

Ivy reddened and mumbled something about needing to change her own passwords.

"So if that's what they were after," said Gideon, "they didn't get it."

"Well . . ." Enid twisted the robe's belt between her fingers. "Maybe I had some notes in my desk drawers. It depends what the thief was after."

"Is there any information in the will and trust that isn't common knowledge?" Tempest asked.

"You all know what's in there," said Enid. "There were no

secrets. Harold never had kids, and he invested his money well, so there's plenty of money in the trust to keep the library going for decades. It includes funds for renovations, maintenance, property taxes, costs associated with running the library, and good salaries for both Cameron and a library assistant. And a modest salary for me is being paid through one year after the library opens. You all already know this."

"Can we see—" Tempest began.

"Sure," said Enid. "But your dad has already seen the details of the trust. He wanted to make sure there were adequate funds for the renovation. Like I said, there are no secrets in there, so I happily showed it to him."

Tempest had been so sure she was right about the intruder needing to get access to Enid's apartment. "Why did you lie to us about why you couldn't come over tonight?" she asked.

Enid opened her mouth to protest, then changed her mind. Instead, she began laughing.

"I'm so sorry," Enid said. "I've muddled things for no reason. I was just so *exhausted*. I couldn't imagine fitting in one more thing. Do you know how difficult it is to run one library and plan another, especially with the bureaucracy I had to go through with Hidden Creek to get the Gray House Library approved to be part of this summer stroll?"

"Wait," said Sanjay. "You were simply *tired*?"

"I'm an introvert." Enid shrugged. "I like people, but I like books even more. People are fun—especially book people—but they exhaust me. A good book and a cup of tea replenishes my energy. I know you two stage performers probably don't understand, but Ivy probably does. And maybe Gideon."

"Definitely," said Gideon.

"Why didn't you just tell us?" Ivy asked. "I would have understood."

"It sounded important to you that we do a proper rehearsal

with an audience. But I didn't think my presence would help. So I told a white lie."

"What book did you read instead?" Ivy asked.

Enid smiled. "A British Library Crime Classics collection of recently discovered bibliophile short stories from the early to mid-1900s. I got through three stories before I fell asleep. And you can find the remnants of my cup of chamomile tea in the sink."

Ivy reddened. "I'm sorry we had to ask."

Enid smiled warmly. "I'm glad you came and asked, rather than skulking around thinking I was a killer instead of simply asking for my explanation for why I lied. Do you know how often the puzzle of a mystery novel would have been cleared up early on if only the characters had spoken to one another?"

"But then there wouldn't be a book," said Ivy.

"Agreed," said Enid. "And what fun would that be? But truly, saying I was tired wasn't a subtle hint that you should leave. It's more that I'm being run ragged running my library and now having to set up a new one."

"You don't want to do it?" Tempest asked.

Enid hesitated. "I wanted to follow through with Harold's dying wish, but honestly? Cameron could have done it with the help of a consultant. It didn't need to be me. I wish Harold had never asked."

☠.☠.☠

"I'm glad I'm not a real homicide detective," Sanjay said on the walk back to where they'd found a parking spot two blocks away. "I don't know how I'd deal with the constant frustration on a daily basis. We're no closer than we were before."

"Aren't we?" said Tempest.

"You learned something?" Gideon asked.

"I believe she was telling us the truth," said Tempest, "which unfortunately gives her a very strong motive. We now know the break-in was related to the Gray House Library, since the nail gun on-site was used—and Enid Maddox didn't want that library to open."

"You can't really think Enid is a killer!" Ivy shouted the words so loudly that a light clicked on in a second-floor window of the house they were standing next to.

Sanjay ushered Ivy into the jeep, and they pulled away before the person they'd woken could take further action.

"I simply think it means we can't rule her out," Tempest said. "We shouldn't be looking at motives anyway. That's what Blackburn does well. We need to focus on what *we* do well."

"Bickering with a bunny at our side?" Sanjay quipped.

"We know how Lucas was killed now," said Tempest, "which anyone could have done, since the house wasn't under observation at that time. Blackburn is looking into people and forensics, but there are *two impossibilities* that haven't been solved."

"The disappearing body," said Sanjay.

"And the reappearing one," Tempest added. "That's what we can solve. It's what we should have been doing tonight in the barn when we got sidetracked."

"You're the one who sidetracked us," Sanjay pointed out.

Tempest scowled into the rearview mirror, but Sanjay wasn't looking her way to see it. "Hey, I solved the mystery of the invisible intruder."

"That's not bad for one night," Gideon said.

Tempest grinned and caught his eye. "Who says the night is over?"

Chapter 48

Tempest didn't actually have a plan. And she didn't have much time to figure one out. There was no traffic on the bridge on their way back to Hidden Creek, so they'd be back in no time. There was something off about their re-creation of the scene of the crime. She wanted to take another look at it.

It wasn't much past midnight when they arrived in Hidden Creek. The main road took them through the center of town before reaching the turnoff onto the side street that would lead them back to Fiddler's Folly.

"Slow down," Gideon said as they drove past Veggie Magic, which was brightly lit in spite of the late hour.

"Lavinia never has her café open this late." Ivy craned her neck as Tempest slowed.

"People are getting an early start on the summer stroll." Tempest pointed at the new Himalayan restaurant down the street with its lights still on. "They must be staying open late for that."

"Pull over," said Gideon.

"You hungry?" Tempest asked.

"Milton and Kira are inside Veggie Magic," he said. "They must've headed there after we canceled the rehearsal."

Tempest pulled over, and they headed into the café.

"There was no way I could get to sleep," Kira said when Tempest and her friends arrived at their table. "Milton agreed to keep me company."

"We were just finishing up," said Milton. There were no plates on the table, but rumpled napkins and nearly empty cups of tea sat on the tabletop.

"Good," said Tempest. "Because we need your help."

☠.☠.☠

Ten minutes later, they were back at the barn workshop at Fiddler's Folly.

"We got sidetracked earlier tonight," said Tempest. "It's time to finish what we started. We're all set up for a rehearsal—"

"*Now?*" Milton scratched his beard. "It's after midnight."

"What's the matter, Milton?" Sanjay asked.

Milton chuckled. "I remember what it was like to be in my twenties like it was yesterday, but I'm no longer up for being awake until three o'clock in the morning."

"Worried you'll slip up because you're tired?" Sanjay clasped his hands behind his back and leaned forward with his eyes narrowed. Was he attempting to look intimidating? It wasn't very convincing.

"W-what?" Milton stammered as he stepped away from Sanjay.

"Maybe accidentally reveal something to your mentee that you wish she wouldn't know?"

Milton reddened.

"What's he talking about?" Kira asked Milton.

Milton's shoulders slumped. He sat down on the bench serving as the futon in their stage reproduction and put his head in his hands. "They said they wouldn't tell you." He gave Sanjay a withering glance, but it only lasted a moment. "I should probably tell you anyway. It's time. I don't want to have to keep pretending."

Kira sat down on the bench next to him and took his hand. "You can tell me anything. Wait, that's not true. If you tell me you've only been pretending to be gay and you're actually trying to seduce me, I'm outta here."

That got a chuckle out of Milton, but he didn't meet her gaze when he spoke. "I'm not a rare books expert. I don't know anything about old books. Or anything interesting. I'm simply a boring old accountant."

Kira squeezed his hand. "I know that, silly."

Milton looked up at her. "You do?"

"So does your daughter."

"She *does?*"

"Milton, you're an even worse liar than you are a 'rare book expert.' Ellie didn't start spending time with you again because of that, but because she missed you. She was angry for a long time because she felt like you split up the family, but that was just her acting out as an emotional adolescent who was upset her family had changed. She doesn't actually blame you."

"How do you *know* all this? You two have been hanging out without telling—"

"No." Kira shook her head. "She's a chronic oversharer on social media. I started following her after we met after that first show she came to."

"You're not angry that I lied?"

Kira shrugged. "Everyone lies about their lives online. You aren't active online except to share new shows of the Creekside Players, so I gave you a pass for needing an outlet to pretend to be good at something you weren't."

"I'm sorry," Milton said. "It was a stupid thing to have lied about, and I didn't know how to unsay it."

"It's all good," said Kira. "Just don't do it again. You don't ever need to lie to me."

"Yes, well." Sanjay cleared his throat from where he stood in the spot that would have been the bathroom if they'd been in Gray House. "I'm glad we got that cleared up. Can we please get to the actual matter at hand?"

Tempest was standing a few feet away from Sanjay, in the room that would have been the dining room, which they'd marked off with blue painters' tape. She followed the line of sight from where Sanjay stood to where Kira and Milton sat on the futon.

"I know what happened," Tempest said. She'd been close to figuring it out when her grandfather's text about Enid had arrived, and now she could see it clearly.

"You really know?" Ivy asked.

"Not just a guess?" Sanjay added.

"I do," Tempest said quietly. "Gideon, could you bring me the large sheet of cardboard on the table behind you? Then I'll be able to tell you for sure if this is about lines of sight. Everyone else, stay where you are."

The four-by-four-foot piece of cardboard swayed as Gideon handed it to her. She placed it on the line of tape of the dining room wall that faced the living room, then slowly moved it around each section of wall they'd drawn with tape. When she was done with the dining room, she moved on to the kitchen and bathroom.

"You're looking to see if there any blind spots," said Sanjay, catching on.

"Sort of," Tempest said. "The arched opening from the living room made us discount the idea that someone could have left the group and moved the body from the living room."

"I was in the kitchen," Ivy said, "where it's a straight shot to see the living room, bathroom, and dining room. I'd swear to the fact that I didn't see anyone go back into the living room."

"I don't doubt you," Tempest said. "But do you remember what you were doing in the kitchen?"

"Of course," Ivy snapped. "I was with Cameron the whole time between when we found the body and when it disappeared. I was helping him open the cabinet to get our cell phones to call the police. I was . . ." She trailed off and gasped. "You're right. If I'd turned my head, I could have seen what was happening. But I was so focused on getting to a phone . . . I was facing *away* from the living room."

Tempest nodded. "The living room and the bathroom were both behind you. And from where Enid, Milton, and I were in the dining room, we could only see the kitchen, not the living room or bathroom. We were all in such proximity to one another that we assumed we were all together."

She should have noticed even sooner. There was only *one person* with an opportunity to slip away. Even though Ivy and Cameron were in the kitchen, they were facing in the other direction.

"There was only one person who was alone," said Tempest. "One person not in our line of sight. We thought we knew where she was, but in truth, we only *heard* her."

One by one, all eyes turned to Kira.

Chapter 49

You didn't," Milton whispered earnestly to Kira.

"She's the only one who could have moved his body." Tempest tossed the cardboard aside and followed the blue tape back to the living room to stand in the spot that would have been the stage in front of the fireplace. "If we agree it wasn't Harold's ghost who moved Lucas's body, it's the *only* answer that's possible."

"She isn't the killer." Milton took a deep breath and looked as if he was about to say more, but Kira spoke first.

"Don't do anything stupid like confessing to a murder you didn't commit to save me." Kira turned from Milton and faced Tempest.

"It's true, isn't it?" Tempest watched Kira's resolute face.

Kira didn't look frightened. Or sorry. Only *relieved*.

"I didn't kill Lucas Cruz," Kira said. "But I moved his body."

"Where?" Sanjay asked as several others gasped. "I swear you couldn't have found an impossibly small hiding spot in my magic trunk."

"The one place we never thought to look," said Tempest, "because normally there's no way a body could be hidden in such a small-seeming piece of furniture. But we forgot one important thing. In addition to the folding chairs, the one other piece of furniture we rented was the *futon*. It was rented from Kira's cousin's company: Storage Solutions."

Sanjay groaned. "*Storage.* It's right there in their name."

"So everything they rent includes extra storage," Gideon added.

"The folding chairs fold up to be flat," said Tempest. "And the futon must've had a hidden storage compartment."

Kira nodded. "The cushion is a lot thinner than it looks. After I threw up in the bathroom, I looked out and saw the body to my right, and Ivy and Cameron to my left—*with their backs turned to me.* I had a flash of inspiration when I saw Lucas lying right next to the futon. It only took a couple of seconds to unlatch the futon's storage section and lift him into the long compartment under the cushion. I might look small, but I'm hella strong from hauling around heavy stacks of books all day, so I knew I could do it."

"Why?" Ivy asked. "Were you covering up for the real killer?"

"No way." Kira shook her head. "I really did think it was an accident. That the props got messed up and it was a tragic accident."

"You thought I killed him?" Milton tugged at his beard.

"Not on purpose," Kira insisted. "I know you'd never do that. I was freaking out at what we'd just seen. While I was throwing up, so many things were flashing through my mind. Not just wondering how the prop gun could have malfunctioned, but also how the library opening would be ruined. My local library is how I got through my childhood. I've seen up close how much both kids and adults use our little public library. Libraries are *essential*. Having another library in town would have been amazing."

Her confession sounded genuine, but there was something in her words that didn't ring true.

"I don't buy it that you'd move a dead body to save Gray House Library," Tempest said.

"It's the truth." Kira rubbed her eyes. "But you're right. That's not the whole story. I was also thinking of myself. How could I not? My boss is a tyrant, but libraries are my calling. I didn't want to leave Hidden Creek . . ."

"You thought you could get the second librarian job that Harold's trust set up?" Tempest asked.

Kira nodded. "I was already trying to impress Cameron with my work ethic, hoping he'd hire me. I knew I couldn't bring Lucas back to life, but I thought I could at least have his body be discovered *after* the city council meeting. I thought someone being killed would mess up the library getting approved, so I only wanted to hide him long enough to get through the city council meeting when the vote was supposed to happen."

"And then the city council decided to postpone the vote," Tempest said.

Kira's face darkened. "I did it for nothing. I know I screwed up. The largest screwup of my life."

"But how did you get his body back onto the floor the second night?" Sanjay asked.

"Were you the person who trapped us in that room?" Gideon added.

"No way," Kira said adamantly. "I have no idea who killed him, how they figured out he was in the futon, or how they got him out of there while trapping all of us in the escape room.

I swear it. I was trapped in there with you! But as for moving his body in the first place to save the library?" She took a deep breath. "I take responsibility for that. I'll go talk to that detective now. I have his card, so I can wake him up. I'll turn myself in to the police for my role in messing with the evidence. He seems honest, so I don't think he'll railroad me into confessing to a murder I didn't commit."

"Let me go with you," Milton said.

"I can do it on my own," Kira snapped. "Don't worry, I'm not going to run away to avoid whatever punishment is coming to me. My whole life is here in Hidden Creek. I hope it's still waiting for me when I get out of jail."

"Let me go as your friend," Milton said. "Wait. I don't mean that."

Kira winced.

"What I mean," Milton added, "is that I want to go with you for *me* as much as for you. I lost out on a lot of years of being a dad, and it feels good to have been able to look out for you these past couple of years. Let me be selfish. Let me be your moral support. Whatever you need, I'm here."

Milton watched her hopefully, and a moment later, Kira threw herself into his arms. When she broke away from the hug, there were tears in his eyes.

"That was a surprisingly touching resolution," Ivy said as they closed the barn door behind Kira and Milton.

"Except it's *not* a resolution," Tempest said.

"Because we still don't know who actually killed Lucas Cruz." Ivy leaned against the barn's sliding door.

"Actually . . ." Tempest bit her lip so hard she drew blood. She hated what she'd realized. But all the clues told her she was right. "I know who did it. Who's up for breaking into Gray House?"

Chapter 50

I can't believe you talked us into breaking into a crime scene."
Sanjay peeked through the curtains.

"It didn't take much arm-twisting for you to agree to it,"
Gideon pointed out.

Sanjay snapped the curtains shut. "Mrs. Hudson doesn't appear to be awake, so let's keep it that way."

"It was still a good idea to park down the street and keep the blinds drawn," said Ivy. "Tempest, are you finally going to show us what we're looking for?"

"The futon really doesn't look like there's room to hide a body." Tempest crouched in front of it.

"You think Kira made it up?" Sanjay joined her at the innocuous piece of furniture.

Tempest shook her head. "Blood was in Sanjay's trunk because that's where Lucas's body was hidden at first, which is why the police thought he was hidden in the trunk once more, and they didn't look further for where else he could have been hidden a second time." She attempted to flip open the futon, but it didn't budge.

"There's got to be a lever somewhere." Gideon knelt next to her and felt around the wooden edges. "Got it."

The cushion lifted upward silently, leaving a shallow space tall enough for extra blankets, books, or a dead body.

"That looks like a little bit of blood." Tempest pointed.

"Don't touch it." Sanjay pulled her away from it.

"I'm not going to."

"Oh no!" Ivy ran to the front windows.

"You heard something?" Tempest followed.

"Not yet, but don't you see?" Ivy looked in horror at the un-assuming piece of furniture. "Kira is telling Blackburn about how she used the futon to hide the body right now—"

"That means the police will be over here soon," Sanjay finished. "Great excursion, everyone! Now let's get going." He hooked his hand through Tempest's elbow, but she pulled free.

"We won't be long," she insisted. "Blackburn will take Kira's statement. We left at the same time they did, so we have time."

"I still don't like it," said Ivy.

"You're going to like what I say next even less." Tempest walked to the fireplace, where she could face them all. "Ivy, I need you to answer two questions truthfully."

"No way," Sanjay said. "You can't suspect Ivy of murder."

"Obviously," Tempest snapped. "None of us is a killer. I know that. But Ivy has two key pieces of information."

"I do?" Ivy zipped up her pink vest and peeked out over the top of the collar.

"Who suggested the restaurant you and Cameron ordered takeout from?"

"You mean the new Himalayan restaurant?" Ivy asked. "I did. Cameron wanted something spicy, and I'd seen this new restaurant but hadn't tried it yet, so I suggested it."

Sanjay caught Tempest's eye. "Sounds like a force to me."

Ivy laughed. "You mean that Cameron made me pick the restaurant without knowing I did?" She shook her head.

"The restaurant itself didn't matter," said Tempest. "But the fact that it was fragrant, spicy food did."

"What are you talking about?" Ivy looked from Tempest to Sanjay.

"To cover up *another smell*," said Gideon.

Ivy's head snapped to Gideon. "What are you all talking about?"

"You'd see it, too," said Tempest, "if you weren't interested in Cameron."

Ivy crossed her arms and glared at all of them. "You're seriously telling me that because Cameron had a food craving, it means he's a killer? Listen to yourselves. That doesn't make any sense. None. Zero. No sense. Because it's nonsense."

"Lucas had been killed more than a day before," Tempest said gently. "His body was starting to smell. That's how Cameron located the body where it was hidden."

"I didn't smell anything," Ivy said. "You were with me at Gray House—"

"I was," said Tempest, "but what better way to cover up the scent than to light a fire and order food that would mask the smell, at least for a short time? The fire would also help speed along the stages of rigor mortis."

"Now you're making even *less* sense," said Ivy. "If he found Lucas's body because of the smell, why wouldn't he simply tell the police? And if he was the one who killed him in the first place, like you're suggesting, he wouldn't have invited us over for dinner at Gray House after finding the body Kira hid. He doesn't even live here. There was no reason for any of us to have come over before he got rid of the body."

"Unless he wanted to create a perfect alibi for himself," Tempest said.

"The escape room?" Ivy said. "Really? You think he set that whole thing up to give himself an alibi? Well, it's the best alibi possible, because it's truly impossible for him to have moved the body from the futon to the floor. I was with him the whole time. I'll swear to that."

"Even when he went to grab the poker?" Tempest asked.

Ivy hesitated. "Yes. Yes! I was on the stairs, with the rest of you."

"The furniture," Sanjay said as he walked around the furniture. "I get it now. *That's* why the furniture was rearranged. Not because of a trick mechanism, but because of the lines of sight."

Tempest nodded. "Cameron moved the furniture so the futon wouldn't be visible from any other room—or the stairs. He had a great excuse to grab the poker, since we thought someone was being attacked upstairs. We were all still close to him, so we'd all *think* he was within sight. But like Kira, he's gotta be strong from moving heavy piles of books, so it wouldn't take him long to step a foot away from the fireplace and roll Lucas's body out of the futon. The fire was keeping the room warm, so he was speeding along the decomposition process, making Lucas's body look distorted when we found him—like he was beaten up, which confused things even more."

Sanjay shook his head. "I should have seen it."

"I thought I came up with the unstable spot to put our phones," Gideon said, "but it's only because he'd covered every surface of that table with food, wasn't it?"

Tempest nodded.

"You're all grasping at straws." Ivy backed away and tripped. Sanjay caught her before she fell, but she yanked her arm away from his hand. "You're all turning against him—and me. Making up a fantasy so that this mess will be over."

"We're not turning against you, Ivy," Gideon said. "Tempest is right. It's the only way everything that's happened makes sense."

"Harold's ghost was a lucky addition to muddle things," Sanjay said. "I'm sure Cameron was thrilled when Enid suggested that idea. She gave him so much great material to work with. And he took advantage of it."

Ivy shook her head. "You've all lost your minds. How did he make Harold's voice call out from upstairs, huh?"

Tempest raised an eyebrow at her BFF. "You're claiming it *was* Harold's ghost working with Cameron?"

"Well, no," Ivy said. "But Cameron's voice is nothing like his great-uncle's, and he knows nothing about AI, but someone had to have cloned Harold's voice to do that, right? I'm sure he'd be happy to let the police search his computer, since he doesn't have anything he could have used to fake Harold's voice. There's no proof about any of this."

"Ivy is right. We don't have proof," Sanjay said. "The facts fit perfectly, but it's all circumstantial. The escape room clues about poison were written in unrecognizable block letters, Cameron has a legitimate reason for his fingerprints being everywhere in this house, and the police screwed up forensics by not taking any that first day when he killed Lucas early in the day before texting me. Oh! What about Lucas's cell phone? Cameron must have been using it."

"Blackburn already told me Lucas's cell phone had been in this house the whole time," Tempest said. "It doesn't tell us who was using it."

"Oh." Sanjay kicked the carpet. "So the only thing we don't have is proof."

"Which you don't have," Ivy said defiantly, "because he didn't do it. What about Harold? Have you all forgotten about him? We heard his voice. He could have—"

"Actually," Gideon said, "I have an idea about proof."

All eyes turned to Gideon. "I was thinking about that voice we heard, before we got trapped in the escape room. It sounded grainy."

"Because it came from upstairs," Ivy said.

Gideon shook his head. "It was more like static." Gideon really was the best at noticing the smallest details, though Tempest couldn't yet see why it mattered here.

Ivy gasped. "You don't really mean I was right and it *was* Harold?"

"Yes and no," Gideon said. "When we were first hired to work on the job site, Tempest talked to Harold to get his vision for the magic he wanted to bring to life here, like she does with all clients. He told you about his career."

Tempest smiled. "He was a curmudgeon, but I have a soft spot for curmudgeons. Especially ones who love books."

"Your notes mentioned what else he was interested in besides books," Gideon said.

"Radio!" Tempest said. "He walked away from a career recording *radio dramas* in the '50s not because he didn't have talent on air, but because he had to work more collaboratively than he wanted to. Radio dramas of the '50s had all sorts of dialogue like that. What do you want to bet we'll find a radio show where Harold's character cried out for help?"

"But that doesn't prove anything," Ivy insisted, though her protestation was less vehement than minutes before. "Anyone could have found that—"

"Did you all hear something?" Gideon hurried to the front window.

"I did," Tempest said. A *click*. But not from the front door. The sound came from the back.

"The police must be here already," grumbled Sanjay. "Come on, they're not here for us, so let's go out the back—"

"Not that way—" Tempest called after him, but someone was already pushing Sanjay back into the living room.

Cameron Gray—with a shotgun pointed at Sanjay's chest.

Chapter 51

Cameron motioned with the barrel of the shotgun toward the empty spot on the living room floor where the trunk and Lucas's body had once lain. "Sit down."

"Cam?" Ivy whispered. "What are you doing?"

The look of utter bewilderment on Ivy's face broke Tempest's heart. Whatever it took, Tempest was going to hold Cameron Gray responsible.

"I was at home in my apartment and got a security alert notification," Cameron said. "And now I've found four burglars at Gray House."

"We'd better do what he says." Tempest pulled Ivy down onto the floor next to her. Gideon and Sanjay followed suit. Sanjay glowered at Cameron as he sat curled on his knees, as if ready to pounce. Gideon's expression was blank, like a stoic philosopher's, and Tempest had no idea what he was thinking. She didn't know which of the two men frightened her more at that moment.

But Cameron wasn't paying any attention to them. He only had eyes for Ivy.

"I'm so sorry, Ivy," Cameron whispered. "It was an accident. None of this was ever supposed to happen."

"Your regrets would be a lot more convincing if you weren't pointing a shotgun at us," Sanjay growled.

Cameron swung the shotgun his way.

"This isn't you!" Ivy shouted. "How can you do this, Cam?"

"Would you believe me if I told you I was possessed by Harold's ghost? No? I didn't think so." Cameron winced as he looked at Ivy's horror. He looked away from her, unable to meet her gaze. His settled on Tempest, and his expression hardened. "Toss your cell phones over to me. All of you. And that hat of yours, Sanjay."

They did as instructed, though Sanjay hesitated for a moment before letting go of his hat.

"I thought I had adapted to the circumstances so well," Cameron said. His voice was cold, but it also shook ever so slightly. He wasn't as calm as he was attempting to project. "I thought of *everything*. I read mysteries and watch crime television. I know how to cover my tracks. I made sure Lucas's cell phone never left this house. I didn't bring anything new into the house when I changed the escape room to get trapped inside with you and give myself an alibi. I'd snapped off a piece of that broken Agatha Christie bust to jam the door. It was the same color as the molding, and if you hadn't been so flustered, you would have spotted it. I didn't think it would even hold that long, since it didn't need to stay in place for long. All I had to do was remove it when you were all behind a bookshelf. I disguised my handwriting. I was so careful that nothing I did was observed. I was so damn careful, and I played on what was happening around me."

"Harold's ghost," Ivy said.

"I half believed Enid when she raised the possibility," Cameron said. "You have no idea how much I was freaking out inside when the body vanished. I knew I hadn't moved it, so who could have? And *why*? But that doesn't matter. Enid gave me a perfect opportunity to sow confusion." He shook his head and laughed. "I thought using Harold's voice from the radio drama was a nice touch. I had no idea it would be my downfall. Even if I were to erase it from my computer, everything is on a cloud backup server."

Cameron's face hardened. He kept the shotgun trained on them with one hand, but lowered his other arm to pull a roll of blue painters' tape from his pocket. He tossed it at Gideon, then went back to holding the shotgun with both hands. "Bind everyone's wrists behind their backs with this."

"What if I don't?" Gideon asked calmly.

Cameron pointed the shotgun at him.

Gideon shrugged and kept his gaze locked on Cameron's. "I've had a good run. My early demise will make my sculptures much more valuable for my family."

Cameron's arms shook. Gideon's ploy had worked to rattle him.

Gideon's jaw tensed. Sanjay shifted almost imperceptibly. They were going to charge Cameron. Tempest had never seen a shotgun blast up close, but she knew this wouldn't end well. Even if they wrestled the gun away from Cameron, if he got off a single shot at this close range, someone was going to be gravely injured.

Cameron must have sensed the subtle movement. He swung the gun away from Gideon—and pointed it directly at Tempest's chest.

Sanjay and Gideon both froze.

"Do we have an understanding now?" Cameron asked. "Tie Sanjay's arms first. Do his in front of his body. I don't trust his hands where I can't see them. Not just once around! He could rip through the tape. Do at least five times around. No, make it ten."

"There might not be enough tape for that," Gideon said.

"Five, then." Cameron's voice shook. "Five is fine."

Duct tape would have worked much better as a way to tie his hostages, but Tempest imagined he was winging it and only had painters' tape on hand.

"What are you going to do with us?" Ivy asked. "You can't really plan on killing all of us."

"Of course not! You think I wanted to do this? *Any* of this? Lucas gave me no choice. It was an accident. I'm not a killer."

"This kinda makes you look like one." Sanjay held up his thickly bound wrists as Gideon moved on to Ivy.

"Tape her wrists behind her back," Cameron directed.

A squeak escaped Ivy's lips as her face darkened with anger.

"You just need to stay tied up long enough for me to get away." Cameron's gaze darted to the front door. "What was that?"

"Nothing," said Tempest, hoping it was the police, although she hadn't heard anything herself. "You're being paranoid."

Gideon finished with Ivy and moved on to binding Tempest's wrists.

"Tighter," Cameron said. "I don't want to hurt any of you, but I will if you give me no choice."

"Why, Cam?" Ivy asked. "You said Lucas's death was an accident. I'm sure the police will understand—"

"Please stop talking, Ivy." Cameron couldn't meet her gaze. He looked everywhere except at her.

"Do you hate me that much?" Ivy shouted. "Everything was a lie?"

Cameron's hands shook.

"He doesn't hate you," Tempest said. "He's in love with you."

Cameron's eyes brimmed with tears. "None of this was supposed to happen! None of it. Why couldn't Harold have just left a normal will like anyone else? Then we could have been happy together, Ivy."

"Uh, I think I missed about five steps," Sanjay said.

Cameron took one hand off the shotgun for a second to wipe his eyes, then trained the gun on Sanjay.

"He's no threat to you," Tempest said as calmly as she could. "Cameron, I know you didn't mean for any of this to happen. You broke into Enid's house last week looking for a way out, didn't you? Something in the details of Harold's trust beyond the parts that applied to you."

Cameron nodded. "Enid was the executor of his will and the trustee overseeing the trust. She was in his confidence and had all the legal documents about setting up his library legacy. They didn't even trust me enough to show me everything. I needed to see if there was a way out."

"A way out of *what?*" Ivy asked. "What are you both talking about?"

"The library," Tempest answered. "*Cameron* is the person who didn't want the library to open."

Chapter 52

"How did you know I didn't want the library to open?" Cameron asked Tempest. "I'm a librarian, after all. And this wonderful house is my inheritance."

"You're also someone with your own free will," said Tempest, "who didn't want your whole life dictated for you. Harold thought you would love the tiny apartment he built into the attic for you to live above the library, since you were always looking at tiny houses."

"Only because I'm a young librarian in California in the 2020s!" Cameron shouted. "How else was I supposed to afford a home? When I was looking into building a tiny house, I was trying to make the best of a bad situation. It's not like most people would choose a tiny house with no privacy and a bed on a loft like that of a child. It's not freedom when we have no other choice."

"He forced you and Enid to go along with his library plans."

"Enid isn't even a librarian." Cameron laughed without humor. "Did you know that? She's a woman who loves books, so she built her own library and hired skilled librarians, but she's not one herself. But Harold still thought he knew best that she was the right person to oversee his vision of a community library."

"A benevolent dictator," Tempest said. "Did you know Enid didn't want to be roped into this either?"

"She didn't?" Cameron looked like a helpless little boy. Or at least he would have if he hadn't been pointing a shotgun at her.

"Enid wanted to find a way out, too."

Cameron laughed as a tear rolled down his cheek. "Harold *thought* he was being so generous, but do you know what he really was? Controlling. Yes, I loved the old guy. I wasn't reading to him because I thought I'd get his house. I'm not that coldhearted. I was the only one of his relatives he liked. And I felt the same way about him. It was a wild surprise when he started hinting that I'd inherit the house, but it made sense. Felt right. Most of my family are extroverts who'd rather be on a Jet Ski or playing volleyball on a beach than reading. I was the outcast. Just like Harold in his generation. I thought it was going to be so perfect, one bibliophile passing down his home of books to another . . ."

"Until you found out there were strings attached." Tempest squirmed in the sticky tape pulling at the skin on her wrists.

"That's an understatement. I get to live in a tiny, modern, cramped apartment with sloped ceilings without enough headroom to stand up in many places, but downstairs, there are two floors of beautiful architectural details filled with amazing books—none of which are mine and all of them need to be shared with people. People who Harold would have hated sharing his space with during his lifetime! It was all spelled out so clearly in the trust . . . I didn't see a way out."

"So you turned to murder?" Ivy glared at him.

"No! That was never planned. You have to believe me. I was honestly trying to give Harold's plan a go. I was grateful for inheriting the house. But the more I looked into the conditions required for me to benefit from the trust he set up, the more I resented how controlling he was. Did you know I'm not allowed to shelve any modern authors' books in the library? Harold never wanted me to read new authors to him at his bedside. Which is fine. But to prohibit the library from stocking them?" Cameron shook his head. "Classic mysteries are fantastic, and I adore them. But it's not like they're better than the books being written now."

Cameron's voice shook, but he carried on. "Harold thought he was being so forward-thinking for giving me a 'tiny house' like the ones he saw me reading about. But did you know he didn't even give me a choice about how to build it? When he knew he didn't have a long time left, he simply made his own plans to convert the attic into what he thought it should be. At least he hired Secret Staircase Construction. That was the one good thing that came of this—that I met Ivy because of it." He shrank back as he glanced at her and saw the hatred in her eyes.

"You *killed someone*, Cameron," Ivy said.

"I didn't mean to do it. I swear I didn't plan for it to happen. He was gathering those signatures to save the library. That morning, when no one else was here, he showed up and said he'd come by to make sure everything at the house looked just right—because he wanted to film the dress rehearsal. He'd been giving teasers to his social media followers about his latest production, so he thought at least one of the videos from our rehearsal would go viral and show overwhelming support for the library before the city council vote."

Ivy gaped at him. "You killed him over a social media post?"

"It wasn't like that! I never meant to hurt him. He was just so arrogant. I didn't mean to do it." He winced at Ivy's cold stare before turning to Gideon. "Hurry up with that tape."

"Already done," said Gideon.

"Oh. Right." The gun was as unsteady as Cameron's voice. "Then hand the tape to Sanjay to bind your hands behind your back. And let me see him do it."

Sanjay took the roll of blue tape with his bound hands and awkwardly wrapped the tape around Gideon's wrists and hands.

"You can do better than that, Houdini," Cameron said. "You could shuffle a deck of cards with your hands tied behind your back."

Sanjay gave up the pretense and wrapped the tape in five smooth circles around Gideon's wrists.

"Happy?" Sanjay asked as he kicked the tape over to Cameron.

"Of course not." Cameron's voice broke. "You have to understand. Harold forced my hand, and then Lucas did. Lucas loved attention and wanted to be the hero who saved the library."

"So Lucas had to die before he could do that?" Tempest said.

"I think I'm going to be sick." Ivy leaned into Tempest's shoulder.

"Don't you see? He would have unfairly influenced the city council," Cameron insisted. "I wasn't doing anything underhanded to stop the library. I hoped, at first, they'd do the right thing and not approve a library in this residential area. But Lucas took away all hope of that. Not only that, but Lucas didn't care about the library at all. He was only doing it to look like a savior and gain followers."

"You pretended this whole time how much you wanted to save the library and have the city approve it," said Ivy, "but that was all a lie. *Everything* was a lie."

"Not everything." Cameron took a hesitant step toward Ivy.

"Don't touch me," Ivy snarled.

Cameron looked deflated. "I know I've ruined everything, but you have to believe me—I never planned to kill anyone. When Lucas told me about his plans to save the library, I just . . . I snapped."

"You picked up the missing ice pick," said Tempest.

Cameron nodded. "I didn't realize what I'd done until the ice pick was already in his chest. There was no way to save him. He died instantly."

"You took his cell phone to make plans to cover it up," Tempest said.

Cameron nodded again. His face was even paler. "The worst part was that even though I knew exactly how I could hide the truth of what had happened, his phone needed his face to unlock it. So I had to look at him one more time and see what I'd done. I almost couldn't move forward with my idea to text Sanjay to spin him a story about wanting to win over Kira with a trick. But Sanjay was so eager to help that he dropped off his trunk on the porch right away, and it was so easy to set the stage for the deception. I thought that way Lucas could be found in a mysterious way that pointed away from me—and that having a murder at the library would shut it down."

"Only Kira wanted to save the library so badly that she moved the body." Tempest gave up on subtly wriggling her wrists. She was only bunching the tape and making her left hand go numb. "She thought if she could delay finding the body and the city council approved the library, that you'd hire her for the one additional position Harold funded."

"Kira?" Cameron said. "*That's* what happened? How did this go so off the rails? I never meant for this to—"

"Just stop!" Ivy shouted.

"I'm sorry," Cameron croaked. He looked forlornly at Ivy. "I did it for you. I knew you were special from the moment I met you, Ivy. If the library was rejected by the city council, at least I could provide a nice house for the two of us. Something we could never buy on two librarians' salaries."

"We were barely dating!"

"But I could tell how special you were. I knew that you—"

"You. Don't. Know. Anything. About. Me," Ivy growled. "If you did, you'd know that I don't care about a big, beautiful house. I mean, maybe a little, but all I really want is to have my loved ones and books in my life. I was starting to think you were special, too. But I was wrong."

"But I did it for you," Cameron whispered.

"Don't put this on her," Tempest snapped. "You don't care about anyone besides yourself. You sliced Ivy's hand open with a razor blade!"

"That wasn't supposed to be Ivy. I tried to stop her from rushing to the book. There was never any poison, but I didn't want Ivy to get hurt, even with a small cut."

Ivy squirmed in her restraints. "Your disappointments aren't my responsibility, Cameron. Harold was paternalistic, but not a bad man. You didn't have to accept his inheritance at all. I was falling for the man you *could have been*. Not this man you've turned into."

"It wasn't my fault," Cameron whispered.

"Why are you still here?" Ivy asked. "We're restrained."

Their bound hands kept them from stopping Cameron while he had a gun trained on them, but as soon as he left, they'd be able to free themselves. Cameron wouldn't have time to truly get away. He must have realized that escaping meant more than getting out of that house. And desperate people do desperate things . . .

"I don't know what to do," Cameron whispered.

A faint noise sounded, but Tempest had long ago given up on thinking the police would arrive to take the futon as evidence. They didn't know there was any urgency.

"I don't know if I can let you—" Cameron began, but with a *thunk* he dropped to the floor.

Behind him, Mrs. Hudson stood holding her massive binoculars raised above her head.

"I've seen that done in movies with a rolling pin or a cast-iron skillet," she said, looking down at the unconscious Cameron. "I've never been much of a baker or a cook, but I started bird-watching when my husband was sick. Oh, dear . . . You don't think I've killed him, do you?"

Chapter 53

The next day, Mrs. Hudson was the guest of honor at an early afternoon tea at the Fiddler's Folly tree house before the summer stroll kicked off. Tempest, her dad and grandparents, her three best friends, Enid, and Abra the rabbit were all there with her.

Ash doted on Mrs. Hudson for saving his granddaughter and her friends and said he was going to name a new recipe for blackberry-lemon muffins after her—Martha's Muffins, which added Mrs. Hudson's preference for lemons to his existing corn bread muffin recipe. Morag painted a thank-you card for Mrs. Hudson that showed the fearless former librarian on a pedestal of books. And Darius had insisted that he'd cover any magical home renovations she wanted, free of charge.

"I didn't want to resort to violence," Mrs. Hudson said for the fourth time as Ash plied her with yet another cup of tea and more pastries.

She'd seen a sliver of light at Gray House when something had woken her in the night, so she'd crept in through the back door that Cameron had left unlocked for his getaway. She ran back to her house to call the police, but returned because she was worried Cameron was about to do something desperate.

"He only has a small bump on his head," Tempest said. "He didn't even need to stay overnight at the hospital before being released into police custody."

Her phone buzzed, and she smiled as she saw a text from Detective Blackburn.

"Blackburn is releasing the Gray House crime scene," she told them. "We're free to move forward with the escape room game and mystery play starting with tonight's opening."

"Do you think Kira will be able to act in it?" Sanjay asked. He'd already said he was willing to take over Lucas's role in the murder mystery play for the weekend, since they were evening shows that didn't conflict with his afternoon magic performances in the courtyard of the Hidden Bookshop and Hidden Wine Bar. But he swore he was never doing anyone a favor ever again.

"Kira is cooperating with police for her role in tampering with evidence," Tempest said, "so she was charged, but Milton is securing her bail right now. As long as she's out, Milton said they'd be there."

"Have you thought more about what we talked about this morning?" Enid asked Mrs. Hudson.

"What did you two talk about?" Sanjay looked from Enid to Mrs. Hudson.

"I think you should do it," Tempest said.

"Would someone please tell me what's going on?" Sanjay asked. "Nobody tells me anything around here."

Ash chuckled. "You were at home sleeping while I made everyone breakfast this morning."

"Of course I was sleeping," Sanjay said. "We didn't leave

the police station until almost four o'clock in the morning. How was I supposed to know breakfast was a let's-discuss-important-plans meal?"

"Ahmed reviewed the documents," Ash said. "There will be a short delay to get it set up legally, but there's no reason the plan won't work."

"Who's Ahmed?" Sanjay asked.

"The lawyer in Ash's magic Rolodex who handled Harold's will and trust," Tempest said.

"Harold didn't anticipate Cameron going to prison," Ash said, "but the documents did specify what would happen to the house and library if Cameron were to die or be otherwise indisposed, so there's a way forward that involves the library being owned by the city while being overseen by Enid."

"But I thought Enid didn't want to take it on," Sanjay said.

"I don't," Enid said. "But I can remain legally in charge while someone else runs the day-to-day operations. Someone who'd be the perfect person, much more so than I ever was."

Mrs. Hudson smiled. "I'm glad it worked out, in the end."

"You're taking over the library?" Sanjay gaped at her.

"I'm so sorry I made a muddle of things by thinking Harold was still alive," Mrs. Hudson said. "He just loved mysteries like that so much that when strange things started happening and we heard his voice, it seemed like exactly the type of thing he could have done. I didn't want to believe he'd died before the two of us had gotten past our feud."

"But you're the main person rallying against the library," Sanjay insisted.

"I shouldn't have done that," Mrs. Hudson said. "I was angry because Harold had once entrusted his books to me, years ago, when he had a health scare. His first heart attack. That was back when I was working as a librarian. A few years later, shortly after I turned fifty, I retired early from my job as a librarian. I hated to do it, but it was important for me to spend every precious moment with my husband as he was battling cancer. Harold was horrified that I chose my husband over books, so he said he'd find someone else who'd properly care for his books. I was bitter that he found someone else to run his library because I know that people are more important than books. I made a poor decision because of that, but I stopped pushing for signatures almost as soon as I started—and I never even signed it myself. I only wanted to make a point to Harold."

"I don't blame you," said Tempest. "I'd be bitter in that situation."

"It's not that I wanted to stay retired," Mrs. Hudson said. "I cared for my husband for several years before he died, but by that time, the world had moved on and forgotten about me. Nobody would hire me. I didn't want to be a library volunteer working at the whim of someone with a fraction of my experience. I wanted to contribute using my expertise."

"Which you can do here at the Gray House Library of Classic Detective Fiction," Tempest said.

"Which is a mouthful," Mrs. Hudson added, "so I think we'll be calling it the Gray House Library as a nice abbreviation."

"*We?*" Sanjay asked.

"I'd like Ivy to be the assistant librarian." She smiled at Ivy.

"Really?" Ivy smiled over the rim of her mug.

"And I do hope that the apartment on the top floor that Harold put so much work into won't go to waste," Mrs. Hudson added. "I know it wasn't what Harold wanted, but Tempest tells me you're currently apartment-hunting, so . . ."

"Yes!" Ivy's tea sloshed over the edge of her mug as she set it down and rushed over to give Mrs. Hudson a hug. "Thank you, Mrs. Hudson."

Mrs. Hudson hugged her back and said, "You might as well call me Martha. But not at work. Since Harold had a collection of Sherlock Holmes works, and I have even more to contribute, our patrons should call me Mrs. Hudson."

"That's perfect," Ivy said.

"But one last thing," Mrs. Hudson added. "I know you want to apply for your master's of library and information science. Your employment will be contingent upon making time to apply."

Tempest's phone pinged. "Kira's out on bail. She and Milton are in for tonight." She stood. "So if everyone has had their fill of my grandfather's treats, we've got work to do."

☠☠☠

Tempest was worried that people wouldn't come to Gray House after what had happened there, but even in a cozy town like Hidden Creek, the allure of a true crime made the events at Gray House even more in demand.

The escape room and the murder mystery play sold out quickly, so they added additional shows throughout the weekend to accommodate the growing demand. Both the play and the escape room were wildly successful, and the weekend summer stroll was a huge hit for all the small businesses that participated.

It was now early Sunday morning, with one more day to go, but Tempest and her three best friends had gathered at Fiddler's Folly to take Gideon to the airport together before they had to be back at the Gray House Library.

"You didn't all have to come to see me off," Gideon said, but he was smiling as he did so.

"Of course we did," Ivy said.

"I'll only be gone for three months, you know."

"But it's the end of an era," Tempest said as they piled Gideon's luggage into the back of her jeep. "My dad and I are figuring out what's next for Secret Staircase Construction, and I know you'll be back, but our lives will never return to being exactly like they were."

"You're always welcome to come back to the team if you'd like to," Darius said, "but there's no expectation that you do."

"You're all living your dreams," Morag said.

"Which is exactly how it should be," Ash added.

"Even shilling for the bookshop's wine bar hasn't been that bad," Sanjay said. "I mean, it taught me that I'll always read contracts carefully, but I'm glad it turns out both that the wine is pretty good and that they're doing some good for the world by giving ten percent of their proceeds to a literacy charity. And after this weekend, I'll get back to planning my next show."

Ash handed Gideon a paper bag of homemade food for the long flight. "Better than airplane food," he insisted.

Gideon accepted the bag with his left hand. In his right, he held a small sheet of thick paper. "This is for you," he said as he handed it to Tempest.

"A sketch of your dragon-mouth mantelpiece?" She ran her fingers over the beautiful graphite rendering of the stone dragon opening its mouth around a fireplace.

"The stone dragon *itself*," he said. "I thought it would fit perfectly in the house you're building. If you like it, I want you to have it."

Tempest Raj didn't usually find herself speechless, but here she was, unable to form words. Gideon was right. The dragon mantelpiece would fit perfectly with the stone walls and cozy gothic vibe she was going for. And the fact that Gideon had carved it made it even more special. But it must have taken him months to make. She couldn't possibly accept the gift.

"She'd love it!" Ivy squeaked. "You'd love it, right?"

"I would." Tempest grinned at Gideon. "But it's too big a gift—"

"It's settled," he said. "Now we should probably get going so I don't miss my flight."

"I'm surprised Abra isn't going with you to the airport to see Gideon off," Darius said.

"I suggested it," Ivy said with a smile, but that smile wasn't as bright as it had been before she'd learned Cameron was a killer. "But between all of us and Gideon's luggage, there wasn't room for Abra's travel hutch."

"It's a good thing a certain bunny is car-trained." Tempest jogged over to where she'd hidden the hutch, lifted Abra into Ivy's arms, then pulled her friend close for a human hug.

"I was really falling for him," Ivy whispered only loud enough for Tempest to hear.

Tempest knew what it was like to be wrong about someone she cared about. "It'll get better," she whispered back. "I promise."

Because it would. There was a lot of hard work ahead of all of them, but her grandparents were right. They were all living their dreams now, exactly as they should be.

Tempest couldn't contain her broad smile as she looked at her beloved friends and family. "Time to get on the road."

RECIPE FOR BLACKBERRY CRUMBLE COBBLER

INGREDIENTS

4 cups fresh or frozen blackberries
½ cup jaggery* or brown sugar, divided in half
1 tbsp cornstarch
½ cup all-purpose flour, sifted
½ cup rolled oats
2 tbsps cornmeal
1 tsp baking powder
½ tsp cinnamon
¼ tsp cardamom
⅛ tsp salt
2 tbsps freshly squeezed lemon juice
¼ cup coconut oil, melted
2 tbsps oat milk (or other milk of choice)

*Jaggery is an unprocessed sugar that's used widely in India and can be found at Indian grocery stores or online. It's a bit less sweet than brown sugar, with a deeper molasses flavor.

DIRECTIONS

Preheat the oven to 400 degrees Fahrenheit.

Place the blackberries and half the sugar in a pan. Heat while stirring the mixture until the sugar dissolves, then add the cornstarch. Stir over medium heat for 3 to 5 minutes until thickened. Pour the blackberry mixture into a 10-inch oven-safe dish, then set aside while preparing the topping.

For the cobbler topping, mix together the flour, rolled oats, cornmeal, baking powder, cinnamon, cardamom, salt, and the remaining sugar. Stir in the lemon juice, melted coconut oil, and milk. Mix lightly, but it should be clumpy rather than smooth.

Add the crumbly topping on top of the berries and bake at 400 degrees for about 30 minutes or until the fruit bubbles up and the crumble topping is baked through.

WANT MORE RECIPES?

SIGN UP FOR GIGI'S EMAIL NEWSLETTER TO RECEIVE A FREE EBOOK COOKBOOK:

www.gigipandian.com/subscribe.

Acknowledgments

Writing a book is a strange combination of a solitary task that takes a huge community to come to fruition. This book wouldn't be in your hands today without the fantastic publishing team at Minotaur Books and St. Martin's Publishing Group, especially my superstar editor, Madeline Houpt (who suggested the revisions to my draft manuscript that fixed the book!), Kayla Janas, Sara Beth Haring, and Mac Nicolas. And thanks to everyone who does so much work behind the scenes: Rowen Davis, Gabriel Guma, Ken Silver, Alisa Trager, and Catherine Turiano. Thanks to the team at Macmillan Audio, including my fabulous narrator, Soneela Nankani; audiobook producer, Elishia Merricks; and Maria Snelling and Drew Kilman in Marketing and Publicity. And Jill Marsal, my incredible agent of fifteen years, I continue to feel every bit as lucky as I did fifteen years ago to have you in my corner!

Huge thanks go to my critique readers and brainstorm partners: Nancy Adams, Ellen Byron, Jeff Marks, Lisa Q. Mathews, Emberly Nesbitt, Susan Parman (a.k.a. my artist and writer mom!), Brian Selfon, and Diane Vallere; and my writing communities of Crime Writers of Color, Mystery Writers of America, and Sisters in Crime.

I'm lucky to have so many remarkable people in my life who inspire me and keep me going in this wild and wonderful career. My editor has told me I don't have the endless space it would take to thank everyone else who positively impacted my life as I disappeared into my writing cave for long stretches of time to write *The Library Game*, so I'll keep this list of thanks short: Leslie Bacon, Greta Lorge, Kelly Armantage, Jen Rojas, Christy Semsen, Catrina Roallos, Eveline Chang, Winona Reyes, Juliet Blackwell, Rachael Herron, Kellye Garrett, Kim Fay, Sarah M. Chen, Naomi Hirahara, Shelly Dickson Carr, Aaron Elkins, and, as always, my amazing family.

To the librarians, booksellers, reviewers, podcasters, and bloggers who promote my books and the works of countless other authors, thank you!

And I'm sending my heartfelt thanks to my readers, each and every one of you. I'm having so much fun writing Tempest and her Scooby gang (or are they the Abracadabras?), and it's because of you that I get to have this career. Regardless of whether you've read all my books or this is the first one you've picked up, thank you for being a reader.

I love hearing from my fellow book people. You can contact me and sign up for my email newsletter at www.gigipandian.com.

☠☠☠

About the Author

Susan Parman

Gigi Pandian is the *USA Today* bestselling and multiple-award-winning author of the Secret Staircase mysteries, inspired by elements from her own family background. She is also the author of the Accidental Alchemist mysteries, the Jaya Jones Treasure Hunt mysteries, and more than a dozen locked-room mystery short stories. Pandian has won Agatha, Anthony, Lefty, and Derringer Awards, and was a finalist for an Edgar Award. A breast-cancer survivor and accidental almost-vegan who adores cooking, she lives with her husband in Northern California.